Someone is trying to kill Katie Taylor.
Does she have information worth killing for?

Amnesia after a car crash leaves her unable to remember a lot, like the fact that she is no longer engaged to Sheriff Grant Campbell.

Men of the Badge continues in Hawk's Peak, a small mountain town in North Georgia, where Grant Campbell, a former Atlanta cop, has returned after many years to be sheriff.

Katie Taylor is the love of his life – the woman he loved and lost years ago. Grant must keep Katie alive long enough to remember the secrets worth killing for, even if it means she remembers she stopped loving him. Even if it costs him, once again, the love of his life.

THE KILLER YOU KNOW

RILEY McKISSACK

ABOUT THE AUTHOR

Riley McKissack is an award-winning journalist. Cornered gunmen, cop killers, a bomb going off in a domestic terrorism incident, Riley's covered them all. Riley spent years chasing stories involving every type of bad guy and cop imaginable, including FBI, Homeland Security, homicide detectives and arson investigators.

Riley sponged up the drama, tension and danger on SWAT operations, hostage negotiations, drug busts and countless other dangerous situations.

That passion and drama spills out onto the pages of Riley's novels, along with the personal stories behind the men and women who stand between danger and the people they love.

Riley can be found at:
https://facebook.com/riley.mckissack
http://rileymckissack.com/
https://twitter.com/RileyMckissack

CHAPTER ONE

The moon sparkled along the dark mountaintops, as if dropping diamonds onto the ridges. Or razor blades.

"Pick up, Grant. I need to talk to you." Kate Taylor gripped her car's steering wheel as if it was Grant Campbell's phone, and she could squeeze a response from it.

But it just rang on and on in her ear, taunting her as if to say what Grant might be thinking, "Oh, so now you want to talk to me?" Finally voice mail picked up.

"Noooo," she moaned. She couldn't leave this information on a recording.

"Grant, call me as soon as you get this message. It's very important. *Very important*," she emphasized. Then added, "It's Katie," as if he wouldn't recognize her voice, hadn't heard it thousands of times. She started to add another, *It's very important*, but instead said, "It's official business." She left her number, then hung up.

Blood rushed from her heart like coyotes with a bloodlust racing through her veins. No one would be impacted by this information more than Grant. He'd understand exactly what it meant. Besides, he was the sheriff. She had to get hold of him, get this information to him.

Would he be at his house or the sheriff's office right now? Actually, he could be anywhere in the county if he were out on a call.

Lights flashed in her rearview mirror from a car several turns behind her on the mountain road.

At the intersection, she hesitated only a second before instinctively turning toward Grant's place, his family's old farm. He might be busy and hadn't picked up the call.

Or just plain hadn't picked up when he saw her number. For sure, he had caller ID. They hadn't had much to say to each other since he'd gotten back to Hawk's Peak.

Or, she'd made it clear she didn't have much to say to him.

Just to be on the safe side, she grabbed the phone to dial the sheriff's office and check on his whereabouts.

Darkness fell so quickly this time of year, the valleys blackening to a smudgy coal-smeared hue.

Lights flashed in her rearview mirror again. She glanced in the mirror. A dark SUV was right behind her and tailing her way too close.

The bright lights blinded her, flashing through the car like a spotlight. She slowed and pulled to the right just a bit in a clear message to pass her on the straight length of road.

The SUV sped up, and she waited for it to pass.

But, instead, her car seemed to explode, filling with light and lurching forward like a missile. A powerful jolt forced her back against the seat and headrest, as if her car was pushed out from under her while it was bashed from behind. The SUV's lights blared so brightly, as if they were inside her car.

The SUV had rear-ended her.

Her car swerved and fishtailed. She pressed on the accelerator, trying to regain control of her little car. Her car raced forward, and the SUV's lights weren't quite so bright as she put space between her car and the other vehicle.

Why hadn't he seen her, crashing into her as if he'd been distracted, texting, or looking down to dial a number on his phone? So many things to do in a car these days besides just look out your front window. She glared into her rearview mirror.

"Are you drunk?" she yelled at the mirror.

The dark SUV accelerated as if the driver had taken offense at her expression in the mirror. The car lights closed on her with the speed of an approaching meteor. She pressed down on the gas, barely keeping ahead of the speeding car, its engine growling like a black panther on her tail.

Her lungs contracted, and it seemed as though no oxygen was getting to her brain. But, her heart pounded in her chest, frantically trying to help her mind understand what was happening.

"What the ..." She peered in the mirror at the dark vehicle, trying to make out the driver's face. But, the car was completely black, no interior glow at all.

Her heart pounded and racketed in her chest like a wild animal trying to get out of a cage. She tried to swallow but her mouth was so dry it felt like she'd gulped a mouthful of sawdust.

The SUV followed incredibly closely, drafting on her bumper like a bicycle going down the mountain road. The driver acted almost as if he didn't realize he had hit her.

Or didn't care?

She was driving the car her fiancé, Hamilton Avery, had bought her as an engagement present. He'd lovingly proclaimed a ring wasn't enough for a fiancée like her.

Was she being carjacked for the expensive vehicle?

Her sleek, cream-colored BMW stood out in the rural area like a neon sign blinking, *Steal This Car*, ostentatious and flashy alongside all the farm trucks and other useful vehicles that populated the rural roads around the county.

A few recent graduates sported fancy cars they'd sunk their entire savings into, or their parents had bought them for rewards. Few as ostentatious as this car.

But, if someone were trying to carjack it, to steal it, they wouldn't want to damage the vehicle.

The way the SUV had crashed into the small vehicle was more like they wanted to kill her.

Was that the plan? Zero to murder in twenty minutes?

Did they plan to kill her because of the information she'd just discovered?

A shrieking scream formed deep inside her, scratching and begging to get out. Her heart rocketed terror and panic throughout her body with a fight or flight message, a fast paced tattoo of panic.

Fight was impossible. The large vehicle could almost roll over hers. She could only flee before the dark monster that loomed large in her rear view mirror.

The lights gained on her again, a metal-eating beast, ready to consume her and her small car in one bite. She pressed down on the gas and tried to escape the approaching, blinding lights.

She gripped the steering wheel with both hands and drove as if she'd been trained in avoidance maneuvers.

The car wasn't what they were after. The

certainty raised her pulse even higher. They wanted to silence her. She was a problem to be dealt with.

Severely. And finally.

She had to get help, had to let someone know what she knew.

Then, she remembered her phone was in her lap. She picked it up and punched in 9-1-1, putting it on speakerphone.

"9-1-1, what's your emergency?" a female voice droned, as if she were a machine, or as if the woman were talking to someone in the dispatch room about something more important than the fact that Kate was about to be killed.

"This is Kate Taylor. Someone's trying to kill me. A car is chasing me."

"Katie, what do you mean?" The voice was Chastity, a girl she'd gone to high school with.

"I'm on Mountain Ridge Road, heading toward the sheriff's place. I'm driving north. I need help. A large black SUV is chasing me. It's rammed me once and . . ."

She shrieked. The SUV's lights flashed brightly again as the vehicle gained on her. She pushed down on her accelerator but the dark car slammed into the rear of her vehicle, pushing her before it like a billiards cue sending a ball toward the hole.

Her car flew out of control, and careened toward the deep, roadside ditch. The BMW spun in a sickening slow motion swirl of light and darkness. The world outside lost all sense of direction, just varying degrees of black.

Over and over again, the world whirled around her in a chaotic spiral.

Then, with a deafening crash, her car flipped, and rolled. The metal creaked and screamed all around her, as it buckled, closing in for a deadly embrace.

Finally, the motion and noise slowed, and her car quit shrieking and moaning in protest.

"Oh my God," she cried on a burst of air, releasing the breath trapped in her chest, held captive when she'd stopped breathing, waiting for the crash to end. She looked around and tried to get her bearings, searched frantically for the black SUV.

Or more precisely, its driver.

Were they coming for her? She was pinned in the car, the crushed metal holding her in place as securely as large hands could have done.

But, at least she was right side up.

She struggled to reach her purse, to get the gun her father had given her, insisting she keep it with her when she drove at night. But, her purse had flown down into the floorboard. Too far away to reach.

Jell-O filled her brain, bringing a woozy detachment. But, she looked to the left and saw the SUV. It sat up at the top of the steep embankment

The headlights glowed like a spectral figure

of death, wanting to add her to its body count for the night. A person loomed in the window, backlit by the moon, peering down at her. To determine if she was dead or if they needed to come finish her off?

"No, please, I don't want to die," she moaned softly, as if they could hear her or would care if they did. Someone who'd just done what they'd done would be impervious to begging.

Finally, the car drove away slowly, as if at any moment the driver might return to complete the job.

"Katie! Katie! Can you hear me?" a voice from far away called to her.

She looked around frantically, searching for the source of the voice, someone who might help her.

"Katie? What happened?"

Chastity. It was Chastity. Somehow the call to 9-1-1 hadn't been disconnected in the massive car crash.

Kate's vision began to dim, as if someone were slowly turning off the lights as she was shoved into a deep cavern.

She had to let Chastity know where she was because no one could see her from the road. She would lie in this ditch until she died, her desiccated body discovered one day in the distant future by a road worker doing repairs on the mountain road.

She needed to get her phone. Reaching

down, she scrabbled for her phone.

But Jell-O oozed through her veins, filling her entire body as if coating her insides with Novocain and Oxycodone.

The darkness outside her car moved in, closing around her, sucking her into its depths.

Finally, she felt herself blacking out into nothingness, with only the distant voice of one of her high school friends speaking to her.

She wanted to respond, but couldn't. Blackness claimed her, pulling her into unconsciousness, into the soothing darkness.

*****

Grant finished milking the second cow, rinsed her off, dried her udders with an old towel as a courtesy, and then turned her out into the field. He only had a couple of cows and treated them like pets, with a personal relationship with each of them.

His phone rang with the special ring tone he'd selected for dispatch and other department calls. Instantly, he picked it up.

"Sheriff Campbell," he said, like he'd answered a thousand other times during his *off hours.* You never really had off hours when you were the sheriff.

"Sheriff, this is Chastity." The dispatch officer's voice was high pitched, stressed, unusual for her since she dealt with emergencies on a regular basis, and usually spoke in a regulated manner even under the most tense circumstances.

"What's up, Chastity?"

"It's Katie Taylor. Something happened to her. She called and said a vehicle was *chasing* her, had bumped her and then she screamed and I heard all sorts of crashing noises, then nothing."

A clutching fist wrenched the air from Grant's lungs. Panic never helped anything. He'd learned that hard lesson in Afghanistan.

But the rush of adrenalin it provided sure packed a useful punch.

He ran toward his sheriff's car.

Katie was alone somewhere and possibly bleeding out. The thought stabbed him with a slashing pain that was worse than when he'd been shot in a fierce firefight with a Taliban group.

He'd seen plenty of horrific things in war.

But Katie's blood? That was another whole level of atrocity. He barreled into his car.

"Where was Katie when she called?" he bellowed.

"She was on Mountain Ridge Road, heading toward your place, from the south. Chastity's voice had regained a professional coolness - she'd gone into *dispatch mode*. As if she realized only one of them could freak out at a time.

"Did she give a landmark?"

"No. Just south of your place somewhere."

He fired up his car, screeching out his driveway, hitting his blue lights just before making a hard left turn onto the main road.

Mountain Ridge Road was a long road. She could be anywhere, alone and hurt.

"Is there still a connection on the line?" he asked, hitting his Bluetooth so he could drive hands-free.

"Yes," Chastity answered succinctly, knowing as he did that words could cost Katie lifesaving time.

"I'm gonna hit my siren and you tell me if you hear it." He pushed the button activating the screeching cry into the night.

Then, he drove silently, waiting for Chastity's answer.

"Nothing," she said, her voice telling more than anything just how worried she was, this from a woman who was trained in hiding her emotions on the phone. "I've got you on a separate landline so I can hear her call through my headset."

He drove for another few minutes, waiting silently for Chastity to tell him when she heard the siren through Katie's open phone line.

"Nothing," Chastity answered his unasked question.

"You sure you've got a connection on that thing?" He scanned the roadside for any signs of an accident.

Then, a large black SUV came up over the hill, like a vampire bat, flying at a rate of speed that almost lifted it from the pavement.

He pumped his headlights but it made no impact on the driver, who merely seemed to speed up even more. If he turned and chased down the SUV, he might give up valuable lifesaving moments to save Katie.

"Chastity, the SUV that hit Katie is headed northbound on Mountain Ridge Road, driving like a bat out of hell, with front end damage on the passenger side."

"We've already headed deputies and an ambulance out your way," she replied. "I'll have them try to intercept the SUV. Turn your siren off and then on again. I just gave Katie's call to another dispatch worker so I could talk to you. She's not sure if she hears your siren or not." She only cared about Katie's welfare, too.

He hit the button to turn it off, then on again. His senses became narrowed and intensely focused on the road in front of him while he looked for any sign of Katie or her car.

God, let dispatch hear the siren come through on Katie's phone. Please God, let her be alive.

He'd dealt with the loss of life many times. He'd befriended many guys during basic and Special Forces training, only to lose them in the mountain regions of Afghanistan to an anonymous bullet.

But Katie's death?

The thought of Katie dying was impossible.

Too horrible to even allow his mind to contemplate.

He'd loved that woman since they were kids.

She was one of the main reasons he'd come home, he finally admitted to himself, though he'd listed a thousand other reasons consciously.

If he lost her now, all oxygen would leave the planet, and he'd suffocate.

A world without Katie? Impossible.

CHAPTER TWO

"She hears it," Chastity blurted into the phone. "Very distantly, but the other dispatcher can hear your siren."

He sped up, driving intently, with purpose.

"It's much louder, she says," Chastity coaxed in his ear. "Getting very loud."

Then, he saw it. A slash of tire tracks careened off the side of the road.

He pulled over.

"I found her," he said, giving directions to Chastity. Then, he hung up, grabbed a flashlight and a handheld radio, and swung out of his car. The blue lights of his sheriff's car blasted the landscape with the color of alarm.

"Katie," he yelled as he ran. At the bottom of a steep embankment, her fancy little car lay crumpled like an aluminum can tossed from a passing car.

So much for the engagement present Hamilton Avery had given Katie.

Fury mixed with the fear that ran through

his veins. If she'd been in her old SUV she'd have been much better equipped to withstand the assault of the black SUV.

The expensive, little sports car Hamilton had given her hadn't stood a chance.

Even before their marriage, that doofus was trying to mold her into the perfect image of a politician's wife.

As if he thought Katie wasn't perfect just as she was, that she needed his finishing touches. His finishing touches might have caused her to be more gravely injured. Or killed.

"Katie." Grant slid down the side of the ditch, barely staying on his feet. Mud covered the vehicle as if the little car had rolled in it.

The top was crushed down so that he had to get on his knees to see inside.

"Katie," he said loudly, keeping his voice modulated, not wanting to upset her further, or feed her terror at finding herself in a ditch, hurt and trapped in a mangled car.

"Yes," a small voice answered from inside the car. "It's me."

He flashed the light at an angle so as not to blind her, then forced himself to look at her, afraid of what he might see.

Her hair covered her face. He reached in and gently pushed it away.

Thank God. A pulse of relief surged through him. There wasn't any blood, no obvious damage to her face or head. Though internal injuries could still kill her.

"Katie, girl, you okay?" he asked in a coaxing tone.

"I'm okay, Grant," she answered in a small voice, as if she were still the first grader he'd gotten his first crush on. She sounded innocent, sweet, as if all he'd put her through had never happened.

As if they still had a chance. A chance for love and everything he'd always wanted with her.

"What's the matter?" Her eyes widened with concern.

"You've been in a car accident, Katie." He took her hand gently, the contact as much for his sake as hers. Her skin felt warm, and she curled her fingers around his. "Do you feel pain anywhere?"

"I feel all right." She looked down at herself. "But, I can't seem to get my legs free."

"That's okay. Don't move too much." He spoke in a soft, steady manner as if it was only a little problem. "I'm gonna get you out."

He put his other hand on her wrist, searching for a pulse. It felt pretty normal at first touch. That was good. Maybe she wasn't going into shock yet.

Just then, he heard the sound of approaching heavy engines. A red pulsing light told him the fire department was here.

He hit his radio. "That you, Quinn?" They'd already spoken once tonight so he knew the captain was on duty.

"It's me, sheriff. Whatcha need down there?"

"Jaws of Life."

"Gotcha, sheriff," the fire captain answered.

Thank God, he'd gotten all the emergency responders on a mutual assist radio band, like they had down in Atlanta, so they could all talk to each other.

After a screeching of brakes, all sorts of rescue efforts kicked into high gear.

Several firefighters were down the hill in moments, with all the heavy-duty equipment needed to free Katie.

Grant squeezed her hand again. "Gonna get you out, Katie."

She smiled weakly. "I never doubted you would, Grant." She rested her face on his arm, sweetly and trustingly.

Just like the old days. The old days that seemed so long ago.

But he couldn't think about that and all they'd lost. All *he'd* lost, he corrected himself. She'd moved on. Gotten engaged to an up-and-coming politician, who was ramping up to run for a United States Senate seat.

Grant was the only one regretting all the stupid decisions he'd made in his youth, before he'd realized you didn't always get an infinite amount of chances with someone.

That you could sever the strings between your hearts so that one of you moved on, never looking back.

That person would be Katie.

He couldn't think about that now. He had to concentrate on keeping her alive, not letting her go into shock. No telling what unseen damage could have been done to her body in the accident.

Grant couldn't bear to watch her blue eyes go vacant as he'd seen so many do in Afghanistan. Even on the streets of Atlanta. Here at home, where people should feel safe, in their own country, life could be so cheap.

The fire captain slid down the embankment with a noisy shuffle of gravel and dirt.

"Hey, Grant," Quinn said, with an easy jovialness as if this were a social encounter. "How 'bout moving back so I can put a neck brace on Katie?"

Katie's eyes flew open and she grasped at Grant's hand. "Don't leave me, Grant," she implored frantically. "Don't leave me."

The captain's eyes jerked to Grant, as if the tone of her voice seemed odd, coming from another man's fiancé. Then, Quinn's face returned to neutral, knowing how frantic people could become during such a terrifying ordeal, grasping onto someone she'd known all her life.

This wasn't about a guy-girl thing, but a life or death situation.

Katie clutched Grant's hand and he returned the pressure. "I'm right here, Katie.

I'm not going anywhere."

She smiled weakly.

Grant moved aside a bit, allowing Quinn to work around him. The captain acted quickly and efficiently, fastening a neck brace onto Katie. Next, he put a blood pressure cuff on her arm and checked the pressure. He flashed a small light at her pupils, checking for concussion.

Several other firefighters came down the hill, carrying heavy equipment.

Quinn turned to Grant.

"Get in there, Grant. Keep her awake," Quinn said quietly into Grant's ear, then he stepped back to let Grant move in closer.

Grant knelt beside the car, touching Katie's face with one hand, his other hand firmly gripping one of hers. "I'm here, Katie," he reassured, though he wasn't sure if she heard it. Her gaze had gone blank and unfocused.

The firefighters began working quickly, as if sensing how close to going into shock she was. They braced large pieces of wood between Katie and the crumpled metal, protecting her as they prepared to use the Jaws of Life.

Katie's eyes slowly closed.

"Look at me, Katie," he demanded. He needed to keep her awake and alert so she could tell the firefighters if they hurt her during the extraction process.

He needed those beautiful blue eyes to stay with him. "Katie," he barked in his cop voice.

Her eyes blinked open, fastening onto him.

"Don't speak to me in that tone of voice," she said, irritably, as if they'd just had a minor spat.

He laughed, despite the situation, and Quinn looked over and laughed, too. But he didn't stop working. Every minute was vital to keeping Katie alive.

"Katie," Grant gentled his tone. "I need you to stay awake. Tell me if you feel any pain, okay?"

Her eyes connected with his gaze, and a shot of electricity sparked through him with a powerful kick.

He gripped her hand tightly, willing his life force into her, willing her to stay alive and not leave him alone on the planet.

"You feeling okay?"

"Emmhmm," she murmured softly, and her eyes drifted closed.

"Stay with me, Katie." He cupped her face with his free hand. "Stay with me, girl."

Her eyes opened drunkenly, and she smiled. "Girl?"

"Woman," he corrected himself, with a playful tone. All he needed was to keep her talking, keep her awake.

"We're gonna exert force now, Grant and Katie," another firefighter he'd gone to high school with said. "Y'all ready?"

"Ready, Katie?" Grant said, making eye contact with her.

"Yeah," she murmured, leaning into Grant's chest, nuzzling in underneath his chin. He wrapped his arm around her, welcoming her there, aching with just how good it felt to have her so close.

Later, when she came to fully in the hospital, she probably wouldn't remember any of this.

But right now, it felt good, just like old times.

Grant looked up to see two of the firefighters watching them, with a questioning look in their eyes.

She was after all the fiancée of another man, a powerful man from a powerful family.

But right now, she was just an accident victim who needed comforting.

"Tell us if anything hurts, Katie," he prompted.

She murmured back and he nodded at Quinn. "Guess we're ready."

"Yeah." Quinn nodded to his firefighters, and the Jaws of Life began exerting pressure on the crumpled metal encasing Katie.

Grant tightened his arms around her. "You okay, sweetie?"

"Perfect." She nuzzled in closer into his chest. "Just perfect."

The metal began creaking and bending back until finally, miraculously, Katie's body was freed from the metallic grasp of the car.

So much for Ham's engagement present,

now on its way to some junkyard.

Grant would have never put a woman he cared about into such an impractical vehicle for driving on these mountain roads, with the snow, rain and icy conditions that regularly made the roads so slick and hazardous.

A new SUV would have been more practical.

But then, with Ham's type of money, practicality wasn't highest on his list of needs.

Ham.

During this whole nightmare, Katie had never once asked for her fiancé, never called out his name in panic or asked that he be called to the scene.

It was as if her need for him had crumpled along with the small, impractical car.

CHAPTER THREE

Katie struggled up out of the Jell-O that encased her mind, and glued her eyelids shut. An antiseptic smell filtered into her senses, the scent of cleanliness and alcohol. A faint beeping nearby annoyed the heck out of her.

She fought against the tiredness and finally was able to push open her eyelids and look around. She was in a hospital bed. Something she should have guessed from the smell.

Why was she in the hospital? Because her knee hurt and she felt bruised all over? Carefully, she assessed the various aches and bumps on her body. Nothing seemed too major. Except for the massive headache that pulsed in her brain.

A memory of rolling down a hill seeped into her awareness. A crash?

Slowly, the memory of her car rolling over and over came back to her. With all the fear and desperation of being inside a crushed, metal cage. When she'd thought she was going to die. Until she'd heard Grant's voice.

Grant. Of course Grant had come to her. He'd always been there for her, her whole life. Dependable, strong and sexy Grant.

A hand on her thigh registered and she looked to her right. The railing on her bed had been dropped so that an armchair beside her bed was almost an extension of her bed.

Grant sat in the armchair, his hand on her leg, his eyes closed, his head tilted back, asleep.

She'd always liked him best that way, asleep, when he was an innocent, clean slate on which she could write her own agenda of expectations.

Asleep - when he had no demands of his own, just the sweet Grant she'd known all through school, her first beau, her only boyfriend ever. The only man she'd ever needed and would ever want.

Few women got as lucky in life as she'd been - finding the man of her dreams while playing with Play-Doh in first grade.

Yeah, life didn't get much sweeter than that.

He slept so innocently. Soon, he'd wake up and start having opinions and ideas of his own, many of which would conflict with hers.

Then, the fun would begin. Because arguing with Grant had always been part of the fun, convincing him that she was right. Or making him work to convince her. That dynamic had always been part of their chemistry.

She looked at the man he'd become and wondered how that little boy she'd known in elementary school had turned into this big, juicy male.

Underneath the hotness, he wasn't all that different, really. The exterior frame was bigger, more muscled, much more guy-like.

But the essence of him was the same. She could stare really hard, with her eyes narrowed, and see the little boy he'd been underneath the veneer of man.

Now, at about six-foot-two, he was big, with dark hair that swept across his forehead and blue eyes that could sizzle with desire, or compassion and humor.

Just then, those blue eyes opened. He took a second to focus on her, then he smiled, warm and inviting, with a heat that had always been there for her.

The electricity sparking between them began to grow, with a kinetic energy. The same sexual attraction that had always played between them.

The tension arcing between them increased, until finally, she couldn't wait any longer. She needed his mouth on hers. Someone had left her bed cranked up, so that she was almost sitting, and only inches away from Grant's mouth.

She leaned forward, pressing her lips against his, taking what she wanted, what she'd always wanted, and would desire as long as she lived.

Grant's hand snaked around the nape of her neck, bringing her in closer, his lips insistent, his mouth opening, his tongue teasing, inviting hers into his mouth, until their tongues were twirling and mating in imitation of what her entire body needed from him.

"What the hell?" A voice barked from the doorway. "Get your hands off my fiancée."

She pulled back to see Hamilton Avery, Ham as she and Grant always called him, standing in the doorway, his eyes narrowed, his hands on his hips, in a comic portrayal of outrage.

Her hand still tangled in Grant's hair, she contemplated Ham's indignation and wondered what was he talking about? She had a private room and the only people present were she and Grant.

But then a lot of things about Ham had never made sense to her.

"Hey Ham, what's up?" She smiled benignly at him.

"Hamilton," he corrected.

He walked toward her, leaned across and took Grant's hand off her thigh and flung it away. She looked at Ham, then back at Grant and laughed.

But Grant didn't laugh. He didn't stand up and ask Ham what the hell he was doing.

Grant just looked at Ham. Kate waited for

Grant to make some smartass comment.

But Grant's face remained expressionless, no outrage, no comic comeback.

He looked almost guilty. The expression he used to get when he lied about something as simple as not doing his homework, or kissing Sara Jane Maple behind the bleachers that time in high school the week Katie had broken up with him.

She'd meant to teach him a lesson.

She hadn't known he'd use the time so efficiently and with such deliberation as to score a couple of kisses with another girl in the short time before they'd made up.

She frowned at Grant, even now a little ticked off at him for kissing Sara Jane.

"What?" he asked.

"Just remembering the time you kissed Sara Jane Maple."

He tilted his head, a slight grin on his face, his eyes crinkling that way she loved. "That was about fifteen years ago. Got any other little grievances in there just waiting to come out?"

She laughed, because it was funny. At pushing thirty, to be mad about something that had happened when they were fourteen was beyond silly. "No, it's okay. You get a pass on kissing Sara Jane. I'm not still mad."

"Thank God, 'cause it's gonna be a long life if I have to keep hearing from everybody in town 'bout stuff I did as a teenager."

She laughed and leaned her forehead against his chest. Out of the corner of her eye, she saw Ham's face · red, strained, tendons sticking out of his neck.

"You're gonna pull something, Hamilton, if you keep that up," she said.

His mouth twisted, and he blew out a gust of air in disgust. She sat up straighter. Ham was like her cousin, and she hated to see him upset.

"What's the matter, Hamilton? What's got your goat?"

He tilted his head, looking between her and Grant. "What's going on here, Katherine?"

"Kate," she corrected. She hated it when people called her Katherine, like she'd done something offensive.

Ham blew out another burst of air, the anger changing to confusion. He looked at Grant. "What's going on?"

Grant drew away from her, dropping her hand. A quick pull of loneliness shot through her, though he was only inches away.

Something inside of her felt like she'd found something she'd lost so long ago and something she could lose again so easily. She reached for his hand, refusing to let Ham's presence alter anything about her life.

Public displays of affection had never been Ham's thing. He thought it was tacky and was never one to kiss a girl in public.

Well, he could just get over it. This was her

life, which she'd realized could end so quickly when she'd awakened alone in the dark car in a ditch. She was terrified and unable to free herself, and she'd only wanted one thing.

Grant.

When he'd appeared out of nowhere, she'd known she was going to be okay. That everything was going to be okay.

She took Grant's hand, grasping it firmly, before she leaned back against the pillows.

"Katie seems to have a little bit of amnesia," Grant said.

She opened her eyes. "What?"

"You were in an accident, Katie."

"Kate," she corrected.

He tilted his head. "Kate?"

"Yeah, I'm over that Katie business, like I'm some little kid. Over it." She sliced the air with her hand for emphasis.

*****

Grant looked at Katie, trying to decide just how much to tell her right now.

She was holding hands again with him, as if they'd never broken up and was speaking to Hamilton as if they'd never been engaged.

All of that was a step in the right direction, for Grant at least.

But someone had run her off the road, and he needed answers.

She'd woken up twice before Ham had gotten to the hospital. And both times, she didn't seem to remember anything about an accident.

He liked this new Kate, the woman who'd forgotten the last words she'd yelled at him before he'd left town for basic training.

"Don't come back here expecting to find me waiting for you," she'd said decisively. "This is your decision to leave. You're leaving me." She'd placed her hands on her hips in that favorite, defiant gesture of hers and said, "And I'm counting myself left for good."

When he'd first come back to Hawk's Peak and run for sheriff, she'd been polite, cordial — all the things an ex- flame should be in a small town.

But this handholding, kissing him till he couldn't think of anything but locking that hospital door, and using the hospital bed for purposes he was sure the designer had never intended? This Kate hadn't met him when he'd returned to Hawk's Peak.

That Katie had looked at him with a chill that said she'd put on ice any heat they'd ever shared.

This Kate was a definite improvement over Hamilton's Katherine who'd made it a point of displaying her affection for her fiancée whenever Grant was present, even though it had obviously irritated Hamilton to have her disregard his no PDA policy.

The doctor had checked Katie out when she'd first gotten to the hospital and alerted Grant that Katie seemed to be missing a few facts about her recent past. The doctor knew

Katie's history well; he had taken care of her as a kid.

So, kisses aside, Grant needed to start grounding Katie in reality. Someone had run her off the road. And they didn't need someone like that riding around county roads.

Drunk or just belligerent, that sort of behavior showed an aggressive disregard for other drivers.

"Kate, do you remember the accident?" Grant prompted.

She looked away, out the window, then finally said, "I remember waking up in a car in a ditch."

She shook her head then touched her temple as if the movement had hurt her brain. "Can't quite recall how I got there. Was it my fault? Did I hurt someone?"

Worry lines formed around her eyes.

"No, Katie, you didn't."

"Kate," she corrected instantly.

"Kate," he agreed. "Do you remember the moments leading up to the accident?"

She looked blankly at the wall for a moment, then back at him, shaking her head. "Nope. Can't say I do. What happened?"

How much should he tell her? The fact that a car had seemed intent on running her off the road was troubling. But it probably was just some road raging jerk, maybe someone who just got fired or laid off, and had gotten ticked off at her expensive car without even knowing her.

Maybe she'd done something to tick him off. Maybe not.

But she needed the information, needed to see if it would jog her memory.

"A large, black SUV ran you off the road."

Hamilton's gaze jerked toward him. "What?"

"She was run off the road by an SUV who hit her car at least twice. She told 9-1-1 it had been chasing her for awhile."

Ham's eyes shuttered instantly.

Grant glanced down at Katie's ring finger, not for the first time, noticing that the gigantic engagement ring Ham had put there was gone.

Ham followed Grant's eyes to Katie's hand, his face reddening.

"Where's your ring, Katherine?"

Grant watched the interaction between the two. Wouldn't have been the first boyfriend who'd tried to crash his significant other's car after a fight. It seems like Katie would have mentioned it was him to the dispatcher.

Maybe Ham had borrowed someone else's car?

"What ring?" She looked down at her hands.

"Your engagement ring."

Katie gave him a blank look.

"Katherine, you're engaged to me," Hamilton said in a deep, commanding tone.

She jerked her gaze to him, looking at him

for a long moment, then burst out laughing. "Yeah, right."

Ham's face reddened further. "It's true, Katherine." He deepened his voice as if to make his point, to emphasize his masculinity and the fact that he was in control of everything in his life, always had been, always would be.

Or so he told himself.

"Kate," she corrected.

There were always so many cars at his dad's place that he could have taken his pick, chasing Katie after a fight.

He'd seemed genuinely surprised to hear about the SUV incident. But he could have planned that reaction. Domestic violence cut across all economic levels.

Ham pulled up a chair close to the bed, sat down and picked up Katie's free hand, then leaned forward to look in her eyes.

"Katherine, the whole town knows we're engaged. Ask anyone, and they'll tell you." He spoke in a soft bedroom voice, and smiled at her with an implied intimacy that turned Grant's stomach. "We had a big party out at the country club to announce it."

"Of course we did." Katie pulled back her hand. "April Fools'."

Ham looked up at him, then quickly away. And not for the first time, Grant began to suspect he was hiding something.

"Where's her engagement ring, Ham?"

"Hamilton," he corrected. "I don't know. Lost in the accident?"

"Or lost in translation?" Katie giggled quietly. "You and I are the last two people in the world that would ever be engaged, Hamilton."

She'd used his entire name. If you were going to laugh in your fiancé's face and deny your engagement, at least you could address him as he preferred.

Katie raised her hand closer to her face, staring at the suntan line that indicated a ring had been on that finger on a regular basis until recently.

Something flickered behind her eyes and she looked at Ham, with what looked like anger and resentment flashing from her sapphire blue eyes.

She raised her hand, showed him the tan line, then unexpectedly slapped him hard.

The smack of flesh upon flesh rang through the room, and Ham pulled back, shock stunning the handsome off his face.

He put a hand to the red imprint on his cheek and stared at Katie.

Ham stood up, towering over Katie in the bed.

Grant strode to his side of the bed, putting himself between Ham and his apparent ex-fiancée.

No ring and a slap added up to a broken engagement in his book.

"What are you doing, Grant?" Hamilton leaned into the hand Grant placed on his chest. "Get the hell out of here and let me and Katherine talk."

"It's . . .," Katie started to correct Ham.

"It's Kate," Grant said before she could finish.

"That's right," she said with relish from behind him.

Ham's hazel eyes flashed with hatred and the impulse to physically attack Grant. He'd seen that look in a man's eyes many times before: in Afghanistan, in downtown Atlanta, and in bars outside Fort Bragg, just before a brawl broke out.

Call it what you would, that look said a man was losing it. Losing the tether to civility that kept people from punching each other left and right whenever someone ticked them off.

Ham needed something to get him back in touch with the rational side of his brain.

"When's the election, Hamilton?" Grant brought up the one subject that would bring Ham back to earth in a heartbeat.

Ham looked at him like he could see right through Grant's ruse, but still it worked, and the rage crept back into its cage, coiling Ham's animal instincts back in with it.

"I think that slap says you need to leave the room, Hamilton." Grant stood his ground but dropped his hand from Ham's chest, wanting Ham to feel like he had some choice in the matter.

Ham looked past him at Katie and nodded at her. "I'm sorry you're not feeling well, Katherine."

Grant could almost sense her mouth opening, but Ham corrected himself, "Kate, I mean."

Ham sucked in a deep breath, and let it out before taking a few steps back. Grant sidestepped so that he could see both of them.

Cause there sure as hell were some undercurrents to this interaction.

Ham dipped his head, trying to make eye contact with Katie, but she assiduously studied the bed sheet, working it with two fingers, twirling and un·twirling the fabric.

Ham sighed softly. "I'll leave my cell phone number at the desk and you can ask the nurses to call me anytime, Kath..." He stopped himself. "Kate, you can call me anytime. I'll come back tomorrow to check on you."

"That's okay," Katie said, still not making eye contact with him, her voice distant and cool. "I'll be fine. I'll have the nurses call you if I need you to come back."

A flicker of pain crossed Ham's face before he got it back under control. "Okay, Kate. Call me if you need me."

Hamilton pivoted on his heel and left, apparently trying to keep his pride somewhat intact.

Grant knew what being dismissed from

Katie's life felt like. It had hurt like hell.

He'd been an ocean, a desert and several Afghan mountain ranges away when it had begun to really sink in that she was done with him, so he couldn't storm back in on impulse and try to get her into bed where they'd always solved all their conflicts.

Bed had always worked for them. Afterwards, neither of them could ever recall what had been so important.

Except for the final fight, when Katie had accused him of abandoning her.

As Ham disappeared out the door, Katie looked at Grant impishly. "Why don't you see if that door has a lock on it." She raised an eyebrow and curled her fingers invitingly toward him.

What sort of a man would take advantage of a woman's loss of memory, of amnesia with a gap of ten years?

A man desperate for what he'd lost, what he'd ached for so many nights alone in a war zone?

All the snipers, roadside IEDs, and other dangers of war hadn't terrified him nearly as much as knowing he wasn't going back to the waiting arms of the woman he loved. Surviving war would be nothing compared to surviving life without her.

She smiled at him with an invitation that said she was clearly willing. But a woman with brain trauma couldn't give consent.

But how she looked in that bed ...

It would require every bit of self-control and sense of honor not to respond as she beckoned to him.

"Shut the door, please, Grant. We need to *talk*. And see if it has a lock."

CHAPTER FOUR

Grant pushed shut the hospital door. As he did, the mirror on the back of the door caught the glare from a nearby light, reflecting it back into her eyes.

The blinding light filled her vision, like another blinding light. Instantly, she was taken back ... to moments before the accident to the headlights of the black SUV, chasing her.

The vehicle closed in on her until she felt like it would roll completely over her and her small car. It might actually have done so, if she hadn't maneuvered to the side at the last moment.

As she did so, just as her car began its crazy swinging spin toward the ditch, her headlights bounced into the other car, flashing on the driver.

She tried hard to remember the face, struggled to concentrate on the blurry image in her memory, but the face wouldn't gel, and finally it faded away.

Something else floated into her mind. She closed her eyes, trying to bring it more clearly into focus: a sticker in the front driver's side of the windshield.

Then, she was rolling down the embankment, her head crashing into her window with every roll, yanking back and forth violently.

Pain shot through her head, like a knife stabbing into her brain.

"What is it, Katie?" Grant's voice infiltrated the pain. "Do you need the nurse?"

She lifted her hand and weakly waved no, not daring to speak. Slowly, the sensation of being back in her car receded.

Thank God, since it seemed to take the pain with it.

Finally, she flickered her eyelids, peeking at the room, convincing herself she could open her eyes without piercing pain.

She opened her eyes completely. No pain.

"What was that?" Grant said when finally she made eye contact with him.

"Don't know," she whispered, afraid if she spoke louder, the pain might return. "I got this vivid recall of the moment before the accident, but at the same time, this horrible pain pierced my brain. As the memory receded, the pain went away. I might have remembered more if I had gutted out the pain. But the pain had its way with me."

"Pain's not good," he agreed.

"Memory loss also not good," she said, with a slight laugh.

"Does it hurt to remember it now?" He peered into her eyes.

She thought for a moment. "No. I can remember what I saw in the flash. But, before it was more like being in the moment, and that was what was so painful. Like a stabbing knife in my brain as I started to roll down the hill."

He stared at her, intently, waiting. He wanted her to tell him what she'd seen.

Suddenly, she looked down at his belt. "What's that doing there?" A star was peeking from just underneath his coat. She leaned forward, to push back the jacket.

She looked at it, then up at him, then back at the star again.

"I'm the sheriff, ya know," he said levelly.

"The heck you say." She leaned back, and was going to laugh but then realized he was serious. "Grant, what is going on? This is like a horror movie. Like a time warp, with you as the sheriff and a man I would never be involved with saying he's engaged to me."

She lifted her shoulders in a massive shrug, as if she could slough off the insanity. Then, she held out her hands as if to weigh the facts, balance out the truth. "Me and Ham? Are you serious? You're the sheriff? Really?"

She laughed with disbelief but it didn't feel at all funny. "How can this be true?"

Grant leaned forward and took both of her hands, looking into her eyes, as if to connect with her, as if to make a big point.

"What?" she asked. What now? What new fact was he getting ready to impart? "Do I have kids, too?"

"No." Grant actually laughed. "No little Hamsters running around."

"Hamsters." She lay back on the pillow and began to laugh. "Oh, you made a little joke. Like Ham's kids, right?" The laughter rolled through her, and even considering the surreal circumstances, she felt better.

"But we would make beautiful kids, me and Ham, right? With his dark hair and my blue eyes. He's got great hair, you've got to give him that."

Grant's eyes darkened to the blue at sunset, intense, with a blackness creeping around the edges, and his jaw tightened.

"They'd kinda look like you," she said, tilting her head to get a good look at Grant. "I never noticed how much you guys look alike. Yeah, Ham and my kid would look like you."

"Spare me the image." He shook his head as if to get the nightmare vision out of his brain.

She knew the feeling. Wanted to shake a lot of images out of her head. If she and Ham were engaged, then they'd probably ... done the dirty.

Oh, man. She put her hand on her stomach, willing back the urge to hurl.

None of this fit any description of normal, and she'd love to shake her head and will it all away.

Especially that last image of her and Ham having sex.

Her ribs hurt with a deep ache that went from the muscle and tendons straight to the bone. In fact, her entire body hurt. But, the ribs were the worst.

As if she'd had a bungee jumping mishap, where everything had gone horribly wrong. She couldn't throw up if for no other reason than the pain in her ribs would explode.

"So, what else am I missing, Grant? What else is the truth that I know nothing about?"

He glanced at her then quickly away.

"What?"

He met her gaze, and shrugged. "I'm not sure exactly what your mind is processing as the truth right now."

She laughed darkly. "That makes two of us. How crazy is this? You would think you would know the reality of your own life, right?"

He nodded.

"You really are the sheriff?"

"Really am."

She met his eyes, wondering was he remembering all the trouble and almost-trouble he got into as a kid. He was always one count away from a stay at juvie. If her dad hadn't taken such an interest in him, supported him in court, vouched for him, and a whole lot of other favors, Grant would have had a record for sure.

"So, you being here is an official visit?"

He tilted his head. "Kind of. Anything you do or say can be used against you. There, you've been Mirandized."

She stared at him blankly for a second before he lifted a hand and said, "That's a joke. You're the victim here, not the suspect."

"How do you know?" She raised a hand to shield her eyes from the bright light of the nearby lamp.

"I know because you called 9-1-1 and said you were being chased down the mountain." Grant stood up and walked to the lamp, adjusting it until most of the light bounced away into the room. Then, he turned to her and his eyes narrowed. "Maybe we could talk about what you remembered a minute ago. If it doesn't hurt you to talk about it?"

She tested the memory. "No pain."

He nodded and sat back down in the chair next to the bed, and waited for her to continue. He'd always been like that, giving her silence to fill up.

"I kinda saw the driver right as my car was spinning out of control. My lights bounced into his car. But, I couldn't make him out." She shook her head with frustration.

Then, like a bolt, something more important took control of her thoughts.

"I was engaged to Ham?" She looked

directly into Grant's eyes. "Are you sure?"

He nodded slowly. "I saw you just yesterday at the Piggly Wiggly, with a big old rock on your left hand. You sort of waved it around at me when you said hello."

"If I'm engaged to him," she sat up straighter, "that means you and I are no longer in a relationship."

His eyes shuttered, giving nothing away.

"Grant." A horrible thought crept into her mind, an unimaginable possibility.

Tears flashed heat along the insides of her eyelids. Could it be true? Please, God, no.

"Are you … ?" She reached for his left hand, pulled it up. No ring. But that didn't mean he wasn't engaged.

"Are you … ?" She repeated, struggling to say the actual word, but couldn't bring herself to say *engaged, in love,* or any other possible words that described the horrifying idea of him belonging to someone else.

The nightmarish thought hung in the air.

She looked at Grant, trying to read the answer on his face before he could put the harsh truth into words.

Say it, say it, say it, she wanted to scream. Not knowing was almost as bad as what the truth might turn out to be. She touched the ring finger of his left hand.

Grant met her eyes and tilted his head. Bracing himself for her reaction?

"There's no one," Grant said flatly. "I

wouldn't have kissed you the way I did if there was."

She felt a blush start in her chest, rising into her face. They weren't even together anymore. Apparently, she was engaged to another man.

But, the way she'd kissed Grant ... What must he think of her?

More importantly, what had happened to them? What could have torn her and Grant apart? She stroked the ring finger of his left hand with its blessedly vacant spot.

"Why, Grant?" She tried to read his face, feeling as if the lights from an even larger SUV were barreling at her, ready to slam into her.

"Why, what?"

He knew what she was asking. He was just skirting around, dodging the question.

"Why aren't we together anymore?"

He looked away, but she reached for his chin, pulling him back to meet her gaze.

"Why?" she asked again, this time the question coming from her gut with a fierce need to understand.

His eyes fastened on her, the blue in them so deep that she could have just leaned into the feelings they inspired. Leaned into the longing she'd always felt for him.

Why had he rejected her? It had to have been Grant who had broken off the relationship, because she never would have walked away from him.

What could have so changed between them that this heat could be smothered? They'd always had a volcanic need for the other.

Had that been a lie?

For the first time, she understood how some people could go crazy. Because this felt like insanity, everything she'd always known to be true was suddenly overturned, gone. This new reality felt like a nightmare.

"What happened to us, Grant?" she implored, begging to be enlightened to things that had happened between them that were now lost somewhere in her mind.

His gaze gentled, like a man who didn't want to reject a woman again, a man who'd explained once that he didn't love her, and didn't want to drive the dagger into her heart again.

"Why, Grant?" she whispered.

"That's a question only you can answer. I never really got it. Still don't."

"You're saying *I* broke up with you?" She gave a disbelieving laugh – at a bad joke. "That never happened."

But, the look in his eyes said it had.

She sure as hell would never have done that. Not with the way he'd always made her feel. That kiss just before Ham had entered the room had been as real as any they'd ever shared.

Everything else seemed unreal. But that

kiss had felt like the real deal.

She needed something real, something to hold onto. Leaning forward, she took his shirt between two fingers and pulled him toward her.

She needed a bit of reality.

CHAPTER FIVE

Like a vision from the past, Katie reached out to him. He'd dreamt about this during those long, lonely nights in Afghanistan when he'd first lost her.

Now, she reached out to him.

Could he take what she was offering, what she'd so long denied him, closeness, intimacy · that heat that could singe the hair from his body with its intensity?

He wanted what she was offering.

But it wasn't right.

He drew back, though every cell in his body called him an idiot.

He wouldn't sleep with a drunken woman who wasn't already his girlfriend, wouldn't have sex with a woman under the influence of drugs.

How was this any different?

If she were in her right state of mind, she'd flutter that ring-encrusted finger at him just to throw it in his face, all that he'd left behind.

It wasn't true that he didn't know the

circumstances surrounding her dumping his ass. But, he hadn't been lying when he'd said he didn't understand it. The key to understanding why she'd cut the cord so completely was buried deep inside Katie's brain.

Wanting herself called Kate all of a sudden was indicative that she wasn't the same person. Almost like an alter ego had emerged, a split personality of sorts.

Ham's Katherine was gone. Grant's Katie wasn't anywhere to be seen.

This new person, this Kate, had emerged.

She looked like his Katie, acted like his Katie, with the obvious heat between them that they'd shared so long ago, but this woman didn't have possession of all parts of her memory and was missing some of the information she needed to make an informed decision.

And until she got in touch with all parts of her brain, he couldn't sleep with her.

It wasn't the honorable thing to do.

Would a few kisses hurt? Probably. Once she realized what he'd let her do, then the pain would start.

With a very adult type of punishment like she'd practiced since he'd returned, flinging that ring in his face, that symbol of her giving herself to another man.

Damn, damn, damn.

Just damn.

Thinking of how she'd tortured him, he decided to give her a little something to think about before she stood in front of the altar, preparing to say her vows to Ham, readying to give him a bunch of little Hamsters.

He stopped resisting as she tugged him forward. Instead, he took charge, moving in for a taste of what he'd dreamt about in those long, lonely nights in the mountains of Afghanistan.

Their mouths met as if in a perfect memory, hers opening instantly to him, inviting him to delve into her heat. Their tongues met in an instant connection to their past, to the hot nights they'd spent learning each other's bodies and what they needed.

A swirling heat filled him, his body responding with an aching need for her.

The kiss consumed them, so much more than a kiss.

She moaned underneath his mouth, her arms sliding up to his chest, inside his jacket, pulling him closer. Closer to the edge.

Closer to locking that door and taking what he'd been denied for so long.

Her kiss said she wanted it, wanted it as much as he needed it. He pulled away to see the misty heat in her eyes, a mist that swirled around them, taking him back to the days when she belonged to him.

Then, he kissed her, kissed her to ease the ache that had lived in him so long, the aching need for her.

"Oh, my." A female voice from the doorway broke the spell.

As if swimming up out of water, he and Katie pulled away from each other, Katie blinking as if it hurt her eyes to open them.

They both turned toward the door.

Katie's Aunt Mamie Lee stood in the doorway, her jaw open. Katie's dad stood just behind her, a slight grin on his face.

"I see you two took up where you left off a few years back," Mamie Lee blustered.

Katie's dad chuckled. "'Bout time."

Katie smiled at the two. "Can either of you two tell me why we broke up?"

"Cause you were stubborn as a mule." Mamie Lee nodded her head profusely. "Uh huh, I said it. It's out there."

Katie laughed. "You've been watching too many of those *Real Housewife* shows, Aunt Mamie Lee."

Katie's dad chuckled. "She does love her Bravo programming."

"You gotta love it," Mamie Lee agreed. "Up here in Hawk's Peak, ain't nobody bitch-slapping nobody. A little voyeurism of other people's self destructing lives can't be begrudged me."

"I do remember a couple of high school parties and nights out at the No Problem Saloon where I thought maybe a couple of reality show cameras ought to be following some people around," Katie offered.

"Well, we ain't talking teenagers and folks with drinking problems," Mamie Lee harrumphed. "Those Real Housewives are slapping and yelling and making a scene and they're grown up. If you can believe people who aren't roaring drunk for a lifestyle acting that way."

Grant didn't add that he saw a bit more reality show type of behavior than he cared for in his job as sheriff. He often felt he ought to be looking for the reality show cameras on half the crime scenes he showed up at.

Most people just didn't know what all went on in the surrounding county around Hawk's Peak.

Like a large black SUV that nearly rode right over Katie.

The image of that blasted through his mind like a gunshot.

No matter the inciting reason, the result was the same. The driver had driven her off the road, then left, not calling 9-1-1, not stopping to render aid.

A simple case of road rage? Or attempted murder?

That tan line on Katie's left ring finger blinked at him like a neon sign. Warning, warning, warning - things are not as they appear.

Katie's mind had so disconnected from reality that he had to wonder was it because of simple head trauma, or something more, something her brain couldn't wrap itself around · like a fiancée who would try to kill her.

So, maybe she'd chosen to forget a lot of details of her current life, to go back to a more simple time.

When her boyfriend was her childhood sweetheart, and the biggest problem she faced was whether to go out for cheerleading or to use the time to work or volunteer at the local vet to get the volunteer/work hours that would be required later when she applied to the University of Georgia veterinary school.

She hadn't needed the popularity points of cheerleading, since her good looks and lively personality won her more friends than she needed.

A part-time job at the vet clinic had won out. Though, she hadn't needed the money, because her dad had enough for his only daughter.

In some ways, she'd gone back in time to a point when she'd had it all, and the future looked good.

Before she'd dumped Grant's ass.

That was the past, though. Now, he needed to find out who'd run a woman off the road, seemingly intentionally, then left the scene.

He needed to find out if Katie was safe, if someone had intentionally targeted her. Like Ham, perhaps.

Hamilton Avery was the first person to investigate, 'cause as they liked to say in the homicide business, in the case of a woman's mysterious death or disappearance, the man in a woman's life was usually the guy involved in her death.

Even if the cops couldn't prove it.

He watched as Mamie Lee and John Taylor hugged on and made a fuss over their little girl, even though she was almost thirty.

The hospital gown made her look a lot younger and more fragile.

"I'm gonna leave you guys to visit for a while," he said. "Gotta do me some cop business." He tilted his head at John to step outside with him.

Then, when Katie made it out from behind her aunt's large hug, Grant nodded at her, trying not to notice her disappointment. Which made him want to stay in her welcoming presence as long as she wanted.

'Cause it had been so very long since she'd looked at him that way.

While Mamie Lee busied herself unpacking some of her home cooking for Katie, John followed him outside.

Katie's dad turned toward Grant, crossing his arms across his chest.

"What happened?" he said. All geniality disappeared, washed away by a wave of parental concern, apparently having been only a front for Katie anyway.

His eyebrows knitted together, emphasizing the wrinkles that had increased on his face and thus the years that had passed since Grant had been a regular at the Taylor household.

"I heard she got run off the road," John continued, without giving Grant a chance to answer the question.

Grant nodded. "That's what it seems like."

"You know who?"

Grant shook his head. "Wish I did, I'd have already been out there with a warrant. They sped off into the night. I saw them leaving as I was heading up the road."

"You kept on toward the accident scene?"

Grant nodded and met John's gaze straight on, knowing his priorities would have been the same as Grant's.

John patted him on the arm. "Good boy."

A warm glow filled Grant. The older man's praise still meant a lot to him.

"You have any idea who might have done this, or why?"

Grant chewed on the side of his lip, trying to decide just how much to say.

John nodded knowingly. "I notice she's not wearing that big old ring Hamilton Avery gave her. You don't think he did it, do ya?"

Grant lifted a shoulder. "Wouldn't be the first ex- fiancé to go crazy on a girl."

John looked at Grant, then raised an eyebrow. "Still, I wouldn't have figured him as one to do that."

Grant met his gaze directly, conceding to himself that he'd been thinking the same thing. The guy had even left politely, leaving Katie alone with the ex-boyfriend he'd caught sucking face with his recent fiancée.

"I know," Grant conceded to John's assessment of Hamilton. "Doesn't seem like Hamster to do that."

John laughed quietly at the derogatory nickname. Couldn't blame an old boyfriend for taking a cheap shot at the guy who'd stepped into his place.

He put a hand on Grant's shoulder, squeezing the way he'd always done when Grant had done something particularly noteworthy. "Always liked you a lot better than any of the yahoos she dated after you went off to the service."

Like there'd been a lot of them. He sucked in a deep breath. It was hard enough to accept Ham putting his hands on Katie, much less a lot of other yahoos.

"I need to check around about this black SUV and maybe go on out to Ham's daddy's place and ask some questions. Understand there was a barbecue there yesterday afternoon and evening. Can you stay here with Katie until I can get a deputy outside her door?" He tilted his head back toward Katie's room.

John nodded. "You be careful though,

Grant. When people start running cars off the sides of roads, it could be dangerous for anyone trying to unearth the truth."

"I know." Grant nodded. "That's why they give us lawmen guns."

John harrumphed. "Yeah, they provide you with good life insurance for a reason, too. 'Cause that star don't make you bulletproof. And sometimes the bad guy gets the drop on the good guy. Why don't you take some backup if you go out there?"

CHAPTER SIX

Grant stood at the accident scene, watching the investigators do their thing. They'd been making measurements and taking photos, their faces grim with the look lawmen got when they thought some perp needed pounding into the ground.

"Ain't looking like an accident." His chief deputy, Luke Bradenton's face was the grimmest of all. He pointed along the path the smaller car had taken before it ran off the road. "No skid marks, nothing showing the bigger vehicle tried to stop. Almost like it intended to drive straight through her."

A chill gripped Grant's body, thinking of someone so callously taking Katie's life.

"Can't imagine who would do such a thing," Luke said. He looked at Grant. "Can you?"

Grant tilted his head and didn't answer. "Has anyone found the SUV yet, or any sign of it?"

Luke shook his head. "Kinda weird that Travis was coming down that road not too far behind you, and he never saw that SUV."

Luke's instincts were good. They were lucky to have him in the department, with all he'd seen during his time working on the Atlanta Police force.

Travis, another investigator, walked up, like he'd realized they were talking about him. A big, broad-shouldered local guy who'd helped his dad bring in a lot of hay, Travis was soaking in everything he could from Luke, their newest transport from the big city police department. Travis shadowed Luke even when Travis wasn't on duty.

Before Luke, Travis had shadowed Grant. Like he was determined to learn everything Grant knew. Grant liked that about him.

Despite the personal loss Travis had recently experienced, he came to work ready to work. As if he could right the wrongs done to his family by finding justice for others.

Grant liked that a lot.

Luke lifted an eyebrow at Travis, then looked back at Grant. "Chastity keyed it on the radio about the SUV, so Travis knew to look for it. But, he never saw it." Luke shook his head.

"What's that say to you, Travis?" Luke asked.

Travis waggled his head again. "The guy knows the back roads, got off that road where officers would be looking for him, back-roaded it around till he came out the other side of the county?"

"Who would do that, Luke?"

Luke raised an eyebrow. This was just an exercise since they both were thinking the same thing. "Somebody local. To know the roads that well. Especially at night."

"Somebody local ran Katie off the road, almost killing her and thus we need to find someone local, with a motive to kill Katie," Travis chimed in, in a matter-of-fact tone.

"A motive to kill our Katie?" Luke looked at Grant like that was the first hard question of the night. "Who'd do such a thing?"

"Don't know. Someone local," Grant answered. "So, guess we need to start listening to every bit of gossip out there."

"The diner tomorrow morning is a good place to start," Travis said. "Somebody can go in there for breakfast. Ya know when word gets out about the accident, people are gonna be talking. Not too much happens round here that somebody at the diner don't know something about it."

"Good thinking, Travis," Luke said with a wink. "See, that's why local guys on law enforcement is so important."

Grant half-smiled at Luke's praise of Travis. Travis turned to him with a wise-ass smile and feinted a punch like he was about to take Luke out. "Don't be patronizing me, dude."

Grant wanted to laugh at the brotherly

relationship that had started between the two investigators. Luke was only about a year older than Travis, but he'd assumed the big brother role cause of the extensive knowledge of policing he'd earned on the streets of Atlanta.

"Listen," Grant said a bit sharply. There was no time for the usual fun. Both Luke and Travis snapped to, as if they'd forgotten for a moment who the victim was.

"We're gonna need to keep an eye on Katie," he said. "And check car repair places from here to Atlanta."

"Atlanta?" Luke raised an eyebrow. "If they go all the way down there, could be hard to track. Isn't Hamilton Avery her fiancé?" Luke asked, with an arched eyebrow.

"I don't know. Let's see what they're saying at the diner tomorrow morning."

"Last I heard he was," Luke continued, ignoring Grant's smartass remark. He turned to look down the road. "Daddy Avery lives in that big old place off the other end of West Mountain Road, which this road comes off of." He looked Grant in the eye. "Almost like she could have been coming from there when this person started chasing her."

"There was a barbecue there, tonight." Grant rubbed his chin for a moment, then met Luke's gaze. "Why would any of the Averys have cause to hurt her?"

Luke turned down both sides of his mouth.

"That's the money question. Why would any of them want to hurt our Katie?"

Our Katie. How many times had he heard that phrase tonight?

Firefighters, ambulance drivers, nurses, doctors, law enforcement personnel. That theme seemed to run through the group.

Shouldn't be too hard to get people talking about who might have tried to kill *their Katie.*

Only thing was, Grant still thought of her as *his Katie.*

Always had.

Always would?

"Listen," Grant said to Luke. "Katie wasn't wearing her engagement ring at the hospital. Claims never to have been engaged to Hamilton Avery."

Luke raised an eyebrow. "A breakup so bad she doesn't even want to remember it?" He huffed in disgust. "There's our suspect. Why didn't you just say so, boss?"

"I don't know." Grant shook his head. "Guess 'cause I find it hard to believe Hamilton Avery would do that."

"Wouldn't be the first time a man goes off the deep end when a woman rejects him. Specially over a woman like Katie." Luke's eyes met his hard, with no disrespect meant toward Katie.

"Another thing y'all need to know. But I don't want it spread around." Grant lowered his voice so other investigating officers couldn't hear. "She doesn't remember that she and I broke up."

Luke's eyes rounded then he gave a low laugh.

Yeah, the gossip mill had definitely filled him in on Grant and Katie's past history.

Travis didn't need to be filled in. He'd certainly witnessed enough when Katie had shown up at football practice, since the cheerleaders had practiced close by.

Travis didn't meet Grant's gaze, looking somewhere off past his left shoulder. He'd been only two years behind Grant and Katie in school.

"What do you plan to do with that information?" Luke asked.

Grant narrowed his eyes, but Luke had built up immunity to Grant's hard stares. One of the things Grant liked best about him.

The implied question was: Did he plan to take up with Katie where they'd left off years ago?

"I plan to go up to ex-Governor Jefferson Avery's place and ask around about what happened this afternoon and early evening that might have to do with Katie ending up with no ring on her finger and almost dead."

"Want me to come with you, boss?" Luke's eyes turned dark and unreadable, but Grant had known and worked with him long enough to know he was worried. "Those rich people live by their own rules."

"No." Grant shook his head. "I want you to find me that black SUV and the SOB driver who almost killed Katie."

And be sure to get a BOLO out to Atlanta," he added. "Hamilton has a place down in the city for when they're in session up there under the gold dome. So put out a notice for body shops down there to be on the lookout for front end damage on SUVs."

"Sure thing." Luke leaned forward and tapped Grant on the chest. "You be careful. Daddy Avery takes his son's run for the U.S. Senate seat seriously. Thinks it will lead to a shot at the presidency."

Travis nodded. "Jefferson Avery's womanizing cost him his chance at the White House." His eyes narrowed into a hard squint. "I figure that man would do a lot to realize his dreams through his boy."

*****

Luke and Travis hadn't needed to tell Grant just how serious *The Governor*, as many still called him, would take any insinuations that his son was somehow involved in an attempt on Katie's life.

Rumors had always swirled about former Governor Jefferson Avery and women. The rumors and ensuing scandals had cost the governor a lot in the way of political currency. He wouldn't want the same gossip to damage his son's reputation.

As the candidate for the senate seat in Washington, D.C., any implications that

Hamilton Avery had anything to do with the crash that had almost killed his fiancée would send gossip and rumor flashing through the hills and mountains surrounding Hawk's Peak like a wildfire.

Phone calls, texts and posts on Facebook and Twitter would explode the rumors across the county.

There were quicker and more efficient ways to spread gossip these days than the old-fashioned party lines the old folks still liked to talk about, where anybody could pick up the phone and listen to their neighbors' conversations.

Grant drove up the long drive leading to the ex-governor's mansion. He hadn't been here more than a couple of times since he was a kid. And then, mostly on official business.

The trees had gotten out of control, arching over the drive, forming a tunnel through the dark woods. The governor was letting the trees have their way with his property.

He ought to get them cut back, brought into a semblance of order, like something a still-powerful former politician owned. Not like this drive that looked as if it would end at a poorly maintained trailer park or run down house.

As he circled into the driveway immediately in front of the house, everything looked different. Here, it looked like the governor's perfectly groomed wife had held sway, with manicured bushes and flowerbeds.

A large number of high-end cars and SUVs cluttered the circle driveway and the parking area to the side of the house.

Nearing midnight, the barbecue was apparently still going on. As he got out, he was immediately captured by the distinct aroma of wood smoke, sharp, acrid, just damned good smelling smoke that spoke of barbecued ribs and sizzling meat.

Laughter and conversation echoed from the rear of the house.

Grant had only walked a few steps before Jocko appeared. The barrel-chested man who'd worked security for the governor for nearly all of his political life. And now in his private life.

"Evening, sheriff." The big man smiled affably. "What brings you out?"

"Need to talk with the governor."

"Oh, he's entertaining tonight. Got some bigwigs here, supporters for his son's senate race." He nodded, like of course the sheriff would know all about that.

"Still need to talk to him for a few minutes," Grant said, keeping his voice polite and non-threatening." Don't want to disturb the party, though. So, maybe you can ask the governor to step out here for a minute."

Jocko's face darkened. Neither he nor the governor were used to being told what to do. They usually told others how it was going to be.

Grant owed a good deal to the governor for his support during his run for sheriff. A fact he was sure Jocko knew.

Politics forced you to mingle with everyone in the county, 'cause even once you'd been elected, you still had to get reelected next time.

Grant was everybody's bitch, as Luke liked to rib him.

So, Grant put a smile on his face as he did his job, whether the person he was talking to was getting arrested for drunk driving. Or was one of the most powerful men in the state of Georgia.

Jocko smiled back, doing the same professional role- playing. "I'm sure the governor wouldn't mind talking to you a minute in his den. Want to come in there while I fetch him?"

Grant shook his head. "Think I'll just wait here."

Again, the miniscule glint of irritation, before Jocko hid it with a smile and went back through the house. Jocko was used to encountering high-level officials and interacting with them in a polite manner.

Jocko drove the car, carried the gun. He was often the first line of defense for the governor. Or the last line in times of danger. Jocko had definitely saved the governor's life at least once, when an attacker had gone after the governor with a knife at a speaking engagement.

Jocko usually stayed pretty close to the governor when there were large groups around. Like tonight. Grant would have expected him to be out back, keeping an eye on the governor.

Someone else should have met Grant at the door, opened it and welcomed him in, then announced his presence to the governor.

Jocko had never met him in the driveway. Tonight, it was almost as if the big man had been on the lookout for him.

Minutes later, the governor opened the door with a wide smile. A pretty quick appearance if he'd been out back with guests.

"Grant, how you doing, son?" He walked out and clapped Grant on the shoulder, then took his hand for a hearty double-handed shake.

Hail fellow, well met, yes siree! The former governor always took up a lot of space and oxygen in any room.

"Good. And you?"

"I'm a little worried." The governor's forehead bunched and lines furrowed between his eyebrows. "Hamilton called and told me about Katherine. She was up here for the barbecue, then said she needed to get home early 'cause of a big work day tomorrow."

Jefferson Avery shook his head. "I can't believe it. Hamilton can't believe it. Who would have thought driving down the mountain she'd get attacked like that? Sounds like something that would happen in Atlanta, with all the road rage down there."

He blew out a burst of air. "That traffic down there makes people crazy, cars cutting you off. People shouldn't move up here if they don't want a slower pace. And if they're visiting, they should respect the way we do things around here."

"That's what you think happened? Road rage?" Grant studied his face for any miniscule signs that would reveal contradicting emotions.

"Sure, what else?" Jefferson Avery's face had the innocence that a born politician could muster in a heartbeat, used to telling each person what they wanted to hear, and making it sound like he actually meant it.

"Katie wasn't wearing her engagement ring after the crash," Grant continued on to an adjoining issue. "Can you shed any light on that?"

"Hamilton mentioned that." The governor nodded sagely. "I 'spect it got lost in the accident. If one of the EMTs or nurses didn't slide it off her finger while she was unconscious. That was a costly piece of jewelry, let me tell you."

It riled Grant that the powerful man picked on hardworking medics and nurses, immediately pointing a finger of suspicion at them. Toward people who were much less equipped than the governor to defend themselves.

"Did anything happen here at the barbecue that would lead you to believe a crime would be committed later against one of your guests?"

The governor arched an eyebrow at how Grant had connected Katie's accident to himself, so succinctly, the way a newspaper article might do later.

"Look, son." The governor edged toward Grant, his chest extending ever so slightly, in a manner that could be interpreted as a bit intimidating. He was a big man and now, he was standing as tall as possible, as if he were used to looking down at smaller people.

The governor and Grant's eyes were just about level, with Grant actually about an inch taller, which the governor seemed to notice, because he stepped back half a foot.

The governor ran his hand through his dark hair, still thick in his late sixties. His hazel eyes flashed with outrage.

"No one in my family, and no one visiting at my house, had anything to do with this accident."

Jefferson gestured disdainfully with one of his large hands. "Hamilton says Katherine can't even remember them being engaged. How can you be so sure what she says about the accident is true? She was drinking up here. My wife told her not to drive. I believe

Hamilton tried to take her keys. Maybe she threw the ring at him then."

He lifted his head, and shot Grant an arrogant glance. "Have you tested her for DUI? That's what a sheriff should be looking at? Not believing what some drunk woman says. Throwing blame all around at anyone but herself. She's got access to drugs at her veterinary clinic. Wouldn't be the first time a doctor uses her position to score drugs. The cabinet got broken into a couple of times and drugs were stolen, I hear, back when she worked there as a teen."

Grant's anger meter went from zero to a hundred, flying off the charts with his need to put his fist through the man's face for saying things like that about Katie.

Then, he remembered · the man was a practiced dissembler. A polite word for liar. That's what he did as a matter of course, throw dirt around at the other party. Get them so mad they lost sight of their original purpose.

"That's pretty good, governor. That's how the article might get printed up. Governor's guest, senate candidate's fiancée, wrecks car after a drunken party."

The governor's cheeks reddened.

"You do know, governor, that a host can be charged if one of his guests drives drunk after his party. There have been cases like that."

Oh yeah, he wouldn't be getting the

governor's endorsement for reelection or any campaign contributions.

That was okay. Things like this were the reason he'd always meant to end up back home as the sheriff, with the ability to look into things, investigate crimes regardless of the person's power or money.

Much different than when he'd been growing up.

The governor got his face back under control. He waved his hand in a manner meant to be placating, but it only irritated Grant more with its condescending quality.

"Now, son, I didn't mean to attack Katherine's character. Just got a little excited when someone started badmouthing my boy. You know how it is when someone's running for office. The other guy wants to take the smallest thing and start talking it up to ruin Hamilton's reputation."

He shook his head, as if remembering from personal experience.

Then, his eyes narrowed and he looked directly at Grant. "People took some pretty cheap shots at you, as I recall. I always stood up for you, for the one I believed in. Told people there was nothing in your past you needed to be ashamed of. Gotta stand up for your people."

A subtle reminder of just how much sway the governor held in the county? Just how much Grant stood to lose if he antagonized the former governor?

Grant's blood began pounding in his ears. This is how it had always been in this county. Since he was a child. *Leave it alone, you don't want to poke the bear.*

The front door opened and Hamilton's mother stepped out, carefully closing it behind her. Her face was perfectly composed, her expression as carefully put on as her makeup.

She was an attractive woman, with her hair tastefully colored a honey blonde, and her thin body clothed in expensive looking outfits. She'd been even more attractive when she'd been younger, a real looker. But her face always took on a chill when she looked at Grant, as if she were remembering some of his teenaged antics.

Nothing really criminal, just stuff like stealing the mascot statue from a rival school's football team and placing it upside down in the giant toilet used by the town's plumbing business as an advertisement out front.

Everyone had thought it had been funny but Hamilton said his mother thought it was tacky. As tacky as that toilet sitting in front of the business, she'd said.

"Mrs. Avery," he said with a polite nod.

"Grant," she answered, with a chilly smile, her lipsticked mouth barely turning up. A muscle ticked in her surgically tightened jaw. "Did you get those blankets and sheets the women's rotary club sent to the jail?"

"Yes, ma'am, we did and the prisoners thank you. We were severely under stocked."

"Saves the taxpayers a bit of money." She lifted her head in acknowledgement of her own contribution. Good deeds needed mentioning often and publicly according to some rulebook for politicians.

She looked from Grant to her husband. "What's going on, Jefferson?"

The governor looked down at her with a benign smile, placing his arm around her shoulders in a protective manner. "Katherine had a car accident."

"Oh, my lord." Mrs. Avery put her hand to her throat, where her pearls lay against her skin. Slowly, she began to finger them, as if counting down to her next facelift. "Where's Hamilton? He'll want to know right away."

Grant looked at the governor, who dropped his eyes, then said quietly to his wife, "He already knows. I just didn't want to upset you or cause drama while our guests were still here."

She looked at him, with a long unreadable stare, then she dropped her gaze to the ground before looking back at Grant. "Was she hurt?"

"She'll be fine, ma'am."

What had that look meant that she'd directed at her husband? What did she know?

"I'd like both of you to come to the sheriff's department tomorrow and give a statement, anything you can remember from the party, any guest who might have gotten irritated at Katie. Anything you can remember might be ..."

"Listen, this has nothing to do with us, our party, or our guests," Mrs. Avery cut him off. "And certainly not our son." Her mouth tightened on the last few words so that deep lines formed around her mouth.

"Now, now, Betsy. The boy's just doing his job. Nothing personal, is it Grant?"

Grant watched the furious stare Mrs. Avery directed at her husband. She might have lived in the same world of politics as her husband, but she sure hadn't learned to let things slide off her back the way they did off her husband's.

"That girl's bad driving has nothing to do with us. I'm going back to our guests." She turned on her heel and disappeared inside.

The governor laughed, slightly. "She takes things personal, always has. I'll be down to the office tomorrow and talk it all over with an investigator about anything I can remember that might shed light on Katherine's state of mind and how much she had to drink. Thanks for coming by, sheriff."

His benign, practiced politician face was firmly back in place.

Grant nodded. "And have Jocko come, too."

The governor tilted his head, and his eyes narrowed. Then, he nodded benignly. "All righty, then. Appreciate your hard work, Grant." His voice was loud and jovial, but a trace of gravel tinged his tone with a hardness that could cut you.

Grant drove away a moment later, with Jocko directing him as if he needed help getting around the cars parked along the driveway.

Jocko rode shotgun on his boss very closely.

CHAPTER SEVEN

Absent mindedly, Kate stirred the soup her aunt had brought to the hospital.

She and Grant had broken up?

She had gotten engaged to Hamilton Avery?

Each of those sentences seemed equally impossible.

She spooned up a bit of soup but stopped just before putting it into her mouth. "Aunt Mamie Lee."

"Hmmmm, sugar." Her aunt was trying to find the Bravo channel on the hospital's television. "These channel numbers are different from at my house."

"Yeah, I don't know if they have the same channels you've got at home," Kate said. "Might be a different service provider, too."

Aunt Mamie Lee clicked through a few more channels.

"When did Grant and I break up?"

Her aunt swiveled to face her.

"And *why* did we break up?" Kate added the most important part of the question.

Aunt Mamie Lee walked to the chair closest to the bed and sat down. She muted the television before placing the remote control on the side table. "That's what I always wanted to know, sugar. You were so adamant about never wanting to talk about it, that I couldn't get a word out of you."

Aunt Mamie Lee shook her head. "Nary a word."

"Really?" Kate tilted her head to get a better look at her aunt's face. "I just showed up broken up from him one day and you got nothing?"

Mamie Lee twisted her mouth downward. "That's what I said. All those after-school cookies I baked for you two and I got nothing. Nothing." She snapped her fingers smartly in the air, as if she'd picked up the habit from one of the *Housewives* shows.

"I think you're supposed to do it like this," Kate said, making the big Z in the air with snaps all the way down.

Mamie Lee laughed good-naturedly. You could always count on a jovial laugh from her.

"Assume I did the big Z, 'cause that's how I felt. Nothing. I got nothing."

"Well, you're no help." Kate looked out the window, musing on what would have caused such a rift in her and Grant's relationship.

"Apparently, I just did it again, dumped a beau for no apparent reason."

"You and Ham broke up?" Mamie Lee

asked. She didn't sound all that unhappy.

"You didn't gather that from the big kiss you walked in on between me and Grant?"

Mamie Lee made a little moue with her mouth. She was picking up all sorts of highfalutin ways.

"Who am I to judge?" Mamie Lee answered. "You ain't married till the preacher says you're married in my opinion." She narrowed her eyes at Kate. "So...you and Ham really broke up?"

Kate nodded. "I think so. Though I don't remember being engaged to him or breaking up with him any more than I remember breaking up with Grant."

"You're just the heartbreaker, I guess," Mamie Lee said, sounding like she only half meant it.

She looked directly at Kate, her expression taking on a new seriousness, all joking gone. "You broke up with Hamilton, and you were driving away from his daddy's house, then you ended up in a ditch after some car almost ran you over?" She shook her head, disgust dripping from her eyes.

"Don't take much cop work to figure that one out. That young Avery is just like his daddy, thinking he can get whatever he wants and nobody better say no to him."

Kate just stared at her aunt. She'd never heard anything like that come out of her mouth.

"Why would you say that?"

"Oh, honey, why wouldn't I? That family has so much money, and they're always finding some crooked way to get more, with ex-politicians of every ilk all up and down that family tree, bending the law to their way, so they can make their little deals."

She shook her head, repeatedly, then she turned away and picked up the remote control. "Now, honey if you get back together with Hamilton, I never said any of these horrible things."

She turned her head to glance over her shoulder at Kate. "*But* if you don't get back together with him, you'll know I'm not all that bothered by the change in circumstances."

Lord, after everything she'd heard today, her head hurt. She massaged her temples.

"Honey, you need me to get the nurse for you?"

Kate nodded. Did they have a pill for a completely screwed up life that made no sense?

Except that crazy race down that road had accomplished one good thing. The thought of that kiss from Grant warmed her entire body, chasing away the headache.

That was a new form of alternative medicine, homeopathic pain control, thinking about the first kiss in years she'd shared with her old love.

Only thing was, it felt like they'd never

been apart, that they fit together exactly as they always had.

A curling want urged her to find out if they still fit well in all the right places.

That kiss said they would, if not perhaps a little better, with a fierce heat, the type of fire that a grown man brought to a relationship.

If it had been years since they'd last been in bed together, they had a lot of making up for lost time to do.

*****

Grant checked in by phone with his deputy Jason who was stationed outside Katie's room.

"Yeah, the nurse said she's asleep," Jason said. "What you and me both should be doing." He gave a little laugh to show he was just joking.

"You got that right, Jason. And thanks for the overtime, I know you must be as tired as I am."

A quiet yawn agreed with him.

"I'm just gonna drop into the diner, get something to eat and see if anyone's talking about last night, if they have any theories, then I'll come relieve you, okay? Can I bring you something?"

"No, boss. But something weird happened last night."

A sinking feeling in Grant's stomach said maybe he shouldn't put anything into it just yet.

"Tell me," he urged Jason.

"The fire alarm went off here last night."

That hadn't happened at the hospital in like ... never. Or at least, not as long as he'd been sheriff.

"What happened when it went off?"

"Lots of scurrying here and there. Most of the nurses left the floor and went running off to the intensive care ward and the newborn ward, in case they needed to start evacuating people."

"How many were left on your floor?"

Jason gave a significant pause before he'd answered, "Only one."

"What was she doing?"

"She started going room to room, checking on patients. So, the hallway leading to Katie's room was empty for quite some time."

Grant sucked in a deep breath. "Would have left time for someone to get to Katie, yeah?"

"Exactly. And something else happened. The stairwell door, the one down at the end. Well, I heard it creak open, just a bit."

This was getting worse and worse.

"When I turned around to look who was coming in, thinking firefighters or something, nobody was there. And the way the door opened, was like somebody was peeking in, checking the hall out."

Grant's heart pulsed blood quickly into his body, readying him for a fight. But with whom?

"I started to run that way, chase the person

down the stairwell, but something told me not to leave Katie's door unguarded."

Just as he'd let the black SUV get away, something said if Jason had gone after a possible suspect that Katie might have ended up dead.

Things weren't looking good for the SUV incident being an accident.

"You did the right thing, Jason. I appreciate your good judgment."

"Thanks, boss."

The thing about Jason he liked best was that the guy really wanted to please. A word of praise went a long way with the guy. Tall and broad-shouldered, he was built to be a deputy. But his soft personality went over real well with the ladies.

His blond hair and blue eyes were also a big hit with women. And the big body did a lot to keep ticked off boyfriends from starting up with him.

Smart and likeable. A deadly combination. Grant had big hopes for the guy's future in the sheriff's department.

"Well, I'm gonna step into the diner," Grant said. "Then I'll be over there to relieve you. Sure you don't want anything?"

"I'm sure, boss."

They hung up and Grant went into the diner, picking up the local paper as he passed the machine. When he entered the diner, a flood of noise hit him.

Not your usual diner conversation, either, from the level of excitement on people's faces.

"Hey, sheriff," the waitress Ruby said. "Is it true that someone tried to run Katie off the road last night?"

"They did more than try," he raised an eyebrow, "they succeeded."

"Oh, Lord." She put the hand that wasn't holding a coffee pot to her cheek, her eyes wide. "What's this world coming to?"

She pointed at the paper in his hand. "Do you think it has to do with that article in the paper?"

She nodded with a knowing look in her eye. "Everyone is thinking so, the case tied up with a pretty little bow."

He sat at the counter and flipped the paper open.

"Coffee, sheriff?" Ruby turned for a coffee mug and placed it on the counter.

"Please." He could hardly wait for her to pour, ready to just grab the pot and drink straight from it. He needed caffeine. Maybe that would correct the damage a sleepless night had done to his brain.

The steamy liquid called out to him, but as Ruby was filling his cup, the headline caught his eye.

Deal Made With State. He read below about the deal to spare former Governor Avery's land from being condemned for the new road right of way. Magically, the state committee overseeing the transportation board had agreed to skirt the road around his land, at a high cost to local taxpayers, but with no apparent gain by anyone but the former governor.

How had that deal been made? Besides the fact that the governor's son was the head of the Transportation Committee?

The article said Hamilton had removed himself from the vote. Still. The guy had a lot of influence up there at the capitol.

Two retired guys who met at the diner every morning for coffee huddled one counter stool away from Grant, and he could hear their conversation from where he sat.

Sam and Hank had the paper laid out on the counter between them.

"Them Averys always get what they want one way or the other, don't they?" Sam, the older one said.

Had killing Katie been part of *the other?*

Like a punch to the stomach, it winded him, the idea that her life might have been so cheap to the them that they would easily sacrifice her if she somehow got in the way of what they wanted, or threatened to expose something unsavory about them.

Sam tapped the counter with one finger. "They might call him the former governor down at the capitol, but he's still the sitting governor in this county."

They both chuckled, not very concerned at

all.

"Hey, guys," Grant said in a conversational tone. "Sounds like you think the governor manipulated things to keep that road from going through his property."

"Manipulated?" Hank looked over at Sam with a wink. "That's a mighty polite word for it."

Both guys chuckled.

"Why would he be so concerned about that piece of property?" Grant asked. "It's not like he doesn't have all sorts of other land spread out all through the county."

Sam looked at Grant like he'd just moved to the county. "'Cause that piece of property is his own private hunting land. Don't nobody hunt out there but him."

He tilted his head. "Now, if you were to ask if you could hunt on that piece of land, he'd say, 'Suuurre,' drawing it out like it was no big deal. 'But, I tell you what,' he'd say. 'I got this piece of land that's much better. If you go on down to Hawk's Nest Road. That piece of land's just full of deer.'"

The man winked. "He hasn't said you can't hunt on that particular piece of land. But you get it. They say he has land set aside for his family and close friends to hunt on, and some other land for everyone else who asks." He tilted his head. "Then, there's that piece of property up there off of West Mountain Road. That's just for him."

Hank nodded, serious this time. "I was driving by one day and saw him up there through the trees, just walking the land, a rifle at his side. But I could tell he wasn't really hunting, just walking. I pulled over to holler at him, but he didn't even notice me."

He shook his head. "Never seen the like from him before. He walked a bit, then stopped and looked like he was talking to himself. Then, he walked a bit more, then stopped."

Hank raised an eyebrow. "I just drove off. Didn't want that man knowing I seen all that." He raised a shoulder. "Maybe he'd had a fight with his wife or his son. But he was definitely working something out with himself."

Sam shrugged. "I don't think he's been *right* for years."

"Emm," the other guy murmured noncommittally.

"You see how he keeps his property. Ever drive up that road leading to his house?" Sam raised his eyebrows. "The one that looks like something from a horror movie?"

Hank took a swallow of coffee.

"That used to be the most beautiful home in all North Georgia," Sam continued.

Hank put down his coffee cup, like he'd finally decided to say his piece. He half turned toward Grant with a serious glint in his eye, a granite hard expression. "Actually, you can trace his change back to when ..."

Ruby walked up, and Hank shut his mouth.

"Y'all getting the gossip straight?" she said with a laugh.

"Nah uh, Ruby, we're waiting to get that from you. Us men, we just talk facts."

Ruby laughed. But out of the corner of his eye, Grant saw Sam gesturing to Hank. Hank nodded, and reached for his wallet.

"Breakfast, sheriff?" Ruby pulled out her pad.

"Thanks, Ruby, two hard fried eggs, toast and some bacon." He smiled at her like it was just another normal day, but all he wanted was for her to leave so he could hear the rest of Hank's sentence.

As she walked off, Grant turned back to Hank.

Hank was pulling some money out of his wallet. "All I've got is a five. Can you cover me this time, Sam?"

"No sirree, Bob. I've just got a dollar and fifty cents for my coffee and tip."

"Then, I guess Ruby will be getting a big tip."

He tossed down the five, assiduously avoiding eye contact with Grant.

"What were you about to say, Hank?" Grant tilted his head toward the stooped old guy until finally, Hank turned his grizzled old face toward him.

"Nothing, boy." He leaned forward to pat

Grant's shoulder. And then, a sudden flash of this same old man at one of Grant's high school baseball games came into the forefront of his memory.

"You still have that old blue Mustang you used to drive back in the day?" Grant said.

Hank's eyes flashed panic for a moment. Damn, why did everyone think of him as the *sheriff* all the time. The same question before he was sheriff probably would have given up some funny story about a crash one night.

With maybe some details that could have gotten him in trouble if the law knew about it.

People sure held back on the gossip when you were the sheriff.

"No, I don't Grant." Hank patted Grant's shoulder again. "No, I don't."

Sam jerked his head toward the diner's front door.

Grant took two fingers worth of Hank's shirtsleeve in hand, just enough to detain him if he were willing to stay but not enough to hold him if he wanted to leave.

"What were you about to say, Hank, about Jefferson Avery not being *right* since ...?"

In Grant's peripheral vision, he could see Sam's face bunching into a tight knot. The guy already looked old, but when his face got all screwed up like that, it was hard to tell he wasn't over ninety yet.

Hank's gaze darted over to Sam, then back at Grant. His expression gentled, as he looked long and hard into Grant's eyes.

"Some things are so long ago, they don't bear talking about, Grant." He nodded like that was that, gently patted Grant again, then turned to follow his friend out the door.

Outside, Grant could see them arguing all the way to Sam's car. Hank had given up driving at his family's request last year, and Sam was his ride to the diner every morning.

Damn. What might he have learned if Ruby had been detained down the counter just another minute or two?

How long since the former governor had been *right?*

He looked back down at the newspaper article about Avery's land. Were there mineral rights up on that land that he was protecting? Did he know there was some valuable resource up there that he was waiting for just the right moment to tap into?

Was it something valuable? Or did former Governor Avery just not like people messing with him and decided to wield all the power he still held?

Grant pulled his phone out of his pocket and called his house to check for any messages there. No matter how many times he told people to call dispatch if they really needed him, some old folks still left messages at his house.

If he didn't check the machine regularly, somebody's cat might not get out of the tree.

Sure enough, there was a voice mail.

Katie's voice spit out from the digital machine, insistent, tense, said she needed to tell him something. "Very important," she'd said.

The date stamp on the recording said it was last night.

She said she had something very important to tell him. But before she'd been able to deliver the message, she'd ended up in a ditch, almost dead.

What had she planned to tell him?

Was it the reason she'd almost ended up dead?

A cold chill ran through him at the image of a world without Katie in it? That was a world not worth living in.

Even when he'd known she'd put another man's ring on her finger, she was still out there. He could see her, talk to her.

Even if she did like to wave that big diamond around in his face a lot.

"Ruby, I'll take those bacon, eggs and toast to go. Can you make it up into a sandwich so I can eat as I drive?"

"Sure thing, sheriff. That seems how you take your meals half the time, driving to some law business." She laughed as she conveyed the change in order to the cook.

This whole place would keep on rolling along if Katie died.

But not his world.

He needed to get to the hospital and talk to Katie, see if anything had come back to her.

Her life might depend on what she remembered.

Or on the fact that other people thought she'd forgotten anything she might have heard.

Before she'd thrown Ham's ring back in his face and fled into the night? Was that how the breakup had happened?

If there'd been an official breakup scene.

Damn. Just too much uncertainty.

That might lead to Katie's death.

CHAPTER EIGHT

Grant spoke with Jason near the elevator, asking about any other notable events on his watch at the hospital, then he told him to go on home and get some rest.

Grant headed toward Katie's room, stopping just outside at the sound of voices drifting through the open doorway.

Hamilton Avery's words were the first he made out.

"Katherine, I'm really sorry I ever took you up to my parent's house. I just had a feeling that wasn't going to go well."

A muffled response from Katie was hard to make out.

"Sorry, I meant Kate."

Grant wanted to laugh at the tone of Ham's voice.

Then, he continued, "Kate, a life with me doesn't have to mean a lot of involvement with my parents. We'd live up in Washington or down in Atlanta, just seeing them for holidays or a few election events."

"Ham, I don't know why you keep talking this way. If you keep it up, I'm gonna have to ask you to leave."

"Okay, okay, okay, Kate. Let's talk about something else. How are you feeling?" Ham's tone was benign, calm, not the tone of voice of a spurned fiancé who might go off the deep end.

To Grant's left, he saw Katie's dad coming up the hall, two sodas in his hands. He nodded and Grant turned and walked to meet him before he got within earshot of Ham or Katie.

"So, any theories?" Grant immediately launched into what they both wanted to talk about. John Taylor wasn't one for idle chitchat.

The older man shook his head. "I never liked that she was involved with that bunch."

Flat out to the point.

"That bunch?" Grant asked.

John shook his head. "Nothing good comes from that man."

"Hamilton?"

"No, his pompous gasbag of a father."

Grant laughed darkly. "Tell me what you really think."

"What I really think?" John's eyes narrowed and a pure, hard, mean look came across his face, such as Grant had never seen from the man.

He'd known him all his life and had never seen that expression. Not even when Grant had gotten a teenaged Katie back home pretty late one night.

"I despise Jefferson Avery and was terrified when Katie told me she was involved with his son. That man had so much power when he was governor, still does really. Seems to make all his problems go away." He shook his head violently. "No dirt ever sticks to him."

Dirt?

"What do you mean, John?"

John's face closed up, there was more he wanted to say, but he tightened his jaw, his mouth pursed closed for a long moment, as if afraid words would fly out that he couldn't get back.

Finally, he said, "Let's just say, I'm not sorry that she's forgotten she ever had anything to do with that fellow."

"That fellow? Our local representative down at the capitol? Possibly our next senator in Washington?"

John growled his disapproval.

"He's beginning to amass a lot of power, isn't he? Just like his daddy," Grant said.

John met his gaze for a long second, then just shook his head. "Just hope he doesn't misuse it like his daddy."

Grant stepped in closer, feeling that if he didn't get the info now, the moment would be gone, and he'd never ferret out just exactly what was bugging John Taylor about the man known still as *the Governor*.

"What do you mean misuse his power, John?"

John was done, though. His expression had dropped the pure hatefulness and returned to the old guy who'd always been just plain normal.

"Let's get on in there. I don't like leaving her alone with that man."

"Mamie Lee's not in there?" Grant looked over his shoulder.

"No, Katie said she wanted a moment alone with Hamilton. She probably thought she could set him straight if they could talk for a bit."

Grant pivoted and headed for the room, pushing the door open. Hamilton Avery stood at the foot of Katie's bed.

Ham raised an eyebrow at him. "Still doesn't remember ever wearing my ring," he said with an ironic tinge to his voice. "Nice to know I make such an impression on a girl."

Ham didn't add that, years later, she still thought she was Grant's girl.

But Grant could see the thought on Ham's face.

"I need to get back to my vet clinic. I've got animals to tend to," Katie said with a dry laugh. "I just hope I remember how to treat them."

She remembered she was a vet and that she had patients to go see. Remembered so much.

But anything to do with Ham? Nothing

about him since they'd been in high school and were just friends.

If Grant had his druthers, he'd kinda like it to stay that way.

If her life didn't maybe depend on her remembering. Or would she be safer not remembering, or at least convincing the whole Avery clan she didn't remember.

Was the threat of her ever remembering enough to make them want to kill the girl who everyone called *their Katie*? Or would they only strike once the threat was apparent?

A nurse came in and began puttering with Katie's IV.

"I've got to get out to Miss Sally's place first thing," Katie said. "Her little dog has liver problems and I'm trying to keep it hanging on for her."

They all exchanged looks. "Everyone knows how much store she puts by that dog," Katie's dad said with a nod. "But, she told me you were by there yesterday."

Perhaps Miss Sally could shed some light on Katie's state of mind yesterday.

"I need to go talk to her," Katie murmured, picking at the bed sheet. "See about her dog."

The nurse piped up, "You know you can't drive, don't you, darling?"

Katie nodded and looked at Grant.

"I can take you," Ham jumped in.

Katie looked down, as if trying to come up with some polite way of saying, *not a chance in hell.*

"I can drive her. Need to talk to her about last night, see if she can give any further description of the SUV," Grant said definitively. He tilted his head toward Katie. "We can do that on the ride out there."

A satisfied little smile crossed her lips.

"Two years out the window." Ham shook his head. "Courting and giving flowers. Dropping by the vet clinic to pick up my mom's dog's meds." He waved his hand. "Out the window."

The nurse laughed along with everyone else 'cause the way he'd said it was kinda funny. Not bitter, not sarcastic, just a guy saying he'd wasted a whole lot of being sensitive on a girl who couldn't remember, thus not retaining points for any of it.

Katie smiled at Ham, the first comfortable smile she'd give him since the accident. "You've always been funny, Ham."

For once, he didn't correct her. As if they'd gone back to high school when he'd never minded being called Ham, or even Hamster, always laughing along with the joke.

When you set your kid up in life for such abuse with a name like Hamilton, the kid better have a good sense of humor about it, or his life in school would really suck.

"Well, I guess I better go on over to the flower shop and set up regular deliveries of flowers to your place." Ham tilted his head toward Katie. "Let's see, I forget, what's your favorite flower, carnations?"

Katie laughed. "That'll do if that's all they have out at the Piggly Wiggly."

He turned toward the door and threw over his shoulder, "I don't think the Piggly Wiggly delivers or else they'd have my business for sure. Support your local suppliers."

He'd left them laughing. A good way for a dumped fiancé to go. Especially one who was a politician running for election to a higher office.

Suddenly, Grant wondered had Ham been as in love with Katie as Grant had imagined anybody would be, or had she just been the obvious local choice for a politician's wife? The pick of the litter?

A man who could joke about being dumped the next day didn't seem like a guy who'd try to run a woman off the road for rejecting him.

Unless the politician in him had learned to cover for any situation.

Back on the list of suspects.

"Miss Sally's your first stop on your veterinary home visits?" Grant looked at Katie, finding her eyes fixed on him.

Those clear blue eyes never failed to jolt him with the connection.

Yeah, he hadn't been so cool-headed when Katie had said they were through. Almost six years of being his girlfriend since they'd both gone through puberty, before that his crush and best friend all through elementary school and middle school.

He hadn't been as classy as Ham when she'd dumped his ass. Not a single funny comment had come to mind.

Nothing had seemed funny about the situation.

Nothing funny at all.

*****

Grant and Katie's dad sat in the hall, waiting for Mamie Lee to help Katie clean up and dress. They relaxed in a couple of armchairs that were close enough that they could see Katie's door.

"Hey, doc," John said. Grant looked up and nodded, standing as the doctor who'd been overseeing Katie's care approached.

"Sheriff, John," the doctor said. He was close to Katie's father age. Grey-haired, but healthy looking, like he took his own advice and worked out and ate right.

John also stood, like he wanted to get eye level with the doctor. "This thing is pretty weird with Katie," John said. "She forgot she was ever involved with Hamilton Avery, thinks she's still involved with the sheriff here."

"Yeah, they were a real cute couple back in high school." The doctor smiled at Grant. "Didn't she used to cheer for the football team when you were on it?"

"Yeah, good memory." Grant smiled. People still liked to bring up his high school glory days as the star player on the football team.

The doctor laughed. "Not really. My girl was on the Junior Varsity cheer team. Had to go to every game to see how the big girls did it."

"Katie remembers some things, yet others she almost seems to have blocked out," Grant turned the conversation back to Katie's amnesia.

"Dissociative amnesia." The doctor nodded, like he discussed amnesia every day. "Some people call it selective amnesia. Kind of like Post Traumatic Stress Disorder."

"PTSD?" Grant thought of Afghanistan. "There was a guy with a group that got hit by a roadside bomb."

"He forget it all?" The doctor looked at Grant with a knowing look.

"Almost all of it. But, he remembered there'd been a dog with them that he and another guy had befriended, a stray dog. Wanted to know if the dog was all right."

"Was he?" John asked.

"Yeah, actually his friend had taken the dog away, walked back with him to secure him so he wouldn't bark. The dog was fine." Grant winced. "But my buddy lost his leg."

John and the doctor both shook their heads. No one said anything for a moment.

"Later, he could remember some stuff, like the dog," Grant continued. "But he just blocked out the whole damn explosion, and the aftermath."

"Thank God," John barked out a harsh laugh. "Some things aren't meant to be experienced, or remembered."

The doctor gave John a funny look, and John shut up.

"What?" Grant looked back and forth between them.

The doctor lifted a shoulder and looked at John, who turned toward the window. Grant waited a moment, and finally John turned back to look at him.

"She may have experienced something like this before." His shoulders slumped and his expression sagged, adding ten years on him.

This was what he might look like as a very old man.

Grant looked at the doctor, whose mouth remained firmly compressed into a tight line.

"Patient confidentiality be damned," Grant said. "If it can save Katie's life, I need to know what's going on."

John looked at the doctor and nodded grimly.

"Katie has a tendency to *forget* painful things, painful experiences." The doctor waggled his hand. "That's why she can remember everything about her vet practice, maybe everything about friends and family that has nothing to do with something dramatically painful like the accident."

John cleared his throat. "It's best to not push her, Grant. Let things come back to her as she wants them to." His eyes welled up. "After her mama left, she became almost catatonic."

He looked at Grant and the doctor hard. "Best not to force memories to come up too fast. I tried that and it went bad real fast."

The doctor's eyes narrowed. "Sometimes, the memory loss is to protect the person from things they don't want to know." He shrugged. "Sometimes, it's simply brain trauma that needs to heal. We won't know for a while."

Just then, the door opened and Mamie Lee and Katie came out.

"What?" Katie said to the trio looking at her. She brushed at her hair, then adjusted her shirt.

*****

Their route to Miss Sally's would take them right along Mountain Ridge Road, and thus past the piece of land that had been mentioned on the front page of the paper.

Before they got there, Grant flipped the paper open and handed it to Katie.

"Does anything about this ring a bell?"

She picked it up, scanning the article. When she'd read it, she looked up at him.

"What, you think I heard something nefarious, maybe about money changing hands?"

He shrugged. "That's what they're saying at the diner."

"Oh, well, then it must be right." She chuckled. "Everyone knows that's where the best rumors start. If people want to pass on gossip that they're not really sure about, to test the theory and see if it flies, they just say 'Let me tell you what I heard at the diner.'"

Grant laughed out loud. "And usually there's some bit of truth, but it's gotten twisted around to make it better."

"Exactly," she agreed. "So many people passing through with little bits of information that usually add up to one crazy wrong rumor."

Suddenly, she sat up straight in the seat and looked ahead at the road.

"This is it, isn't it?" she said, fear tingeing her voice. Her face paled and she reached across for his hand.

*****

They were coming up on the crash site. She knew that much.

Kate began to feel like she was viewing the approaching landscape through a piece of thick glass. Everything looked so familiar yet so strange, as if her mind wanted to go back to the moments just before she'd found the SUV on her tail.

Then, her vision blurred into a dark fog of memories from last night. Touching Grant's hand felt like her only connection to the present. He squeezed tightly just before she spiraled into a full-blown memory of a black SUV crashing into her, sending her spiraling toward the ditch.

"Katie. Katie," a voice murmured vaguely

near her. She heard the voice as if from very far away.

Then, more louder came her name as she liked to be called now. "Kate."

That finally entered her consciousness and the memory of crashing vanished.

"What?" She snapped her head around to find Grant staring at her, his eyebrows furrowed together, his eyes narrowed.

"Are you there, Kate?"

She half laughed, with a sound that scraped at her throat. "Was I gone that long?"

They were sitting on the side of the road across from where she'd crashed. And she didn't even remember Grant pulling over.

"Wow," she said in disbelief.

"We're here." His eyes were reassuring, like she and Grant had never been apart. Like this was just a continuation of ten years ago.

Before everyone said they'd split up. How could that be true? Because she was sitting here beside him, their hands clasped just like old times.

She couldn't feel the distance she should feel if they'd gone on with their lives separately from each other.

Everything seemed crazy since she'd woken up in the hospital. People telling her things that couldn't be true.

But, one thing she did remember was that car coming after her like a demon from hell and the black night sucking her away from her body.

Then, finally, like a miracle sent to save her, Grant's voice pulling her back into the world. *Stop thinking about it. Stop thinking about it.* Every time she thought about last night and tried to remember more, her brain pulsed with pain.

She opened the car door and got out. Fresh air blew on her face, bracing, helping to lock her into the present, to push back the terrible fear of the crash. Wrapping her arms around herself, she looked up at the sky, so blue now, so black last night.

That much she could remember, lying in the ditch, looking up at the heavens, and wondering if those were her last moments on earth.

"He stopped and looked out the window at me." The memory came back to her, like the quick flash of a photograph.

CHAPTER NINE

"Who is he?" Grant was standing beside her, his voice low, as if hoping not to shake her out of the memory.

She felt hypnotized, as if someone had put her under in order to recall the event.

As if the words weren't coming from herself, she managed to force out, "He was large. A large white man. Big through the chest, like a body builder almost."

"What did he do?" Grant touched her arm lightly. That brought her immediately to the present. The physical contact was a mistake if he'd meant for her to stay in the memory.

She focused on Grant, his eyes, his mouth, the way he was looking at her right now.

"What happened to us for the last ten years, Grant?" She inhaled his scent, that smell she'd missed so much.

Wait, she remembered missing him. With a visceral punch that shook every cell of her body, with a pain that was like rolling over and over in the car last night.

"We were broken up," she said, searching for more memory, more parts of her past, more clues to what she'd missed for the last decade regarding herself and Grant.

Grant ran his hand along her shoulder, probably meaning to reassure her, because the touch was light, stroking the way you'd pet an animal.

But the effect was anything but calming, stirring the bottom of her feelings, bringing up anger that had settled. "Don't do that, touch me like that," she said. "You left me."

Resentment, abandonment, bleakness. All of that swirled up into her gut, into a solid mass of emotions from long ago.

Those feelings made even less sense than the accident.

Grant met her gaze and his eyes gentled. "I went away to serve my country, Kate."

He'd used the name Kate. She didn't know why that name felt so much better than Katie, or Katherine. Those names felt like they belonged to someone else.

As if they were the person before the accident, and before Grant had left her.

This new person, the one she was now, was Kate. She just needed the memories of those two other people in order to fully understand her life. To figure out what she wanted to take forward with her into Kate's life.

She looked at the slashing tire marks across the embankment, and walked to stand above the exact spot where she'd come to land. "If he'd really wanted me dead, he could have just shot me."

She waved down the slope. "I was lying there helpless, pinned in place. Why didn't he just shoot me if he wanted to shut me up?"

Grant shook his head. "I guess that's one of the million dollar questions."

She nodded. "Do you really see the governor trying to kill me even if I had seen money changing hands?"

It just didn't seem like Jefferson Avery. He was too good a liar, so well practiced from his time in office.

She waggled a finger in the air, arguing with herself more than making a point. "He could have just denied it, the way he's done ever since that rumor started about how he was gonna stop the road."

Grant tilted his head. "You remember that, him denying it?"

She looked at him, and realized she did. Her memory was spotty, with bits and pieces completely gone, while other parts were completely intact.

"There's no rhyme or reason to what I remember," she said.

"I remember the hoopla about the road controversy but I don't remember being at the governor's house before the crash. That's where I had been, though. Right?"

"Seems that way." He nodded. "You know

you called me last night, before the crash."

"No. I don't know that. What did I say?" A blank again. Almost like anything she didn't need to know to survive was there. But anything important or relevant to why someone would chase after her in a car and run her off the road?

Nothing.

He raised an eyebrow. "Just that you really needed to talk to me. Had something very important to tell me."

"I did?" She looked at him. "What time did I call you?"

"About nine."

"Nine?" She shook her head. "My Aunt Mamie Lee says I went out to the Avery's for a barbecue at about four. That's a long time between the start of the barbecue and a frantic call to you."

"Not frantic. Insistent," he corrected. "Not like somebody was chasing you yet."

"You still have the call?" At his nod, she nodded toward his phone. "Let me hear it."

He called his home phone and she listened to the message twice. "You're right. I don't sound terrified, like running from an SUV scared. What do you think I wanted to tell you?"

He raised a shoulder. "I assume it was something to do with law enforcement since you made it clear that it was official business. You wanted to be sure I didn't interpret it as a personal call." He half-laughed. "Not that you would have needed to make that known. Cause you'd already sent me that message loud and clear."

She smiled at his rueful expression. "Sorry. I just wish I knew what I wanted to tell you."

He nodded. "Wish I knew that, too."

She looked at the long gash in the embankment where her car had tore into the earth with a savage force. "Looks like it might be important."

He reached for her, pulling her underneath his arm, and she leaned into him, wrapping both arms around his waist, resting her head against his chest. It felt so good, so right, so safe. She wanted to stay there forever.

But another distracting thought tore her from that safe place and she stepped back to look Grant in the face. "My aunt said I was driving a BMW." She snorted slightly at the absurdity of the image.

"Really? Me driving a BMW? She said it was a present from Ham." She raised both hands as if trying to measure the weight of that absurdity. "Something doesn't fit here."

He nodded.

"Where's my SUV?" she continued. "I need that for work, not some stupid fancy pants car. And given to me by my *fiancé*, no less?" She pointed a thumb at her chest. "Does that sound like me?"

He shook his head. "That's what I said

when I saw you driving it around, with that big old ring hung out the window. Then I heard Ham gave it to you. Kinda fits the name Katherine."

"Katherine?" she said with a slight laugh. "Get over yourself. Katherine? Who did I think I was, a princess?"

His eyes darkened. "Might as well have been. That family's good as royalty 'round here."

A dart of pain shot through her, remembering just how poor Grant's upbringing had been, with an aunt supporting him as a kid, his dad's sister.

The military had probably been a good choice for him, a springboard into life. Even though she'd always thought he would be with her at the University of Georgia.

UGA had wanted him to play football for them, offered him a full scholarship.

Things could have been so different for them. But, apparently, he'd wanted to serve his country in the military. And, instinctually, she knew she'd broken up with him because he'd chosen that route rather than accompanying her to the University of Georgia.

That had been his choice, an honorable choice, and she should have respected it.

"I'm sorry," she whispered to him.

His head tilted as if he was listening but he didn't look at her. "For what?" he finally asked, his voice quiet like hers.

"For whatever I said to you, however I hurt you." She stepped closer, feeling the ancient pain rolling off him. "We were so important to each other since we were like what?" She waved her hands trying to remember the actual first time she had thought how much she liked him, how sweet he was, how much they got each other's sense of humor.

"Five, I think is when you first said I was your boyfriend," he said. As if the memory of them was indelibly imprinted on his psyche the same as it was on hers.

"How could we have broken up, Grant? It doesn't make any sense to me. Does it to you?"

He shook his head, then pulled her close, wrapping his arms around her waist, burying his nose into her hair. "No. Never did," he said, his breath blowing strands of hair all around her face, the air tickling across her neck.

Just like old times, just like always. For almost as long as she could remember, he'd been there, so close, the smell of him so familiar.

He held her very tightly for a long moment, then put her away from him, stepping back. "We need to get on over to Miss Sally's, see about that dog of hers. You know how she prizes that pooch."

He laughed as if it were a joke. But she sensed something more. The hurt she'd caused him?

Would he ever let her close again? Or had she killed what might have been between them?

CHAPTER TEN

"Oh lawd, it's good to see you two together again, just like old times," Miss Sally crowed as she shuffled onto her front porch, with three glasses of iced tea on a little tray.

Kate held Miss Sally's little mixed breed dog in her lap, as she swung on the front porch swing. Miss Sally set the tray down on a little table, then sat in the rocking chair that was always her favorite spot. She said the rocking motion gave her a head start on getting out of the chair.

"Me and Lucky?" Kate demurred, knowing Miss Sally had been talking about her and Grant.

Miss Sally arched an eyebrow then called out to where Grant stood by the front gate. "Grant, you don't need to be troubling yourself with that."

Grant bent over the gate's hardware with a screwdriver, tightening something. The gate had near 'bout fell off its hinges when they opened it.

"Oh, let me be useful, Miss Sally," Grant called back to the old lady. "I can go all day telling myself what a nice guy I am, fixing my neighbor's gate."

Miss Sally met Kate's eyes with a crinkled up smile that Kate felt all the way to her heart. The old lady was a cheerful sort, very welcoming to the vet who kept her dog ticking.

Though Kate had heard talk of her chasing strangers off her property with a shotgun. City folk, she'd said when Kate had asked her about it.

"Is Lucky taking that liver medicine like we talked about?" Kate felt along the little dog's ribs to see if he'd put on weight.

"Oh, lawd, yes. I puts that in a little pill pocket and he gobbles it down. Thinks it's a special treat."

"Is he eating?"

"He's pickier than the governor up there when I used to fetch and tote food back and forth from the kitchen for him." She raised an eyebrow and looked back up toward the governor's piece of land.

She still called him the governor though he'd been out of office for almost two decades.

You never stopped being the president, you never stopped being the governor. The power and connections of that position lasted a lifetime.

"You know what Lucky likes the best? A gas station hot dog." Miss Sally cackled like it was the biggest joke. "When he was well, I made him stick strictly to dog food. Now that he's on his 'last leg', he gets whatever he wants. A fast food hamburger? You got it, Lucky. A service station hot dog? Okie dokie."

She raised an eyebrow at Kate. "Is that cannibalism, a dog eating a hot dog?"

Kate groaned. "Bad one, Miss Sally."

Miss Sally cackled obligingly.

Then, she pointed at Kate's ring finger. "You made the right decision, missy. Getting back to your original fellow. The governor may have wanted you for his first son, but you're really better suited to his second son." She nodded her head knowingly.

Second son?

"What?" Kate stared at her.

Miss Sally looked at Kate quickly, her eyes focusing as if she'd only just realized what she'd said.

Kate's heart jumped. Something inside of her felt as if she'd just heard another truth she'd forgotten.

Miss Sally picked up a glass of ice tea and extended it to Kate as if nothing had just happened. "Tea? It's half sweet and half plain, the way you like it."

Kate met her gaze for a long moment, then took the glass, swallowed a huge gulp of it, then set it down on the table nearest her. "Thanks, Miss Sally."

"How you feeling, sugar?" Miss Sally looked

at her, concern crinkling her face. "Heared you took a big knock to the noggin. Are you ready to be running round checking on pets?"

As if she hadn't made a verbal blunder.

"I'm good," Kate answered.

Miss Sally went back to talking about her dog, what he would eat one day and not the next.

Kate looked at Grant out by the gate. Was it possible?

The history of his parents was so far buried in the past that Grant never talked about it. As a child, she'd only known they were gone and had thought very little about it. Grant had talked even less about them.

She leaned in close to Miss Sally, making eye contact, and speaking in a low voice, "What did you mean, his second son? You're not saying Grant is the governor's son, are you?"

Miss Sally's eyes sharpened to a razor edge then she looked away.

"That's what they said up at the diner, back in the day." She laughed quietly, as if she too didn't want to attract Grant's attention.

She shrugged. "You and me both know how that diner talk can go, either a bit of the truth, or just some wild speculation."

She looked up at Grant. "You never know which." She narrowed her eyes at Kate then. "Nobody talks about all that anymore, though. Best just let sleeping dogs lie."

Her expression sharpened as she looked at Kate again, almost as if she couldn't help it, as if the thoughts inside her cut deeply. "Even if you remember certain things, it's best to keep 'em to yourself till you figure out if it's useful information or not."

Was she talking about Kate? And what she might have learned last night before someone ran her off the road?

A chill shot through her, as if Miss Sally were giving her a warning. That Kate might have some information that Miss Sally thought might have incurred the wrath of whoever had tried to take her out.

The expression on the old lady's face said maybe it was something more than just some road-raging jerk on the road, who'd run once he'd realized just exactly what he'd caused to happen and how much trouble he might be in.

A few priors or a warrant out for somebody, and the threat of going to jail could tax a person's sense of humanity.

Their own sense of self-preservation could cause them to run, leaving a person alone to die in a cold, dark ditch.

Thank God, she'd had the phone nearby and had dialed 9-1-1 by instinct.

Or Miss Sally might be saying a few words over Kate's grave about what a nice lady she'd always been, checking on her little puppy like he was her own.

"You think my dog's looking better?" Miss

Sally tapped her own leg and Lucky jumped up and tried to leap the distance between the swing and Miss Sally's lap.

Kate laughed and caught him before he could take the jump that he definitely would not have been able to make. She handed him to Miss Sally. "I think he looks great. Just great. Those hot dogs are working the trick. You've done wonders with him."

"You, me and the Lord, all working together to take care of our Lucky dog. And I guess we should credit those service station hot dogs, too."

From a dirty little stray, Kate had picked up on the road one day, washed and presented to Miss Sally as a possible pet, to this little lord of the manor. He was one lucky dog. Half Pekingese, half mutt, every inch of him loved. The blond dog had fallen into the lap of luxury, the center of Miss Sally's world.

"You done good, Miss Sally."

Miss Sally smiled and held him up to her face in a cuddle.

Kate pulled out her cell phone and quickly snapped a shot as the little dog just grinned with happiness at the old lady who doted on him. "I'll print you out this photo of the two of you, Miss Sally."

"Thank you, girl."

Suddenly, a flashing image of her and Miss Sally sitting on the front porch crossed her brain. She was wearing the same clothes as she'd worn in the ambulance after her accident.

She'd held Lucky.

And her ring finger had been blank. No engagement ring anywhere.

Was there a logical explanation for that, such as she'd taken it off to wash her hands and inspect Lucky? Or had she already given it back to Ham?

If she'd given it back to him. Since Ham seemed determined to act like she hadn't.

She met Miss Sally's eyes. "I came by here after the barbecue at the governor's yesterday, didn't I?"

Miss Sally looked away. "Why yes, you did. Checked in on me and Lucky. And now, you're here again, so soon?"

Grant walked up then and she and Miss Sally both shut up, almost as if in collusion on a secret. Grant shot a look back and forth between them, then said, "I'm gonna go out back and check on your chicken pen, Miss Sally. See if it needs tightening up."

"You're a good boy, Grant. Always have been. That's why I voted for you for sheriff. Tea?" She held a glass toward him.

He grinned, reached for the glass and took a drink. "Well, let me go check that pen. Gotta do what I can to keep my voting constituency happy."

He looked back and forth between the two again. His eyes narrowed but he said nothing, just walked away.

"He's the one for you, Katie. Always has been. You two were destined for each other, since birth, really."

Since birth? That was stretching it a bit. Like they'd seen each other in the newborn ward and winked over the bassinets, *See ya in first grade.*

That was a real stretch for sure.

But something in Miss Sally's narrowed glance at her said she meant it, that they'd been born for each other.

Since birth? Really?

*****

Grant and Katie drove slowly back from Miss Sally's along the road Katie had driven last night. Grant had wanted to take another route, worrying about taxing Katie's brain too much.

Katie's father's warning came back to him.

"Do not push her," he'd said. "She will remember what she wants, when she wants."

And the expression on the doctor's face.

How much did the doctor know?

Had she talked in a state of semi-awareness, saying something to the old man?

Grant had listened to John and the doctor's advice and planned to act on it.

But, he hadn't planned on Katie. She wanted to know, needed to know. The same as she'd been since she was a little girl.

Nosey little Katie, her aunt had called her. Her dad would just laugh when he caught her going through stuff she had no business poking into.

Her dad had treasured her, for herself, but also as a lasting remembrance of her mother. From the photos that were sprinkled all over their house, she was an exact duplicate.

Once, Katie had told Grant a story about looking at a photo of herself at about five that she'd found in a drawer at her Aunt Mamie Lee's house.

"I don't remember this photo of me being taken," she'd said, walking into the living room where her aunt and her dad were watching a television program after one of her aunt's great dinners.

Her aunt had taken the photo, turned it around to show Katie's dad and laughed. "Because that's not you, it's your mama."

The two of them had looked so much alike that Katie couldn't even tell it wasn't her. Those were some powerful genes.

He'd heard from old folks about how beautiful Katie's mom had been, the most beautiful girl in the county to hear some old men speak.

They always shut up about it when any of the old women came near. Her beauty was so legendary, they still talked about it.

Many of the older folk would look at Katie from time to time and say, "Just like your beautiful mama. You look just like her." And they'd smile.

Katie would try to keep her contempt for that comment to herself. When they'd walk away, she'd consistently sniff in disgust, "I'm nothing like her. She ran away and left her family. I would never do that. Never."

Katie looked out the window as they drove past the accident site, saying nothing. But when they'd left it behind, she looked over at Grant.

"Grant," she said, her tone tentative. "What do you remember about your life before your parents left you?"

He looked at her quickly, making eye contact for a moment before breaking it off. What he'd remembered was one of the reasons he'd come back to Hawk's Peak.

One of the reasons he'd run for sheriff, though he was the youngest man to ever hold that position in the county's history.

His military service and his time in the Atlanta police department had been great credentials.

He never said that the military service had scarred him for life, that if anything they shouldn't want such a war- damaged person for sheriff.

He'd just let everyone believe he was the hero the military said he was. It wasn't that he wasn't a hero, just that he'd only done what anyone would have done to save their buddies.

He flinched, narrowing his eyes at the memories that threatened to flood back.

Forgetting stuff was a skill he'd had to practice, almost envying Katie's ability to just wipe from her mind stuff she didn't want to remember.

The ability to selectively forget? Any normal person would choose to forget the horrors he'd seen in Afghanistan.

But his earliest childhood memories were something he'd held onto, a loving dad, an equally loving and wonderful mother.

All of that had made it difficult to connect to the reality of how his parents had left him, not able to face up to the hardships, financial and otherwise, of raising a kid, according to his aunt.

How could the people who'd spent the first six years of his life being the best parents possible be the same two who'd walked away with no notice, not looking back?

It was inconceivable. Impossible to understand.

And he should know, because he'd spent a lifetime trying to understand it, to figure it out.

He'd made it his business to start accessing as much information as he could find in sheriff department cold files about the disappearance of his parents then the later discovery of his father's body down near the south side of the county.

Rumor had it his father had been living down in Gainesville, drinking heavily, then fallen in with the wrong sort who'd put a bullet in his brain over a bad debt, or for some drugs he hadn't paid for, or some such low-life doings.

That image had never matched up with the father he'd loved.

They said he'd gone off the deep end when his wife had left him one night, had gone looking for her, then just drizzled away his life.

"It's okay, Grant," Katie's voice infiltrated the distressing memories. She reached for his hand. "You don't have to talk about it. You don't have to think about it."

He flashed her a grateful look, before returning his eyes to the road as they neared a dangerous curve. "I do have to think about it, Katie. I mean Kate." He tilted his had in an apology.

"I've had to think about it all my life. Now's not any different." He didn't tell her that it was the driving force in his life, to not be like them, but also to achieve the type of power that would allow him to understand and to investigate his father's death and his mother's disappearance.

As a kid, he'd had no power, no ability to access information. Everyone had just told him he shouldn't dwell on it.

They might as well have just said, *Move on, son. Forget those losers. You're better off.*

The same fury swept through him as had

accompanied the lack of drive in the locals to solve his father's murder. A single bullet had sat in the evidence bag along with a thin case file that showed just how little effort had been used to solve the crime.

Fury, pure fury swept through him every time he looked at that evidence of how quickly the entire town of Hawk's Peak had forgotten his father. As if he'd never existed.

"It's okay, Grant." Katie gripped his hand tighter. The feel of her hand in his sent a surge of heat, want and long-repressed desire through him.

For so long, he'd wanted this, Katie beside him, so near, so willing, touching him like she'd done so naturally, so often, so long ago.

The urge to have her in his arms, her mouth against his, her body pressed against him, became overpowering, like a wall of water rushing down the Chattahoochee after a rainstorm, a flashflood of desire that he was powerless against. He'd been denied this for so long, and now she was willing.

Her memory was selective. She chose what she wanted to remember, and now, she remembered they'd been in love, in lust, in want, every word that described two people wanting each other so bad that they'd lived for moments alone.

It wasn't wrong. Not if she wanted it. Not if she chose to remember them as a couple.

He took a hard right onto a dirt road that

led into the Avery's property, and drove far enough that they weren't visible from the main road, then pulled the car over and put it in park. On this lonely, untraveled road, they might have been in the middle of the wilderness.

As if through magnetic attraction, as if he couldn't have stopped himself, he pulled Katie into his arms, dragging her to his mouth.

He needed the connection to life she'd always given him, the connection that had brought him back from Afghanistan alive, even though she'd sworn she wouldn't be waiting for him.

Savagely, he took her mouth, forcing her lips apart, delving into her warmth, her heat, as if looking for a safe place to escape gunfire.

She responded as fiercely, with such need, such desire that he almost took her right there. He unfastened his seatbelt.

Katie leaned across him and hit the latch to push his seat back, then slid onto his lap, both knees surrounding his hips, her center pushing against him, as if she couldn't get close enough to him.

As if she wanted him to take her right there.

He pushed into her, their clothes the only thing keeping them from actually making love. "God, I want you," he moaned into her mouth.

"You've got me," she whispered, her voice

husky with want. "Anytime, anywhere."

He pushed her back several inches, needing the space, or he would find himself unbuckling his pants and sliding up under that skirt she was wearing.

Instead, he slipped his hand underneath her skirt, then, into her panties, feeling her wet, ready. Sliding his fingers into her, he took her with them, kneading her, imitating what he wanted to do to her in a bed, alone, with the privacy they needed. He slid his thumb to her most sensitive spot just above his other fingers.

She moaned, and rode his hand, sliding up and down in time to his motions, leaning into his thumb, with her hair falling forward across her face, her eyes closed, a flush crawling from her neck to her cheeks, until finally, she shuddered and clenched around his hand.

He stilled, feeling her climax, relishing the intimacy he'd been denied for so long.

How long had it been since he'd actually felt her, all of her? A lifetime. That was how it had seemed.

There'd been other girls, other women, ones he might have even made a life with.

If memories of Katie hadn't eventually ruined any chances for him with other women. Cause women sensed that type of thing.

No matter how tenderly you treated them, no matter how many nights spent passionately in bed, eventually they could sense if they weren't *the one,* as they liked to say.

Katie was the one. Always had been, always would be.

He just needed her to remember everything, to remember why she'd decided *he* wasn't the one.

CHAPTER ELEVEN

Kate clung to Grant, relishing his hand there at her center, although she held his arm, telling him without words not to move, that she couldn't stand anymore.

Just having his fingers still inside of her was enough. Though she wanted more, much more. And soon.

She wanted a bed, plenty of time. And Grant. Inside of her for a really long time.

They deserved it. Though she didn't understand why they'd been apart, she knew that nonsense was over.

Nights and mornings-after lay ahead of them, trailing out toward infinity.

She giggled.

"What?" Grant looked up at her, his hand still so intimately placed, against her naked skin. "What could possibly be so funny right now?"

He smiled sensually, with an erotic heat that said he hadn't just found the same release she'd experienced. The coverage of her skirt had leant a sense of minimal decency allowing her to experience him almost as if they'd been making love.

She pulled his hand away, then pushed her body against him, so hard and ready underneath his pants.

"Don't," he groaned, with a husky laugh, stilling her with both hands on her hips. "Just don't."

"Cause you don't want it?"

His gaze met her eyes with a shimmering heat that denied that idea. "No, 'cause I'm the sheriff, this is a county vehicle, and we've already gone way too far. But, we got lucky and nobody's seen us yet."

He glanced back behind them, where the main road couldn't be seen. "Let's keep it that way."

With one last playful grind, she stopped resisting his hands as he pushed her back toward her side of the seat. Falling back, she adjusted her underwear.

"Now, I need a shower," she said, with a laugh. "And a cigarette, if I smoked."

His eyes were still simmering with desire. "Do you think it's wrong to use my blue lights to get to your house as quickly as possible?"

"Feels like an emergency to me." She laughed, relishing the easy humor they'd always shared. "Hit that siren, baby. Maybe stop by the convenience store for some condoms, too."

He narrowed his eyes at her as he readjusted his seat and fastened his seat belt.

A smart-ass retort seemed ready on his lips, but it was cut off by a sharp cracking sound that shattered the forest's silence. Bark flew from a tree near the car.

Instantly, Grant grabbed for her, pushing her down toward the floorboard. A second snapping noise and the windshield crackled on her side of the car, the web of cracks spreading out like a tarantula. A shriek tore from her lips as her heart accelerated straight to panic, racketing inside her chest.

Grant threw the car into reverse and barreled backward down the dirt road.

Another gunshot sounded through the woods, pinging off rocks to the side of the car. Grant pressed the accelerator, turning the steering wheel sharply, taking advantage of a wide spot in the road she'd noticed as they drove in, spinning the car around like a stunt driver, and speeding out of the area.

Kate peeked up, trying to see out the window, but Grant pushed her head down again. "Stay down," he growled, with an authority in his voice she'd never heard from him before.

His face was fierce, anger flaming off him like a forest fire sparked by lightning.

*****

Grant watched as Luke pored over his car inside a garage at the sheriff's department. Jason watched Luke's every move, taking down the notes as Luke called them out.

It was Jason's off day but still he'd come flying in when he'd heard the report on the scanner of shots fired at an officer.

"Looks like we can get some good ballistics off this one." Luke held a bullet between forceps. The slug had been pulled from the seat not far from where Katie had been sitting.

They'd already traced the trajectory between the windshield and the entry point on the car seat, deciding that the shooter had to be very high above the car, probably on the ridge just above where the car had been parked.

"What were y'all doing parked there?" Jason looked back at Grant and asked innocently, then his head snapped up, and his face reddened. "I didn't mean to use the word *parked*."

Grant shrugged casually. "I didn't think you did. We'd just driven past the accident site and pulled out of traffic, so I could question Katie before her memory could fade, thought it might have been jogged loose by viewing the scene."

All very innocent and logical. At least coming from your superior officer.

If you were as young as Jason.

Luke, who'd been to hell and back with Grant, kept his eyes on the bullet they'd pulled out of the car.

Making no eye contact whatsoever, with Jason or Grant.

"I think it was a rifle," Luke said. "To travel that distance with that type of accuracy, would almost have to be a rifle, wouldn't it?"

"Like they were aiming for her?" Grant looked at Luke.

Luke raised an eyebrow. "I didn't say that. But, if I were a betting man, that'd be the way I'd go. Cause why would they be shooting down the hill like that? Most any self-respecting deer would have probably been long gone with you guys pulling in there."

Except they had been parked there long enough that a deer might not have noticed them and had run across the road.

But anyone who was sighting on a deer would have to have also noticed the car.

"They could have been just trying to scare her," Jason said. "'Cause it seems like if they'd been on that hill, with a rifle, they could have finished her off."

Luke and Grant both turned as one to look at Jason. Luke smiled at Grant, who raised an eyebrow. "You got promise, Jason," Grant said. "I've always thought that."

A dark feeling rose up in his gut. "I hope you're right that whoever took that shot was only trying to put a scare in her."

"You don't think old man Avery might have done it, do ya?" Jason said. He hadn't called him governor. "I heard she broke up with his son. Maybe he was mad and just wanting to kick her butt a little?"

Luke blew out a burst of air. "Or Ham Avery, ticked off 'cause she dumped his ass." Luke made eye contact with Grant. His expression said that would be his bet, versus the older Avery.

"It's always the angry boyfriend or husband," Luke said the often repeated expression among cops.

"Even if you can't prove it," Jason added the ending of the adage.

"By damned," Grant growled. "If it's either of them taking shots at Katie, we'll damned sure prove it." Fire rose inside of Grant at the thought that anyone could threaten her life that way.

Then, he remembered all the years he'd known Ham. "Ham's been dumped before," he said to Luke, knowing the guy had the historical knowledge to understand Hamilton Avery much more than Jason ever could. No matter how many interviews the younger investigator conducted on the matter.

"That city girl came up here one summer. Dumped his ass flat. He was in love with her. He never responded anything like this before, even though he was a lot younger and more hot-tempered. Never used violence, intimidation or revenge all the years I've known him."

Luke raised a shoulder. "Yeah, but he's

never been dumped by someone like Katie before."

Grant knew the pain of that. Knew the desperation losing Katie could unleash in a guy's gut that would gnaw at his self control until all tether to civilized behavior could run for the hills.

If anyone could understand what Ham was going through, it was Grant.

Luke looked at him, and instantly, Grant knew he was thinking the exact same thing.

Grant grinned and an answering one spread across Luke's face.

"What?" Jason looked back and forth between them. "What's so funny?"

Luke turned to deposit the bullet into a small plastic bag and labeled it.

Grant picked up his phone and began to dial.

"What, you guys?" Jason said again. Neither of them responded. Some information you only got by living it.

Besides, Grant was much more intent on what had almost happened to Katie twice in two days.

Not another damned attempt would happen while he was on it. Road rage? Hunting accident? Two accidental events in two days?

Hardly.

A deputy was stationed outside of Katie's dad's house. Grant had dropped her off there and waited until a deputy arrived before he'd brought the car back to the garage for processing.

"We'll bag these up and send them down to the GBI lab for processing," Luke instructed Jason, who was still looking at them with a slightly miffed expression.

Jason might not have been around as long as Luke and Grant. There might be some information he'd have to pick up second hand. But, as he'd just shown, he was a quick study.

"See if the GBI will put a rush on the ballistics analysis," Grant said to Luke. "Tell them the shooting happened on the governor's property."

Luke winked and grinned at Grant. "That'll put a fire under them."

The GBI ballistics file, an incredible resource for connecting crimes all over Georgia.

He'd sent another bullet down there to be processed and catalogued.

The single bullet that had been found in his dad's body was already in the GBI database, sent there as soon as Grant had become sheriff.

Interestingly enough, nobody had done that before, opened up that old file and processed the bullet. Though many other cold cases had been sent down to Atlanta and solved since that database had become available, long after everyone had given up hope of ever finding a suspect.

The previous sheriff hadn't thought it was important enough to process his father's cold case bullet.

Or had he been told it wasn't important enough?

He picked up his cell phone and called Travis who'd gone to the scene of today's shooting. "Hey, Travis. You find any shell casings out there yet?"

The answer was the same as the other times he'd called. "No," Travis' deep voice growled through the phone. "Ya know, if somebody had been hunting up here, they wouldn't have been so careful as to cover their tracks and pick up the shell casings."

"Right," Grant answered. Injustice really got under Travis' skin. He lived to make things right, to bring the bad guy to justice. And until it happened, Travis was bound to be irritated.

Good. The more people ticked off about what had happened to Katie, the better.

"You know, sheriff, I think I can see right where the person was when he shot at y'all." Travis paused and took a deep breath. "I'm on top of the ridge, and it's almost like they braced themselves against this tree here, 'cause I swear I think I can see some powder traces on the tree, down low near the ground."

He waited a beat. "And there's indications in the dirt that someone had been there, it's scuffed up quite a bit, as if they'd kneeled to get a steadier aim."

"Really?" Grant absorbed the information. Just how close had he come to losing Katie? "How far away do you figure that tree to be from the skid marks leading out of the scene? Could you get an official measurement for me?"

"Sure thing, sheriff. You know what else?" Travis didn't wait to be asked what, but spit out, "This road is almost exactly where that proposed highway would have run if they'd put it in. Almost exactly."

Grant looked out the window, wondering if someone would have taken that shot because of the road. The committee had already voted to circumvent the governor's property, so that seemed unlikely.

"From up there, do you think the shooter would have known for sure that I was driving an official vehicle?"

Travis hemmed and hawed for a minute, then said, "I ain't so sure, sheriff. Your vehicle being unmarked. Do you think the shooter might have thought it was some nosey reporter type or some county official still trying to stir up trouble about it?"

If Grant were that good a psychic investigator, he'd just go ahead and get a warrant based on his feelings. Too bad it didn't work that way.

Cause usually his instincts turned out to be right.

"Evidence, Travis, that's all that counts."

Travis gave a half-hearted laugh. "I know that's right. I'll let you know if I come up with anything hard, sheriff. I'm taking some shots of this disturbed area and gonna see if we can pick up any gunpowder for processing."

"Thanks, Travis." He hung up and looked at Luke and Jason. "If y'all are done photographing and all, I think I'll just wait till tomorrow to get that windshield replaced. You think that will hold till then?"

"Yeah, boss," Jason said. "I can put some tape around it to make sure."

"Good."

He looked at that bullet entry point not too far from where Katie had been sitting. Accident or not, warning shot or not, he wasn't taking any chances.

Katie wasn't going to be unprotected until he was certain all of this wasn't one giant attempt toward putting her away so any secrets hidden inside her head could never resurface.

Run off the road, a gunshot so very close to killing her. A betting man's money would be that someone was trying to kill her.

Trying to shut her up? Or just a spurned fiancé? Cool on the outside, boiling fury on the inside?

Was that Hamilton Avery up on that ridge with a rifle, maybe just out hunting? If so, what he might have seen in that car just moments before the gunshot would have been enough to drive the most normal guy insane.

His just barely former fiancée sitting on an ex-boyfriend's lap.

That would be enough to drive a guy to take a few pot shots just meant to put the fear of God in her.

Hamilton or not, it was pretty clear *someone* had a grudge against Katie. Someone had hurt her. Perhaps wanted to kill her.

"I'll be damned if that's going to happen," he said vehemently, then realized he'd said it out loud, because both Luke and Jason turned to look at him.

The thing was, they both had the same conviction on their faces.

"I'm up for all the overtime you need," Luke said.

"Me, too, boss," Jason said, his face hard and angry.

Grant bit back the string of curses scratching to get out. Nobody was gonna kill his Katie.

His Katie? Did he have the right to think that way because of what had happened in his patrol car just before a bullet had shattered the moment?

Did Katie have true feelings for him? Or was he just a jerk, plain and simple, for letting that happen when so much inside of her head was still muddled?

Yeah. He was a jerk.

CHAPTER TWELVE

Kate sat in her dad's living room, rustling through a box that held all the oldest family photographs, the ones that had fallen out of old crumbling apart albums, and the ones that had never made it into photo albums.

Or had been taken out?

She was looking for one that had come to mind after her conversation with Miss Sally. She'd seen it so long ago, that she'd almost forgotten it.

But, today, clear as a ringing bell, it had popped into her mind when Miss Sally had made her slip of the tongue regarding Grant's paternity.

"There is it," she murmured to herself as she pulled out an old black and white photo. A woman with two little girls sitting on her knees.

She turned it toward the light, peering at the faded image. Much younger, much more light-hearted, the woman holding the little girls on her lap and laughing at them was

Miss Sally.

"Dad, who are these little girls?" She held the photo up for him to see.

He laughed. "Why, that one on the right is you."

"Right." She smiled at the old joke, their code for meaning it was really her mother.

The joke had started the time Kate had mistaken her mother's photograph for one of herself. After that, whenever she'd show her dad one of her mother, he'd say that same old joke.

"Miss Sally was so young," she said in awe, staring at the face before all the years had wrinkled and changed it. Underneath the tracks of time was the same face.

Her father's face filled with confusion. Kate realized she'd never recognized Miss Sally in any photos before, even though she'd been sprinkled throughout the family photos.

Kate had never asked who the woman was, always assuming she was an older relative before Kate's time.

"Why is Miss Sally holding Mama on her lap?"

Her father rustled his newspaper, turning the pages as if he were looking for something specific.

"Daddy?"

He glanced at her and said distractedly, "Miss Sally used to take care of your mama when she was little, before she went to work for the governor's family."

"Miss Sally babysat Mama?"

He nodded. "On a regular basis."

She peered at the other little girl on Miss Sally's lap. "Is this Aunt Mamie Lee?"

Her father flipped a page or two, and huffed as if she were disturbing his reading before looking back at her. "Nope. That's Grant's mama."

Grant's mama and hers held together on the same lap?

"Daddy." She waited for him to look at her. "Were my mama and Grant's mama close?"

"Katie," he said, exasperation sneaking out from around his carefully arranged expression. "You need to stop all this."

All this?

"All this what, Daddy?"

His eyes rounded, as if suddenly he realized he'd given more away in that second than all the simple answers could have done.

"All what, Daddy?" She stood up and walked closer, pulling a wing chair nearer to his recliner. "All what?"

He ran his tongue over his lips, then picked up the remote control. "I've started watching this program that Mamie Lee keeps talking about. She's gotten me watching it."

He laughed as if it was dumb of him, not his usual television fare, then he flipped the television on and to a reality show that was just starting.

The phone rang and Kate picked it up. "Katie," Aunt Mamie Lee's voice came through the lines. "Is your daddy there?"

"Speak of the Devil." She handed over the phone and watched her dad smile at something Mamie Lee said.

"Yes, I've got it on. I'm betting on the blonde housewife to come out ahead in this tiff. She's a sparkplug, that one."

Almost purposefully, her father kept his eyes on the screen, and his ear to the phone.

So that he didn't have to answer Kate's question?

She picked up the box of photos and headed toward the front porch, toward her favorite thinking spot at her dad's house, the place where she'd always gone when she was upset, the place where her mother had last rocked her on her lap, before she'd disappeared along with Grant's mama and daddy.

"Katie," her dad almost yelled, sitting forward in his recliner. "What are you doing?"

She turned to look at him, caught off guard by the level of alarm in his voice. "I'm going out front." Why was he acting like his own front porch might not be safe?

"You might oughta wait till Grant gets here. See what he's found out." He held the phone away from his ear, intent on her response.

"Why is everybody suddenly acting like the whole of Hawk's Peak is a CSI movie set?" She narrowed her eyes at him. "I've had it with this. I am not going to be held captive inside my childhood home. Besides, that deputy's right out there. No one would try anything now."

Her father's expression relaxed. "Sorry. Just kinda het up with all the goings on."

She half-smiled, turned and walked out to sit on the front porch swing. As the noise in her head stilled, she heard her father's voice through the windowpane. He'd never caught on to just how much she could hear through that window.

Her whole life, she'd picked up inside information about things like what she could expect for Christmas, what her daddy really thought about Grant, and how he hoped they'd get married one day.

All sorts of stuff that was surprising.

But nothing like what she heard next.

"She is asking all sorts of questions," her father said. "I don't know what she thinks she knows, but this thing is escalating."

He was quiet for a moment, then he said, "We could never prove anything then. Why should now be any different?"

Kate sat up straight. It was true, everyone was hiding things from her. Was the governor Grant's father? If so, Ham was Grant's brother.

Was that the big secret Ham or the governor wanted to keep quiet? That they were willing to kill over?

The governor surely didn't have any further political ambitions. Would something like that cloud his son's senate race so his future would be dimmed by the information?

A thirty-year-old dalliance? That hardly seemed worth killing over. Maybe the governor just didn't want any more scandal dirtying the Avery name.

How far was the governor willing to go to silence that little tidbit of information?

Her head began to hurt and she leaned forward, rubbing her temples with both hands. Man, she wished she could massage away everything that had happened the last two days.

A car motor alerted her to activity on the road. She sat up as Grant's car pulled in behind the deputy's vehicle.

No, she was wrong about wishing away the events of the last few days. They'd given her back Grant. Although she couldn't remember ever not having him.

And tonight, she wanted to have him at her house. To *have him* in every sense of the word.

The danger being aimed at her was reason enough to entice him to stay over with her. Though he was reluctant to take advantage of the situation, as he'd said.

She couldn't remember why they'd split up, why she'd been such a stupid idiot. But, she'd be damned if she let that other woman, that

Katie, the one who'd made so many decisions for her the last ten years to influence anything that happened in her life from now on.

Grant's eyes met hers just before he got out of his vehicle and Kate vowed one thing.

He might be here in a professional capacity.

But, tonight, Grant was sleeping in her bed. And there'd be nothing professional about the encounter at all.

Nothing.

CHAPTER THIRTEEN

Kate walked inside her dad's house and grabbed her purse, the box of old photos tucked safely underneath one arm.

"I'm gone, Daddy. Spending the night at my house. I'll be careful. Thanks for everything," she called back over her shoulder, just before she shut the door behind her.

Using the same techniques as she had as a kid. When she knew he'd disagree with something, or say no, she'd always just acted like he'd given permission, making him run after her, to say, *Heck no, get back in here.*

This time, he knew she was too old, could make her own decisions. Still, she didn't want to hurt his pride by directly going against his wishes. So, she just pretended they'd already discussed it and he'd agreed.

She breezed toward Grant's car. He was speaking to the deputy who'd guarded the house, then turned toward her.

"Thanks," she called to the deputy as he put the car in gear and drove away with a wave.

"Nice ride." Kate stopped to inspect Grant's windshield. She could look straight through the windshield to where she'd been sitting. "Almost like somebody was gunning for me."

She blew out a burst of air in disgust. "Nobody's got any guts anymore. Nobody walks up to you and tries to blow you away close up, so at least you know who's got it in for you. This anonymous grudge stuff is really low."

Grant looked at her over the hood of the car, then walked around to where she stood by the front passenger door. "Careful what you wish for, it hardly ever comes in the form you're thinking of."

"Devil's in the details," she agreed.

He placed his hand on the door, as if to stop her from getting in, and looked down at her in what he probably thought was some type of authoritative, sheriff manner.

It didn't work. She laughed dryly. "What's that look about, sheriff?"

"I thought you were going to stay at your dad's till this whole thing blows over."

She shifted the box of photos to free one arm, then brushed his hand off the door handle and opened the car door. "That's what you thought. I thought different."

She plopped down in the front seat, fastened the seatbelt, then looked straight ahead.

Grant looked at her through the window for

a long moment, then up at her dad who'd walked out on the front porch.

"That blow on the head didn't change her all that much," her dad yelled to Grant. "Still stubborn as all get out."

Grant nodded. "Yeah, why can't you order up the type of head trauma you want? Give me a little bit of personality change, maybe a bit more pliable."

John laughed.

"But, no." Grant shrugged. "We get selective amnesia, and the same old stubborn as a mule Katie."

She shot him a look.

"Kate, I mean." He looked back up at John. "Did she tell you she changed her name?"

John just smiled.

"She wants to be called Kate now."

"Changed her name, but not that stubbornness." John laughed. "Yeah, I'd say that amnesia thing is pretty selective."

Kate deadpanned her father a look through the open window on the driver's side. She'd heard every word, as they'd both meant her to. She gave Grant a *Can we go now* motion of the hand, waving him toward the front seat.

Grant shrugged at her dad, then walked around to get into the car. "Where are we going, Miss Bossy Pants?"

"My place if you don't mind," she said in an overly sweet voice, and gave him a fake smile.

"Blue light, or no blue light?" he said with a

grin, taking her right back to the moment when she'd sat on his lap, with him touching her so intimately.

Just before the gunshot had disrupted their activities.

As if he'd just remembered that too, the grin fell away. But he started the car and drove away with a two-fingered salute to her father.

"That's not happening anymore, by the way," he said. "Till we get this whole case solved and your memory back."

"What's not happening? You pleasuring me?"

He tried to hide his laugh. "Did you get that expression from Mrs. Green's English class or a romance novel?"

"Either way, it's very descriptive." She ran a finger down his forearm. "Since I was the only one really ending up enjoying myself."

He half turned, looking down at her, and his eyes were heated, the same look as when she'd straddled him earlier.

"There," she pointed up at him. "That's the expression I want to see more of."

He closed down his face, going all cop on her, hiding any attraction he might have just felt. Did the desire, the naked want he felt go away, or did he just hide it better?

She'd wait until they got to her place, and some privacy, before she investigated it.

"Yeah, like I said, *that*." He motioned

toward her body with a little circling finger indicating all of her. "*That's* not going to be happening any time soon."

"We'll see," she said.

He turned right, accelerating out of town, toward her place. In kind of a hurry, she noticed. In a big hurry to get to her house, where *nothing* was gonna happen.

"What'cha got there?" He motioned toward the box on her lap.

"This?" she said, opening the top flap of the box and looking inside. "This is a trip down memory lane, in a convenient boxed format."

"Okaaay," he said, then drove like a cop, sharp turns, accelerating quickly out of the stops.

And looking in the rearview mirror and the side mirrors often. Actually, he seemed on alert for danger from all angles.

"I've got my pistol and a rifle at my place, too, Grant. In case of snakes or coyotes, or anything. My dad made me take it when I moved out there on my granny's old farm."

Grant nodded. "That's good. Can't have too many guns in this situation."

How had her life gotten so messed up? One minute, she was a country vet, the next, someone was gunning for her. Could that be right?

She looked out the window, a wave of bleakness washing over her, threatening to pull her down in a deadly undertow of fear and the need for caution.

"It's okay." Grant reached across to take her hand, squeezing it. "Every deputy in the county and every cop in the city limits is keeping an eye out for anything that seems wrong. We're going to figure this out."

She half smiled at him, grateful for his attempt to comfort her. "Thanks, Grant."

Then, for the infinite time since she'd waken up after the car crash, she wondered what could have made her tell him they were through. It seemed so incredibly petty to tell a man to choose between her and what he saw as his duty to his country.

It's me or your country, babe. Your whole damn country. Choose.

"How could I have said that to you?" she blurted out. "What sort of a person does that?"

He just gave her a sideways look but said nothing.

"I mean," she continued. "You thought it was your duty, right, to join the military?"

He lifted a shoulder. "After 9/11, I was just waiting to be old enough to go. To defend my country from bad men who wanted to hurt people I loved."

She nodded. "What were my exact words to you about it?" Maybe it would jog her memory? "I am so damned tired of not remembering stuff." She leaned her head back against the headrest. If only it really would rest her head, because her brain felt like it was about to explode.

"What a headache, literally," she said. "Every time I start trying to remember something I've forgotten, my head starts to hurt." She looked at him, pleadingly, beseeching him the best anyone could with just a look.

"So, just help me out here," she said. "Tell me what sort of bitchy things I said."

He sucked in a deep breath. "The thing is, you weren't really bitchy about it. You weren't mean. Just almost hysterical, yelling, 'How can you leave me alone like this? I need you. How can you leave me alone?'"

He narrowed his eyes. "Over and over, that's all you would say. Wringing your hands, twisting your mouth up and yelling those words at me. Then, you ran out, got in your car. And wouldn't take my phone calls anymore."

He slashed his hand across the air, sharply. "Wouldn't take any messages I tried to send through your dad. Your dad told me any letters I sent you at his house, you burned, unread."

"Wow," she said. "I was dead serious. That just sounds so unlike us, Grant. We would fight sometimes, but it was never crazy drama like that."

He nodded emphatically. "I hear that. Back then would have been a good time for a name change, 'cause it was split personality city."

"Sounds like." She took his hand and squeezed it. "I remember always thinking we were going to go to UGA together, you with that football scholarship they said would be waiting for you, way back in your junior year."

She smiled sadly. "You were quite the football hero. Maybe I was just so selfish that I wanted what I wanted?" She released his hand.

He shook his head like it had been a mystery to him too, why she'd reacted so extremely.

Then, he tilted his head. "I should have been more sensitive to the fact that your mother left you as a little girl and there I was leaving you."

A firebrand stirred inside her, with the painful memory of lying in bed crying for her mommy. Tears filled her eyes with a quickness that surprised her. Grant reached across the seat for her hand.

"I was young," he said. "And kinda insensitive to your feelings. I just expected you to be proud of me. Never thought how much it probably tapped into your abandonment issues."

The fact that he could put his finger on such a deep psychic wound now touched her. That he understood her. Still, she owed him an apology.

"I'm sorry, Grant. I was wrong. Even if I don't remember anything about what happened, I was wrong."

He slid her a sideways look. "Thanks, Kate. I appreciate that." He clasped her hand tightly, the contact conveying more than his words how much the apology had meant to him. "I guess we were both young."

She smiled. "Yeah, we were young."

The sentiments they'd just exchanged hung there for a long, tender moment.

Then, Kate looked down at the box in her lap and then back at Grant. "Did you know we knew each other before first grade?"

He jerked his head quickly to look at her, his expression shocked, then quickly back to unreadable. "Yeah, we knew each other for as long as I can remember, Kate. When did you think we met each other?"

She shook her head, wishing she could get her memory all worked out. "In first grade. I remember looking over at you, thinking you were the cutest boy I'd ever seen."

He smiled. "You were right about one thing at least."

She smiled back at him, warming in her center again, the dismay and darkness she'd felt moments ago disappearing. Leaning across the seat dividers, she laid her head on his arm.

Grant drove silently for a few moments before glancing down to meet her gaze. "I really do need you to remember what happened the other night. But some parts of this memory loss thing are turning out to my advantage, it seems."

She nodded. "I gotta admit, I'm liking the part about not remembering we ever broke up. But it bothers me, 'cause why don't my memory parts match up. I never thought I'd known you before first grade. And, now, I can't remember being engaged to Ham, and can't remember breaking up with you. Seems like maybe I had memory problems even way back as a kid."

Grant didn't say anything for several miles, just drove in silence. Finally, he cleared his throat.

"You probably need to see some kind of specialist, Kate. Maybe you suffered some sort of brain trauma as a kid and this just exacerbated it. Maybe some brain guy can shuffle everything back into place, with some exercises or something."

He sighed heavily then, only half jokingly. "Just hope it doesn't reshuffle me back out of the loop."

She smiled, then leaned back against the seat, trying to match her memory up to the photos she'd seen that she ought to remember. People usually had full memory back to at least five, some memories back to three or four. Most of hers seemed to start at six.

Except for wonderful, loving memories of her mother. Her mother and father, kissing, laughing, hugging. Her mother putting her to bed, singing to her.

So many possible future memories had ended when her mother had left. The two images of her mother didn't match up, a loving mother and the cold woman who could leave her husband and child and never look back.

Maybe Kate was like her mother, split personalities that didn't match up. The woman who'd loved Grant and the one who'd broken his heart and apparently never looked back, were like two separate people.

Finally, they reached her place, sparing her any more painful soul searching.

They turned into the little dirt driveway in front of what had once been her granny's place, that she'd bought and made her own, insisting to her dad and Aunt Mamie Lee that she pay them for it, knowing that at least Aunt Mamie Lee could use the money.

"Your partner still picking up the slack for you at the clinic?" Grant said.

"Yeah, lucky things are kind of slow."

He nodded.

As they pulled in, she saw her SUV sitting in front of her house as if she'd never had the BMW.

"There's my little SUV," she crowed. "There's my car. Why was I using that impractical BMW if I had my SUV?"

He shook his head slightly as if having to explain things to a child that everybody else understood. "You use the SUV for work mostly. Then, I guess when you were going to see Ham, you'd take the BMW. Or that's how it seemed anyway."

He'd known a lot about her comings and goings for someone who'd moved on.

She shuffled in her purse for her keys to the house. What would she find when she went in, with all this new awareness, with all the things she'd noticed as if with a different person's memory the last twenty-four hours?

This would be the first time she'd been in her Granny's house with Grant in ten years, if she believed what they were telling her. She'd be alone with him, with all the powerful emotions he inspired in her, with this mad attraction as if they'd only just met.

If he was protecting her, then who was going to protect him from her?

Because she felt downright predatory toward him right now.

CHAPTER FOURTEEN

By the time Katie had warmed up dinner and set two plates of food on the table, Grant was sound asleep on her couch. He'd washed up and offered to help but she'd told him to kick back for a few minutes till supper was ready.

Snoring lightly, he looked like he might sleep there till morning. He'd even kicked off his shoes to get more comfortable. She went to check the front door and saw that he'd already locked up. The curtains were drawn too, so no one could look in on them.

She pulled a chair up under the front door, then went to set the alarm her father had gotten installed when she'd first moved in. No one was getting in this house with her unaware.

Grant looked so comfortable there on the couch, as if it had been sized just for him. She stopped for a second. Had she really done that, gotten an extra long couch thinking of him and his height?

So much she didn't remember. And why? Which of the things she couldn't remember was important?

She kept having a niggling little feeling like she was getting ready to remember something important, but the headaches would come and she'd back off searching inside her brain for the connection.

Pain was a powerful motivator.

She took Grant's plate to the kitchen and wrapped it with plastic wrap and put it in the refrigerator.

From the looks of him, he might sleep all night. A sick little feeling of frustration crept through her, at the thought that she might have to wait longer for what she craved so badly - him.

She walked into the living room with its dining table off to one side. Pulling out a chair, she sat down to a plate of meatloaf and mashed potatoes her Aunt Mamie Lee had left in the refrigerator.

So many nights, she used to eat and do paperwork at this table as she watched television. Alone.

What sort of a life had that been?

How many nights had she told Ham she was busy just so she didn't have to have dinner with him? Suddenly, the memory of that had come back clearly, as if she'd never forgotten it.

Was that why she'd kept putting off setting

a wedding date? Because secretly, her unconscious mind knew she wasn't ever going to get married until it was Grant waiting at the end of the church aisle for her?

It almost seemed like she'd put her life on hold since she'd broken the connection with Grant. Because now, she could imagine so many nights sitting here, laughing and joking with Grant over dinners and breakfasts.

Had she gotten engaged to Ham because he was Grant's brother? If you could believe the scenario Miss Sally had put into her head. Had that been what had drawn her to Ham, the genetic similarity to Grant?

Both tall, that same dark hair. And damned if she hadn't begun to notice the similarities in their facial structure. Both with the same strong jaw line. At the hospital, it had just suddenly crystallized in her brain how much they looked alike.

Almost as if Miss Sally had discussed the matter with her yesterday afternoon, putting the idea in her brain.

Now, Grant was sleeping on her couch, looking so perfect there.

She owed two men a sincere apology. Grant had already gotten one, but deserved so much more of making it up to him. Which she was willing to start tonight, up in that bed, if he was willing. If he woke up.

Hamilton? He'd accepted her rejection, but as part of her amnesia.

The thought of the friend she'd had throughout her childhood being hurt by her was unbearable.

Tears began to cloud her vision, and she used her napkin to wipe at them.

Seems like Katie and Katherine had been real bitches. So, why had both of these men been willing to put up with her?

She took a bite of meatloaf. "Mmm," she hummed in appreciation. Nothing like her Aunt Mamie Lee's cooking. She took a bite of mashed potatoes and hummed in appreciation again. Equally delicious. The comfort foods of her childhood.

Her Aunt Mamie Lee often dropped over to put cooked food in her fridge. She always said, "Katie girl, you're gonna blow away if you don't eat something."

The only time Kate ate like this was when she ate her Aunt Mamie Lee's cooking. It seemed a good compromise to eat ultra healthy otherwise, 'cause she knew she couldn't resist her aunt's down home cooking. She'd steamed some broccoli tonight as well, a concession to healthy eating.

After the first initial onslaught of hunger was satisfied, she opened the box of photos she'd brought from her dad's house and began sorting the photos into separate piles.

For many of them, she had to peer at the faces of much younger versions of people she knew now as middle aged or old folks, in order to recognize them.

There was Ham, playing with her and Grant. Funny, she didn't remember that picture. Hadn't realized she'd known Grant before first grade. And apparently, she'd known Ham as well. Couldn't remember him before first grade.

There was Ham's mother. And Kate's mom. So pretty. So lively. Kate continued leafing through the box.

Then, she stopped dead at one photo, dropping her fork onto the table. It looked like a candid shot of them at a cookout.

With both hands, she turned the photograph toward the light, leaning closer and scrutinizing the image. A photo of her dad and her mom, arm-in-arm, looking as in love as they'd always looked.

There wasn't a photo of them that they weren't gazing at each other instead of the camera, as if they couldn't take their eyes off each other.

To the side of them was Ham's mother, laughing at the camera, with Ham's daddy, the governor, standing beside her, his arm around her like a good husband.

But it was the expression on his face and who he was looking at that were the shockers.

His eyes were fixed on Kate's mama, with an apparent longing that was so wrong that Kate couldn't believe someone hadn't ripped up the photo yet. It was documented adulterous longing.

Maybe no one had ever noticed it because everyone in town had looked at her mother that way, just not with such blatant indecency.

Her mama had been pretty, everyone said so. And it wasn't just because Katie saw her through the eyes of a daughter. The photos proved just how beautiful she was.

Shockingly beautiful.

And the way the governor had looked at her, showed the power her beauty had on him.

Katie set it at the bottom of one of the stacks of photos, as if she'd found pornography. The insight into the governor's private thoughts had felt so dirty. Like she'd seen something through a neighbor's open curtains that she'd try immediately to forget.

She sorted through the photos and noticed photos of Miss Sally with little Katie on her knee, sometimes Katie on one knee and Grant on the other.

Kate knew that was after her mother and Grant's parents had run off, when Aunt Mamie Lee and Miss Sally both helped her father out with childcare.

Miss Sally had become something of a second mother to both her and Grant. That was good for Grant, since his aunt, who was Grant's father's sister, hadn't had a well-defined mothering gene.

Still, Kate had to give her praise for

stepping up at all, to take on the care of a little motherless and fatherless boy.

Poor little Grant. The look on his face said it all. The happy little boy had turned into a sad child. Those sad images lasted until much later when he'd returned to something of himself.

Then, by high school, it was almost as if he'd never been abandoned in the first place. Football hero, loved by the entire town. He'd embraced the position of importance in the community that being an athlete had given him. Almost as if the whole town became his family.

A stray photo of Katie and Grant dressed up, going to the prom showed just how much in love they'd been. Something about the way they'd looked at each other reminded her of her parents in photos. Dressed up so nicely, happy, she and Grant had looked like the perfect all-American boy and girl.

If you didn't know about the being abandoned by their mothers, and in Grant's case his father as well. Then the uglier part about his father showing up on some country road with a bullet in his brain.

Yeah, if you didn't know about that, you could look at Grant and say he'd had a golden life.

The way he'd picked himself up by his bootstraps, making something of himself, was an American success story. A painful kick of guilt hit her at the thought that she'd punished him for serving his country, doing what his conscience demanded.

What a bitch, no matter how Grant tried to excuse her.

She set the last photo of the two of them on top of all the others and carried her plate to the sink, rinsed it off and set it in the dishwasher.

On her way upstairs, as she passed Grant, she was tempted to lie down beside him, or wake him and take him upstairs.

But the thought of the last ten years ate at her, until she just turned off the living room light and went upstairs.

*****

"No! No! No!" Screams sent shockwaves through the darkness.

Grant sat straight up, instantly alert, though for a second, he couldn't place where he was. Then, it hit him. He was in Katie's living room and she was upstairs, screaming.

He pulled his pistol and bolted up the stairs, only stopping to look quickly around the corner before he entered her bedroom.

The hall light gave enough light for him to see that Katie seemed to be alone.

She was sitting up in bed, yelling "No," over and over. Her eyes were open but with a strange glazed look that told him she was still asleep.

He sidestepped into the room, checking it, the closet and the bathroom for intruders just in case.

Then, he set his gun down on the dresser and approached her slowly, speaking in a comforting tone. "It's me, Katie. It's Grant. Wake up, sweetie."

Slowly, a sense of time and place came back into her eyes. She looked at him, making eye contact.

"What's going on?" she asked as if he'd been the one yelling in his sleep.

He gave a low half laugh. "You were having a nightmare."

He sat on the side of the bed and stroked her arm, hoping to help bring her back to reality. He'd talked down other crime and accident victims from the shock.

But, none of those people had been Katie. None of them had shared the kinetic attraction that had always existed between them, like an explosion of tectonic plates coming together, with an earthquake of physical and emotional impact that he'd never found with any other woman.

Slowly, her skin warmed beneath his touch, and as if their flesh melded, he couldn't take his hand away from her shoulder. She turned into it, dipping her head so that his hand so naturally moved to her face.

"Hmm," she murmured, then lifted her face to his, her lips only inches from his mouth.

She looked into his eyes, fully awake now, but with memories washing through them.

Memories of them so long ago.

Thoughts of what could be again?

Just admit it, damn it, he thought. This was his fantasy of coming home to Hawk's Peak, this moment.

Would it hurt so badly, to take what she was offering, to take what he wanted so fiercely? She was remembering more and more, all the time.

When would it be acceptable to step into the passion that washed over them every time they were together, that raged beneath both their skins like a fever?

"Stop thinking," she ordered, her voice husky, her eyes clouded with passion. "Just kiss me. Kiss me, Kate." She laughed at her own little joke.

And he smiled back at her. This sure seemed like the same woman, the woman he'd left for the army. Just before the screaming hysteria had started, he corrected himself.

He drew back at the reminder of why he couldn't move into the passion, but she snaked her hand around the nape of his neck and pulled him in. "Stop thinking. This is me, this is what I want, am offering. If you want it too, then just take it, take me."

Her eyes flashed with passion and want, their heat melting any resistance remaining inside him and he pulled her fiercely to his mouth, kissing away all of the last ten years, all of the loneliness, all of the repressed want for her, the bottled up desire.

"Yes, baby," she said underneath his mouth, as he rolled her over onto her back, and slid into place between her legs, the thin nightgown and his jeans were all that was keeping them apart.

He pulled aside the straps of her cotton nightgown, exposing one breast, that beautiful mound of creaminess that had taunted him in memories.

He lowered his mouth to it, taking the tip in, mouthing it slowly, urged on by her moans, running his hand over the soft skin, feeling what he'd missed so much.

He slid his other hand underneath her nightgown, underneath the top rim of her panties, and straight into her slick center.

"Oh, Grant," she cried out as his hand slid across her, two fingers stroking her. She arched up, her back pushing her breast closer into him and he sucked harder, began to stroke harder with his hand.

This was what he'd missed more even than his own release, being able to see her like this, being able to bring her to this point of ecstasy, sharing this intimate passion.

She was ready to explode, pressing into his hand, driving him on with her moans, until finally, she shuddered, clutching at his shoulders, pushing her pelvis against his hand, wrapping her legs around his hips as if he were making love to her. Her mouth molded to his, her tongue snaking into his mouth, as if she couldn't get close enough to him.

Finally, she fell back, grabbing his hand to still it.

"This is getting to be a habit with us," she laughed weakly.

He looked down at her, her breast naked to him, her nightgown pushed up so that he could see his hand there in her center, see that lush area that had beckoned to him in his dreams.

It was a lie to say he'd missed giving her that ecstasy more than he'd wanted to be inside her, because now, that was all he could think about, all he wanted.

As if nothing existed in the world but being between those legs and pushing into her.

She looked at him from beneath her eyelashes, and laughed softly, huskily, a sexual laugh that beckoned to him. She reached for the top button of his jeans and slowly, naughtily, unbuttoned it, then unzipped his jeans.

She flashed him a wanton smile, a seductress' smile, that couldn't have been more promising, more teasing.

Pushing him over onto his back, she took his jeans and pulled them down his hips and then down his legs as he helped kick them off.

Then, she began kissing her way back up his legs, her hands and mouth trailing fire along his skin.

God, she wasn't gonna do that. He didn't know how long he could last if she did that.

Her eyes were hooded with desire, as if she wanted this as much as him.

Slowly her mouth proceeded, teasing him with want, the desire growing into a hungry frenzy in his belly. His hands itched to bring that mouth to him, to have those velvet lips encase him.

Finally, she reached his oh-so-ready *guy part* as she'd called it when they were young. A slight grin crossed her lips as if she too remembered her younger, innocent language. Though it had been a reference she'd kept up even when they'd progressed past the point of all embarrassment with each other.

Then, as if other memories of long ago lovemaking pushed out the humor, her eyes became clouded with passion, and she took him between her hands, slowly lowering her mouth.

Until he couldn't think of anything but that mouth.

Her hands and mouth became all that existed in the world.

Slowly, excruciatingly, she obliterated the world.

Just her and that mouth.

CHAPTER FIFTEEN

Katie filled her travel mug with coffee, grabbed her purse, then dropped a key and a piece of paper on the table in front of Grant where he sat drinking his coffee.

"Lock up when you leave, will you? That's the code for the alarm. Just hit *away*, these numbers, then *away* again, and get out the door within two minutes." She laughed lightly, attempting for nonchalant about this whole leaving bit.

"If you do take too long leaving, the alarm company will call me and I'll tell them it's okay."

He stood up, following her toward the front door. "Where are you going, Kate."

She wasn't up for a confrontation but she wasn't going to lie either. "My doctor said I just needed to wait twenty-four hours before I could drive."

"Yeah, but your sheriff thinks you ought to wait till we figure out what's been going on with this whole shooting, and running you off the road business before you start driving willy nilly through the county."

"How 'bout if I just cut out the willy nilly part?"

He arched an eyebrow and lifted his head. "What's up, Kate?"

She met his gaze and decided to just tell him. "Ham called. He wants to see me."

"What? And you're meeting him? Where?"

"Yes, I am." She nodded determinedly. "At the little picnic spot, in that turnout a couple of miles before you drive into town."

"No." He shook his head like he had the final decision. This sheriff job had certainly firmed up his sometimes- authoritative streak.

"Look, Grant." She laid a hand on his arm. "Ham is not going to hurt me. You know him."

He took her shirtfront by two fingers, shaking her lightly, in no way threatening but just to make a point. "How many crimes have I covered where the woman has said, 'It's only so and so, they wouldn't hurt me'? But, you don't hear it from them, you hear it from their friends and relatives *after* the woman's dead."

He shook his head again. "No."

She took a deep breath, determined not to lose her cool with him. "You're the sheriff, Grant, I get it. But I still have free will."

He just kept shaking his head, over and over. "Kate."

"Grant, I owe him this. Hamilton Avery is a decent guy, always has been."

"People get crazy at certain moments of high emotion, Kate. Someone ran you off the road, someone took a shot at you, up near Ham's daddy's property by the way, where Ham goes a lot."

He picked up her hand, holding the ring finger in front of her face. "No ring, Kate. Those three things add up to a suspect or person of interest, no matter what I can prove. I don't care how long we've known Ham, I'll throw his ass in jail just as quick as I would a stranger if he thinks he can murder someone."

He didn't say *murder her.* Almost as if he couldn't. As if it were too painful a thought for him.

She turned her hand, which he still held, turned it so that she grasped his hand. "I know, Grant. I know just how worried you are. But I owe Ham an apology. I can't live with myself until he gets it."

He pulled his hand away. "I'm following you." He tilted his head when she started to speak. "I won't let him see me. But I will be close, and I plan to have a rifle trained on his head the whole time. Got it? So, if he starts anything, just hit the ground, or go limp, so I'll have a clean shot."

She shook her head, laughing darkly, and walked out the door. "Got it," she threw over her shoulder.

Before she'd even gotten into her car, he was walking out the front door, putting the alarm code paper into his pocket, and locking the door after him.

The guy was so stubborn. Guess it was an asset as the sheriff - the boss man. But it would be a long life if he thought he could get away with that with her.

A long life, as if she just assumed they'd be married.

Maybe the guy didn't want that with her anymore. Sure, they'd slept together last night, with a passion and need that had singed itself into her memory for life.

Nothing could ever damage that perfect memory of them -two people locked in love.

Maybe that had just been the built-up heat between them, just some sense of resolution after all this time. A deep sigh pushed from her chest, to think last night might be the last time she made love with Grant.

She'd needed him so, and he'd showed the same desire, with a passion that couldn't be faked.

But, whatever it was, it didn't mean the guy wanted a lifetime with some crazy bitch who'd dumped him and walked away cold for so many years.

He'd always have to wonder in some part of him, if it wouldn't happen again. If the woman who'd turned him into a stranger wouldn't return.

God, she worried about that herself. It seemed there was someone hidden inside of her, who could suddenly take over and change her life on a dime.

It had happened with Grant. It had happened with Ham.

And she, Kate, sure as hell didn't understand any of it. But she would. If something had happened the other night to freak her out, to cause her to cancel her engagement with Ham, she'd find out.

She turned her SUV toward town, planning to resolve things with at least one guy today, the one who'd cared enough about her to put a ring on her finger.

*****

"Katherine, you have to end this right now."

Ham's first words weren't really what she'd expected. Instead, she'd expected maybe some entreaty to resume their relationship? Or was that just her ego talking?

But, he'd launched into a tirade about accusations against his family.

She turned to sit down on a picnic table's bench seat. A lively, little creek bubbled clear water along the edge of the picnic spot.

Where was Grant? Somewhere with a rifle pointed at Ham as he'd said he'd do?

Kate put Grant out of her mind, because there was no way she could focus on Ham right now, with Grant in her head, watching her and her former fiancé. Because thoughts of Grant only brought memories of their night together.

She took a deep breath, then, looked up at

Ham. She met his gaze steadily, looking for anything in him that would have sparked enough interest that she'd agreed to marry him.

"This is throwing suspicion on me and my family. My father said Grant was out there at his place, questioning him and my mother."

She looked straight into his eyes. "This is what you called me about?"

Enlightenment came over Ham's face and red crept up into his cheeks. "Well, I did want to discuss the engagement as well." He coughed nervously. "That was the main reason really, but I got distracted by my father's phone call about Grant's visit."

"Of course," she said dryly. His lack of concern about their broken engagement kinda hurt her pride. "Guess I'm a bit of a princess, thinking any man would be devastated to lose me." She flipped her hair back dramatically and sniffed in what was meant to be a comic fashion.

Ham looked at her for a long moment, then sat down on the bench across the table from her. He took a breath, looked at the little creek that ran through the picnic area, then back at her. "Look Katie, let's just be honest and not pretend we were anything different than we were, okay?"

What had they been?

He met her eyes seeing the unspoken question. "What we were, was an easy place to land for both of us. You were never gonna be over Grant." He shook his head emphatically. "Never. And I didn't really care. I wanted the perfect wife. Or at least, my dad wanted that for me."

He laughed sarcastically with a dismissive shake of his head. "I can't believe I ever thought that was a good idea. I guess I was just so ambitious that when he pointed out all the advantages of you for a wife, I went for it." A dry humorless smile twisted his mouth.

He met her eyes with pure honesty. "We would have been a marriage waiting for an affair to happen. On your part or mine. There were gonna be ugly headlines one day, probably at the most inopportune time." He drew a finger through the air as if writing headlines for a newspaper. "Senator named as baby daddy of . . ."

He stopped for a second before continuing, "Someone. It wouldn't have really mattered who, 'cause it was bound to happen, when two people start a marriage under false pretenses. The perfect wife and the undemanding husband?"

He narrowed his eyes and leaned across the table, taking her hand, holding it gently. He wasn't demanding, angry, vengeful. Because she was pretty sure she'd be able to feel it underneath whatever pretense he might have put on.

She'd always been great at that, perfecting

the ability to read people from an early age.

"Katie," he said, as if to get her full attention. "That's all I was to you." The fact that he'd reverted to calling her by his childhood name for her said a lot, instead of using the pretentious Katherine.

"Kate, I mean." He smiled. "It's okay that you weren't really in love with me, Kate. We were friends, always had been. So, it was okay that neither of us was looking to marry the great love of their life."

He nodded succinctly again. "But, that's not what I called you here to talk about." He took a deep, shaky breath. "I called you here to tell you that you need to stop this gossip about my parents. About them being involved in whatever happened to you in that crash and whatever happened yesterday afternoon as well."

He paused a moment, then looked up at her. "And, I need you to help put a stop to talk about that road deal."

She looked at him blankly. What was he talking about? She didn't give a damn about the road.

He tilted his head. "Do you really have amnesia, Kate?" He peered into her eyes, as if trying to peel back any pretenses she might have. Searching for the real her. "Come on, please be honest with me. We've known each since... forever."

Wait a minute, that photo of her, Grant

and Ham had sparked something.

"Ham, did we know each other before first grade?"

"What?" He sat back, letting go of her hand. "Why are you asking me that?"

She blew out a burst of air, searching for something not crazy sounding to say.

"I saw this photo of you, me and Grant, and your dad was behind us and we had to have been about four at the most." She fumbled in her purse, then pulled out the photo she'd stashed away last night and had brought with her, planning to show it to him.

She held it in front of Ham. "I don't remember that photo being taken. Do you?"

He looked down at the photograph, then at her for a long moment before answering, as if searching for the right words, as if talking to a small child about something difficult.

She was getting really sick of that look from people. The nurses at the hospital, the doctor, Grant the other day, and her dad.

Even Miss Sally had talked to her like a child she could deceive and distract.

"Do you remember that, Ham?" She begged him with her gaze - *please help me out here, and let me know that forgetting things doesn't mean I'm crazy.*

"No, I don't Kate."

He was lying.

And that made her feel crazier than if he'd said, *Of course I remember. I'm sure there are other photos I don't remember though.*

What all didn't she remember? She was beginning to feel like huge chunks of her life were missing.

That was normal, though, right? Lots of people didn't remember early childhood.

Not crazy, right?

Then, she noticed Ham studying her, trying to decide if she was lying. Trying to decide if she'd really had amnesia about whatever had happened before the crash.

What didn't he want her to remember?

He kept his expression purposefully bland, the perfect dissembling politician. He'd go a long way in that business, able to step up to microphones and spin the topic whatever way he wanted it to go, giving it just the right curve that wasn't really a lie, but emphasized the information he wanted out there.

"Okay, Katie." He tapped the table. "We're square, you and me, about this engagement business."

He smiled and tipped his head. "If anyone asks, I'm just gonna tell people we realized we were better off as friends." He nodded at her for confirmation.

"That's a nice way to say it." She smiled, for once glad of his politician's ability to turn a phrase. "I'll use that too."

The perfect politician.

She smiled into his eyes, her childhood friend, she and Grant's childhood friend. The one she remembered since first grade.

Even if she didn't remember so many of the toddler and kindergarten pictures she'd seen in the box last night.

Why didn't she remember those photos? Had she always been like this, losing portions of time? Was she a classic split personality?

Ham raised a shoulder and smiled at her with that smile he'd always had ready for her. "It's the truth, after all. We've always been friends."

He reached across the table and took her hand. "We always will be."

He sucked in another long shaky breath before adding, "That's why I say, Kate, that even if later on, you think you might know some things."

He tilted his head at her, making strong eye contact. "Maybe in little towns, some things are best left unsaid, undiscovered. In a town this small, some secrets are best left alone."

A cold chill crept through her body. Ham wasn't threatening her personally; he was just conveying a message as her life-long friend that certain things could be a threat to others.

And some people were willing to kill to keep their secrets hidden.

Because it was a long life living in a community as small as theirs.

Not meeting his eyes again, she stood. "Thanks, Ham. I'll see you around town."

Then, she walked to her car.

Quickly.

Because every nerve sensor in her body told her to be on alert. That she wasn't safe.

Ham might not be the source of the danger, but he'd definitely been the messenger that her actions, her memory, could cause her harm.

After the events of the last couple of days, the evidence was clear that the man wasn't lying about that at least. She got into her SUV, hitting the lock key immediately, hearing the secure latching of all the doors. She fired the car and put it into gear, wheeling quickly out of the small rest stop.

As she drove off, she glanced in her rearview mirror. And saw something even more disturbing than anything Ham had said. The man was walking and talking to himself in the small dirt parking lot, gesturing with his hands, as if arguing with someone.

Someone whose ideas and thoughts Ham found very disturbing.

Then, something clicked, something she'd half-noticed as she'd gotten in her car. Something about Ham's vehicle.

CHAPTER SIXTEEN

After Katie had left Ham, Grant drove past the picnic area where Ham and Katie had their rendezvous. He was ready with a casual wave for Ham if the guy looked his way.

The wave would say, *I wasn't just up the road with a gun trained on your head, ready to blow away a hometown boy, a guy I've known all my life.*

The wave would say, *Morning, dude, glad you're alive. Glad I didn't have to kill you just now.*

But, he never got a chance for the casual greeting because Ham didn't even notice Grant riding by. Ham walked and talked in the dusty parking area of the picnic grounds. He gestured wildly, as if talking to someone right in front of him.

Was he on a Bluetooth, having a conversation? Or was he crazy, talking to himself? So hard to tell these days with all the phone connection devices that couldn't be seen from a distance.

Used to be easy to tell the crazies from the *normal* people. Now, not so much.

Grant continued driving toward town, determined not to go back and confront Ham. He wouldn't go back.

Luke had agreed to interview Hamilton since Grant was way too conflicted about talking to the man who'd been with Katie for the last few years.

So, Grant drove toward town, determined not to go back and press Ham for answers, to look into his eyes and see for himself what lay there, what lies he might not be able to hide from Grant.

Luke could handle the interview. He was getting way good at ferreting out the truth from local people. Even people who considered themselves of a higher echelon than law enforcement, who condescended to give interviews. Like former governors and sitting state representatives.

Luke could handle it.

Still …

Ham was a politician, raised by a politician, possibly the most practiced form of liar around. Grant needed to look the man in the eye. And see if he had murder in his heart.

Grant braked, swung wide on the road, bumping onto the median, kicking up dust and gravel as he turned his vehicle back toward the rest stop.

As he approached the rest stop, he could see

another vehicle had pulled in. He strained to
see who it was.

Buford Gafney.

Of all people to happen up on Ham at this
spot, where they could talk without fear of
being recorded.

Buford and Ham's heads both jerked
around, looking in the direction of Grant's
approaching vehicle. Then, Buford bee-lined it
for his car, getting in and pulling out in the
other direction. Did he hope Grant hadn't
already identified him?

But, he had seen him. Buford Gafney, the
man who'd been mentioned in the front page
article on the supposedly corrupt
governmental decision to cost the taxpayers
loads of money – the main proponent of the
initiative to take the road around the
governor's property, rather than right through
it.

As Grant hit the parking area, dust still
swirled from Buford's departure. Grant drove
through it, like smoke rising up from the fires
of hell, obscuring his view for a second, until
Ham appeared out of it.

Like the devil himself, Ham stood, his
hands on his hips, his feet apart, as if bracing
for a fight. A fight Ham had no intention of
running from. From the tilt of his head, it
actually looked like he relished the
opportunity.

Grant braked and unbuckled his seat belt.

Ham headed toward his side of the car. Grant jumped out and to his feet, ready for whatever Ham was bringing.

"You," Ham growled. "You are the lowest form of man, snaking a man's girl away from him, when she can't even think straight."

The accusation stung, because it had truth behind it. He'd thought the same thing about himself when he'd gotten up this morning. And last night, after he and Katie had sex · several times in a row.

The man had a point.

Still, why had Ham lured Katie to this isolated spot? And why had Buford Gafney shown up immediately afterward? Was he supposed to have been there just a few moments earlier? When Katie had been there?

What would have happened if Buford had shown up when Katie was still there?

"Where's all that laissez faire attitude we saw at the hospital, Ham?" Grant met Ham's gaze as if his accusation hadn't hit home.

"Laissez faire?" Ham said, twisting the phrase as if they were curse words. "Where'd you learn that sort of talk? Overseas? When you dumped Katherine, leaving her here crying and alone?"

Damn, the guy was good at hitting at Grant's weak spots, his points of self injury, where he'd stabbed himself with guilt.

Grant leveled a smile at Ham, his eyes narrowing. "Leaving you the opening you wanted all through high school?"

Ham flinched. They both knew each other's weak spots. Ham had always hung around Katie, craving any contact, any crumbs of attention left over from her time with Grant.

Ham might act like he wasn't devastated by Katie's rejection, but Grant and Ham both knew different. The guy had slunk around after Katie ever since Grant could remember.

Grant had decked him once, when they were about thirteen.

"Well, you left her wide open, didn't you?" Ham continued picking at Grant's scab, the scab that covered a wound that would never heal. "Took her years to get over it, Grant. Now, you swoop in after the woman has a head injury, a concussion?"

Ham gestured wildly with his hands. "Hell, the woman shouldn't even be signing contracts right now. Much less, making other life-altering decisions."

Grant narrowed his eyes. "You mean, like naming names in corruption charges that could get you thrown in jail?"

Ham's face flushed blood red. He punched a finger at Grant's chest. "There is no truth to that at all."

Grant knocked Ham's hand away. "Yeah, then why are you meeting Buford Gafney out here in the middle of nowhere?"

Ham flinched.

"Not to mention, luring Katie out here."

Ham's eyes narrowed.

"Then, Buford shows up. An accomplice? What were you two planning?"

Ham began to breathe hard, quick pants like a cornered coyote. "What are you insinuating, Grant?"

"You're not a stupid man, Ham. There have been two attempts on her life, both out around your daddy's property, one time at least when we know you were out there. For your daddy's barbecue."

Ham's mouth began working as if he was just waiting for Grant to finish his set of accusations before he jumped back into the verbal fight.

"Buford's name has been linked to the corruption allegations that were on the front page of the newspaper. With some sideways insinuations that you might have been involved."

Grant pointed down the road toward town. "Everyone at the diner feels the same," he concluded with a touch of irony, because neither he nor Ham were in the mood for joking.

Spit flew out of Ham's mouth along with his denial. "That paper is setting itself up for a lawsuit for slander."

"Really, Ham? Cause last I heard, the truth is a pretty good defense." He stepped forward, into Ham's personal space. "Is that why Katie slapped you at the hospital, because on some level, she knows you tried to kill her? And she knows why?"

Ham's hands shot out before Grant could bring his up to stop him. Ham grabbed Grant's shirt, latching onto him, pushing him backwards.

Like a wild animal, Ham yelled words Grant couldn't make out. Ham screamed as if in pain, as if Grant had stabbed him with the truth.

"You, you, you snake," Ham hissed finally so that Grant could make out his words, his face inches from Grant's, spit flying in all directions.

The man had lost all control, no longer the rich boy from the mansion up on the hill. He was every bit as off the chain as any tobacco chewing, brawling, high school drop out fighting for his lost honor in a take no prisoners fight at the No Problem Saloon on the outskirts of town. The bar was a favorite of guys with a chip on their shoulder and a need for a Saturday night fight to get their aggression out.

Ham's maniacal reaction only confirmed what Grant had suspected.

Grant stepped backward and to the side, letting Ham's momentum continue to take him forward till Ham lost his balance, falling on the ground. He rolled, ending up flat on his back at Grant's feet.

Grant kept his eyes trained on him,

stepping back further, putting distance between them, his hand on his gun in case the guy came up shooting with some unseen weapon.

Ham scrabbled on the ground like a crab on its back, trying to regain his footing and his dignity, although that train had left town.

Finally, he flipped himself over and jumped to his feet.

Pointing a finger at Grant, Ham barreled toward his car, half stumbling across the dusty parking lot. "You better come with a warrant, buddy, next time you've got something to say to me. You know who my lawyer is."

"The highest priced liar this side of the mountains?" Grant called. "Yeah, I know that guy you and your daddy favor. Bring him with you down to the station 'cause Luke is just itching to get your statement."

"And you." Ham whirled and stabbed a finger at Grant, as spittle flew wildly from his mouth. "You need to keep it in your pants until Katie's gotten over her concussion. You making moves on her now is wrong on so many levels and you know it. Everybody in this town knows it." He jabbed at Grant one more time with the truth.

Grant merely narrowed his eyes and watched until Ham got into his car and spun gravel from his tires as he tore out of the small, dirt parking lot.

Yeah, that man had very little in common with the spurned lover they'd all witnessed at the hospital, the casual guy who'd demonstrated his gentility in front of Katie, her family and the hospital staff.

People his daddy's lawyer would call as defense witnesses in court, if called to testify in a case about what had happened with Katie.

This man Grant had met in the picnic parking lot, this crazed jealous man was at the core of the animal inside that civilized man seen at the hospital. Ham wanted to kill Grant for taking his place in Katie's bed.

Maybe he'd wanted to kill Katie when she'd told Ham he wasn't gonna be welcome in her bed anymore.

Or maybe on a more thinking level, he or Buford Gafney had wanted to silence the woman who could send them both to jail for a very long time.

What had Katie found out that night when she'd phoned him, leaving that message that she had information for him? Correction, she'd said she had information for the *sheriff.*

He got back in his car, and headed toward town, to talk in person with Luke, to let him know about this meeting between Buford Gafney, a county commissioner, and Hamilton Avery, their area's state representative.

As if on cue, Grant's phone rang, and he hit his Bluetooth, talking to the air, driving around in his car having a conversation seemingly with himself. Like everyone did nowadays.

"Sheriff," Grant answered, per his usual habit. Even a childhood friend got that greeting till they'd made it clear they were calling on personal business.

"It's Luke."

"Hey."

"Think we've found the dude who ran Katie off the road."

"Really!"

Was the perp friends with Buford Gafney, someone on his payroll?

"Found him down on a side road off the main road to Gainesville. Big black SUV with front right end damage. A white guy is sitting in the driver's seat." Luke paused for a moment. "He's got two bullets in his head."

"Dead!"

A dead guy in the SUV that had almost killed Katie?

"Emm," Luke made an unintelligible sound.

Grant knew exactly what it meant. Luke was thinking, dead men didn't talk. Couldn't roll over on anyone.

"Wonder who put those bullets in him?" Grant thought out loud.

Luke barked a laugh. "Knew those would be some of your first words."

"And why did he get two bullets in the head?" Grant laughed dryly. "Cause he didn't do the job well enough? Or 'cause he could lead the cops back to the guy who hired him?"

"Probably both," Luke said, with a burst of disgust. "That's why he got *two* bullets."

Grant liked working with the guy 'cause their brains were on the same loop.

"The dead guy's got a lengthy record of criminal offenses. Never murder, but you just don't know if something got bargained down from murder. Criminal assaults. Robberies, burglaries. DUI's, hit-and-runs," Luke rattled off. "Got a bad habit of violence and a poor driving thing going on, so would be perfect. He's still young, I mean, *was*, but his record started when he was only thirteen, according to a Gainesville cop who knew who he was as soon as he heard his name."

"The GBI processing the car?"

"They're arriving as we speak. Do you think you can get Katie down here to look at the car, see if it rings a bell, and maybe get a look at a snapshot of the dead guy?"

"Make it a clean looking photo," Grant said tersely. "Don't want to traumatize her any more than she's already been."

Some cops just lost touch with a normal person's sensibilities. They'd seen so much that it was like watching a *CSI* show on television to them. Didn't understand the average person's need to hurl after seeing evidence that cops saw routinely.

Course not as much crime up here in

Hawk's Peak as he'd seen in Atlanta, where every day was another joy, another guy with his head shot up.

"Gotcha, boss," Luke said and hung up after giving Grant directions to the scene. Luke had been around. He didn't really need to warn him about being discrete in the photo he planned to show Katie.

Grant was just being careful. Katie had been through a lot in the last few days. Hopefully, this dead guy was gonna bring an end to the threat to her.

He could only hope.

*****

By the time Grant and Katie pulled into the scene, the body was gone but the SUV still sat on the side of the road. Huge, black, hulking, it looked as if it could eat a small car like Katie's BMW for lunch and keep on driving.

Katie got out of her beat-up, old SUV. She'd insisted on driving separately, saying she needed to get some things done afterward, acting like she hadn't been targeted twice in the last couple of days.

The dead body wasn't looking good for things returning to normal anytime soon. Or maybe it did, if it ended the search for Katie's attempted killer.

"The body's gone," Luke said when Katie got close enough to hear.

She nodded. "How close can I get to the car?"

"Just don't touch it. The area around it's

already been processed but they're going to take the vehicle back to the GBI lab to look at it in detail."

The GBI guys always provided support for big cases in their area. And all they had to do to get speedy reports on this case was to mention it might involve the former governor.

Even if it might be to prosecute him or his son. The GBI techs didn't need to know that.

Ham's behavior at the picnic parking lot had given Grant a lot to think about. The way he'd looked talking on that phone as Grant drove by.

A powerful image of a man driven crazy by his own actions? Or of a man arguing with men driven beyond the realm of human decency by ambition and the desire for political power?

Then, Hamilton meeting with Buford? And his fury against Grant, like Katie was still his?

All adding up to Ham wasn't the gentleman ex that he wanted to seem to Katie.

Katie walked to the right of the vehicle toward the passenger side, to the angle she would have seen it from as it passed her. She continued all around the vehicle until she reached the front driver side. She walked closer, peering at the windshield.

Then, decisively, she shook her head. "This isn't the vehicle. Can I see the photo of the man, please?"

Luke shot Grant a look then walked to her, hitting a button on his phone. An image came up and Katie and Grant both leaned over to look.

"Poor kid," Katie said.

"Poor kid?" Luke raised an eyebrow. "He might have tried to kill you."

Katie shook her head. "This looks like a thin person. Right?" She glanced at Luke.

"Small built," he agreed.

"This isn't the vehicle and that's not the guy I saw." She waggled her finger dismissively at the SUV, then again at the phone.

"It was dark, and crazy that night, Katie," Luke said. "You couldn't have seen much and so much of your memory's muddled right now."

"The man I saw was large, not this slight built guy."

Grant watched her eyes. She was holding something back, wasn't telling them something.

"What, Kate?"

Her eyes flashed to his.

"What aren't you telling us?"

She shrugged. "Look, I've got to go. That's not the car, that's not the guy. Sorry you guys wasted your time."

"No problem, Katie." Luke smiled benignly. "We would have had to process it and work it anyway, just hoped it was your guy. Maybe get some clues."

Katie nodded and left without further comment, driving away with a kick of dust.

"Tough girl, that Katie." Luke laughed roughly. "Lots of people, men and women, would be crying under the covers after what she's been through. Not her. She's all business. 'Gotta go', she says." He laughed again, but without much humor.

He'd seen something in her eyes, too.

Grant looked at Luke. "What do you think she's not telling us?"

Luke shrugged. "Don't know. But, I bet we get a chance to find out soon. This is all moving real fast."

"Damn." Luke looked in the direction Katie had driven. "We didn't put a car on her tail. No telling where she'll go."

Grant smiled, held up his phone. "I put a little thing underneath her car, yesterday. Got it tracing her even as we speak." He looked down at his phone. "Let's see, she's heading toward town."

Then, he looked again. "Damn, she turned left, heading out on West Mountain Road, direction of the governor's place. What the hell is wrong with her?"

He ran to his car.

Luke just shook his head as Grant put the car into gear. Because he knew, just like Grant, that danger was tailing Katie, close on her heels, just waiting for another chance to nip at her.

Katie was driving out that road, just like normal, just like she'd done several times a week before all this had started.

Before there'd been two attempts on her life.

CHAPTER SEVENTEEN

Kate drove toward Miss Sally's, her hands clenched onto the steering wheel as if it could anchor her to the earth. So much information ricocheted through her brain, so many random images not making sense.

She felt as if she were on drugs. Mind-altering drugs meant to defuse her ability to think, to process reality.

Flashes kept coming at her. As if from long ago. She was running, running through the woods, trying not to scream, terrified.

Then, reality suddenly wiped out all imaginary images. Her SUV careened onto the red clay on the side of the road. The vehicle slid violently before she jerked her steering wheel to the left, jolting back onto the blacktop road.

She slowed and looked back in her rearview mirror. She'd veered around a curve so fast her car had almost gone off the road down a steep embankment into an even deeper ditch than the one she'd been pushed into by the crazy SUV driver.

Because she'd been distracted with all the images in her mind. The events of the last few days might be the death of her yet. And if she'd just crashed, everyone would think she'd been murdered. Rather than just a distracted driver.

She drove on and tried to keep her mind on the road, but again, one image flashed into her thoughts, the sticker in the driver's side windshield the night she'd crashed.

She'd seen it before. And she'd seen it again today. It looked like a government parking sticker they used up at the state capitol. As a state representative, Ham was entitled to special parking.

The sticker on the SUV that had chased her looked an awful lot like that.

Her heart clenched in her chest.

Had Ham chased her? Could that possibly be true?

Was she such a bad judge of character that she didn't even recognize the possibility for violence in a man she'd been engaged to, someone she'd known all her life?

She tried to still all the noise in her brain, to use only logic to solve this problem of who might want to hurt her, and what could be their motive.

A spurned fiancé? An overheard conversation that could send someone to jail or ruin a political career?

She needed to figure it out so she could get her life back, a normal life, with no drama.

Waking up in hospital beds with parts of her memory missing, getting glass in her hair from bullets through windshields. It was getting more than a little annoying.

Yeah, it was a big pain.

Not to mention the terror part of the whole equation.

She laughed to herself, as she had her whole life, to try to defuse powerful emotions.

Finally, she pulled into Miss Sally's driveway, got out and walked to the front door. She rang the doorbell.

"Round here," Miss Sally's voice came from the back of her house.

Rounding the corner, she saw Miss Sally stirring a large black pot over a wood fire. Steam rose in the air, swirling out the aroma of salty, boiled peanuts. The wood fire tinged her nose with a curling acrid bite. The aromas spoke of fall.

"You want some boiled peanuts?" Miss Sally held out a ladle full of the steaming legumes. "I think they're cooled enough."

The scent drew Kate forward. Something about the smoky smell always made her nostalgic - nostalgic for a time when everything was right in her world.

When was that time, she often wondered, when the feeling came over her?

She took a peanut, split the shell and

popped the chewy insides into her mouth, sucking on the saltiness. "Emm, good," she murmured.

"Nothing like 'em, fresh from the pot, huh?" Miss Sally smiled over the steam.

Kate looked at her, tilting her head, seeing something different about Miss Sally through the steamy mist. Kate narrowed her eyes and all of a sudden, a memory from the distant past emerged full force.

Miss Sally, younger, thinner, looking at her across the swirling steam of another boiling pot of peanuts.

"You were boiling peanuts up at the governor's house that day."

Miss Sally's hand jerked and several peanuts fell to the ground, splashing into the dirt. "What?"

What day was that when Miss Sally had been boiling peanuts at the governor's house? And why should she suddenly remember that image, something that had never come forth before?

Miss Sally's eyes narrowed, and hardened. "Katie, you got to let it be."

As if Miss Sally knew exactly which image Kate was remembering.

"What are you talking about, Miss Sally?"

The old woman's face closed down as if she'd been caught doing something wrong. She shook her head.

"Miss Sally," Kate said insistently. "Help

me."

Miss Sally narrowed her eyes again. "I'm trying to, same as I've done all these years. Haven't I always had your best interest?"

"There's so much happening that I don't understand, and I've got the feeling you understand it all, Miss Sally. Why do I have that feeling?"

Miss Sally set the ladle back into the pot of boiling peanuts and began walking toward her house. Kate caught up to her and put her hand on her arm, gently stopping the old woman who was like these mountains.

Same as the mountains, the old woman had always been a part of her life.

Stable, strong, grounding her to the earth.

Slowly, Miss Sally turned to stare into Kate's eyes. "Katie, girl. There's lots of things you can know in the world, but not all of it you got to talk about, some of it you just need to let lie."

She pursed her mouth together, as if trying to hold back words that could cause harm. "You think you remember some things, Katie girl? It's 'cause you do. But you've forgotten things your whole life because it was to your best benefit to forget them."

Miss Sally shook her head and looked up toward the governor's mountain, his land separated from hers by a ribbon of asphalt. Then, she looked directly into Kate's eyes, with a hard, purposeful expression. "Some things is just too powerful, that they'll drive you crazy if you remember them."

With another meaningful nod, she pulled her arm away from Kate and shuffled toward her front door.

Kate watched her go, the old woman who'd been like a granny to her, kind, standing between little Katie and harm, whether it was a Billy goat that took umbrage with Katie and charged at her. Or a rooster who'd flown at her, wings flapping like a giant hawk, ready to peck her to death.

Miss Sally had gotten between Katie and the rooster. Once they were both outside the pen, Miss Sally had laughed so hard and so long, that finally Katie had joined in, laughing at what had scared her.

It had seemed like, together, the two of them could stand against all odds.

And suddenly, Katie remembered a flash of herself terrified, in the arms of Miss Sally.

Slowly, her gaze drifted toward the ridge beyond Miss Sally's property, toward the governor's land.

Somewhere up there was the answer to what she'd forgotten two nights ago. And teasing little flashes told her there was more up there, more to remember.

Like the sudden memory of her as a very little girl, five or six, running to Miss Sally, running into her arms, crying hysterically, holding onto her, wrapping her arms and legs around her like a small monkey latching onto its mother.

And Miss Sally running, holding her, both of them afraid, running as if for their lives.

Kate's heart began to pound, blood pulsing through her. She looked up at the woods and hills just across the road and headed toward them, as if drawn by some supernatural force.

Answers. She needed answers.

"Katie, where you going?" Miss Sally called out as Kate walked down Miss Sally's driveway, crossed the asphalt road and disappeared into the trees, the sound of the old woman's voice fading as Kate moved into the tangled overgrown property. "Katie ..."

Once she'd entered the wood line, everything stilled, noise almost nonexistent. The further she walked through the mulchy undergrowth, the further back in time she seemed to go.

Leaves crunched under her feet as they'd done when she was five.

Time didn't exist here, in the woods, but stood still so that she could be five, fifty-five, or eighty-five and it would all be the same, the trees with their leaves mingling with various shades of orange, red and yellow, stretching upward to the bright blue sky.

She just walked, not knowing where she was going or why she was doing it. Then, the sound of leaves rustling and footsteps shuffling through them filtered through the trees.

She stopped and stood completely still.

Muttering. Someone muttering as they walked.

Instinctively, she knelt down, making herself smaller, a less visible target.

Then, she saw the source of the noise. Through the trees, she could make out the governor.

Walking, a rifle down to his side, as if ready if he saw a deer, he walked aimlessly, shuffling, muttering, his eyes seemingly unfocused. A glaze over his face.

A chill crept through Kate, and she began shaking.

Something unnatural about the sight of the old man struck her. He kept obsessively talking, almost as if possessed by the spirit of something he couldn't shake.

Slowly, he passed on by, going over the ridge, until finally Kate couldn't hear him, couldn't hear those strange mutterings.

Then, she began backing up, heading in the other direction, an innate sense of self-preservation kicking in, telling her to get off his property. To get off the governor's haunted land.

The governor was a ghost of himself, drifting through the woods. He wasn't the genial old man who would have been her father-in-law. Loud, boisterous.

This gray ghost wasn't him.

She backed up until she was certain enough distance was between them that he couldn't hear her, then she began to run, fleeing through the trees. Somehow knowing her survival depended on it.

Her mind flashed to another time, another time she'd been running through trees, crying, desperate to get away.

She tried to focus on the memory but even as she did, it fled, as if it were only a story she'd heard before, not something she'd actually experienced.

Finally, she burst free from the trees and the sun shone onto her face, as if welcoming her out of the dark forest. It blinded her for a second, sending prisms of light into her brain, along with tiny stabbing knives of pain.

She closed her eyes for a second, fighting against the agony inside her head. When the pain receded, she opened her eyes and focused on safety, sprinting across the road.

"Kate." Grant stood by his car, his gaze on her, shocked. He drew his gun and ran forward, pulling her behind him, backing up until they were behind his car, then he pulled her into a crouch so they were protected by the bulk of the SUV.

"What the hell?" He poked his head up to look toward the woods on the other side of the road, as if he expected someone to emerge.

After a moment, he fastened his gaze on her. "What was that?" He pointed toward the governor's property. "What were you doing up there?"

How could he understand if she didn't even understand it herself? Her breath came in gasps, her heart beating so loudly she expected the governor to emerge across the road, yelling at her for trespassing. As if he had heard the noisy racketing in her chest and head of blood pulsing through her with a panic driven fury.

What had she been doing up there? Seeing what no rational mind could reconcile with the known image of the governor.

"I don't know," she wheezed out. She had to gasp for air, sucking it into aching lungs, before she could continue.

She stood and leaned her hands onto her knees for a moment, gulping in oxygen. Then, she turned and looked toward the tree line on the other side of the road. "I just felt like I needed to go up there."

"Suicidal impulse?" Grant took her by the shoulders and turned her toward him, studying her face, as if trying to decide if she needed to get back to the hospital right away.

Then, his expression softened. He holstered his gun and pulled her into his arms. "You scared me, Kate."

His arms felt so good, almost like the arms she'd run to as a child. So long ago, when something had happened up there.

She pulled back to look into his eyes.

"Grant, do you ever think about our childhood? About that summer when your parents and my mother all ran away?"

He started and his eyes rounded.

With an expression in them, almost as if he'd felt this moment coming.

CHAPTER EIGHTEEN

"What do you mean?"

She averted her eyes and gazed off into the distance, toward the wooded ridge that ran between Miss Sally's property and the governor's house.

Dark and foreboding, the dense trees knitted themselves into a solid mass that absorbed sound and light, an almost impenetrable barrier to reaching the governor's house.

Or getting away from it?

High above the trees, a hawk circled, riding the wind drafts that swirled him into the heights.

"There's always been such a mystery around it, all three of them running off like that." Her mouth narrowed into a hard line. "I mean who does that? Not one parent but both of yours and my mother with them? No one ever talked about it. They just faded into history."

She swiveled her head to peer into his eyes.

"Why is that, Grant? As if *everyone* decided together never to talk about it." Her clear blue eyes looked as deep as the lake on a sunny day. The depths of that lake held a lot of secrets.

She turned full face to look back up into the trees. As if hypnotized, drawn by a force she couldn't resist, she took a step toward the ridge.

He grasped her by the arm. "Kate, what are you doing?"

He turned her toward him again, looking into her eyes. Eyes that were vacant and unseeing.

The sound of a creaking screen door behind him alerted him to the fact that Miss Sally had come outside onto her front porch. "Get her out of here, Grant. She's talking crazy talk."

He looked into Miss Sally's eyes and saw secrets misting in her eyes. The answer to the mysteries Katie had just spoken about? "What's going on, Miss Sally?"

She shook her head, her face blank. Unnaturally so, the way criminals made their faces blank so you couldn't read any reaction.

Suddenly, it seemed the whole town was tilting on its axis, leaning toward crazy. For Katie as a child, Hawk's Peak had been a safe and comforting place.

Not for him.

He'd been the poor, abandoned boy, brought

up on a shoestring by his aunt. Life hadn't been so easy for him. He'd wondered incessantly about his parents' whereabouts.

His aunt had told him his parents loved him but had been forced to leave him. That hadn't been good enough for him. But, like a child does, he'd buried his questions.

Because none of his aunt's answers had been good enough. So, finally, he'd stopped asking.

When they'd found his father shot dead just this side of the county line, he'd had a concrete end to wondering about him. He'd always felt his mother had been killed too, but that her body hadn't been discovered or properly identified.

Then, the need to know who had killed his father had become a central, driving force in his life.

He'd determined he would know, one day, who had killed his father. And why.

He'd vowed to make the person pay. No matter how long he had to wait for justice for his father.

In doing so, maybe he would also finally find out conclusively what had happened to his mother.

He looked into Katie's tormented eyes, seeing nightmares fighting to come to the surface of her memory.

What did she know? Could they access it, without driving her to the point of insanity, causing an entire mental breakdown?

The misty glaze across her face made him wonder if she needed to know the truth as much as he did? She'd lost her mother that day. The day the trio had gotten in a car and left.

What was so bad that they'd all run like a herd of spooked sheep?

What was so bad now that someone had tried to kill Kate, wanted to make her run just like their parents had?

Because he'd never bought the theory that all three of them had gone bad the same day, influencing each other to run away to a carefree existence, leaving their responsibilities behind. Like some kids taunted him about in middle school, when some kids get mean, and he hadn't gotten his size yet.

He turned toward Miss Sally, standing on that porch, gazing intently at Katie. There was no mistaking that she was looking at Katie, as if to determine what Katie would say next.

Was the truth somewhere inside of Miss Sally, too? Or at least part of the truth? Sometimes, it seemed the hardest part of a sheriff's job in Hawk's Peak was separating immediate, new information from old histories between people.

Katie sighed restlessly, her feet shuffling as if his hands on her were the only things keeping her from heading back up the ridge.

He'd have to come back to question Miss Sally later.

Some innate cop sense told him she knew something, a piece of the mystery of why all of this was happening right now, why Katie's mind seemed to be unraveling so quickly, with indiscriminate bits of information missing.

It felt like Katie knew things she couldn't even admit to herself. What did she feel the need to protect herself from?

"Give me your keys." He put Katie into his car then drove her car out back of Miss Sally's house, so it couldn't be seen from the road. Or from up on the ridge.

With a final glance at Miss Sally standing silent and grim faced on her front porch, he got into his car.

"Put on your seat belt." When she didn't move, he leaned across and buckled it for her.

Then, he started the car. He couldn't get her away from here fast enough.

As they pulled out the front drive, a hawk plunged, suddenly, quickly toward the earth, toward prey that wouldn't know the hawk existed until its talons were piercing into its back, cracking its spine, wringing the life out of it.

A shiver ran through him, and Katie likewise wrapped her arms around herself, looking toward where the hawk had disappeared into the trees.

"Who's the hawk in this town? Who's the hawk in Hawk's Peak?" she intoned, turning her clear blue eyes on him, saying the words almost like some Shakespearean actor.

A shudder ran through him at her tone, dark, foreboding, as if from a deep, dark part of her mind.

"Yikes, Katie." He tried for lightness. "You're really scaring me."

"Don't call me, Katie." Her eyes narrowed, but still remained unfocused as if seeing inward. "Katie's that little girl, that scared little girl in the woods."

He slowed the car, knowing there was more, waiting for it to come out. When they were children, she'd alluded to scary things in the woods.

But, then, he'd figured, didn't all kids?

Scary things under the bed, in the closet, in the woods. The same, universal, scary things.

"I'm not Katie, not Katherine. I'm Kate." The way she said it was as if trying to convince herself.

Then, as if coming back to herself, her eyes focused and seemed fully present. She shook her head and looked around.

"Where's my car?"

Her car? As if she didn't realize how she'd gotten here, several miles down the road from Miss Sally's.

"You're really freaking me out now. We need to take you back to the hospital, get some scans done on your brain. The doctor said to watch for unusual behavior."

He choked out a harsh laugh that rattled across his vocal chords with a painful rasp. "This qualifies."

"I'm sorry, Grant. I just keep blanking on things. It's like I've got so much going on in my head that I can't concentrate on all of it at once. I'm okay, really."

"I don't think so."

She laid her hand on his forearm, stroking it softly. "I really am. Better than I've been in years."

"Better than you've been in years?"

"Yeah. It's like I'm finally cleaning house in my head, straightening things up. Getting unengaged with Ham, so there's room for you if you're still interested." She laughed slightly. "No pressure."

Room for him? Words he'd wanted to hear for years. But not like this. Not in the middle of all this insanity.

He sighed. "You want to come over to my place?" To the farm his parents had owned and his aunt had managed to hold onto, God knows how.

A beautiful smile spread across her face. "Yeah, I would. I haven't been there in years."

Not since she'd yelled at him for leaving to go into the service. Not since she'd acted like some crazed person, so different than her usual self. Kinda like now, as if some alter ego, some hidden personality had come out.

The way she'd changed her name was almost as if she were saying she was a different person altogether. As a child, she'd been Katie, with Ham she'd been Katherine.

Now, she was Kate?

Who was this Kate?

And why did she feel the need to dispose of that younger self, that little girl? Was it as simple as the childish-sounding name not fitting this grownup, mature woman, who people turned to for help when their animals were injured or sick?

She held the answers so many people sought for the pets they considered part of their families.

This grownup Kate was definitely different than the Katie he'd known. Her skinny teenaged frame had become rounded curves, with a voluptuousness that drew him to her, even more than the young woman he'd left behind.

This new, soul-singeing fire between them was a grownup kind of passion, deeper than their teenaged heat, all the shared history between them made even sweeter by time apart.

As teens, they'd taken their passion and their love for granted.

Now?

He looked at her and wondered how he'd ever been able to survive without her? How had it been possible to draw breath with that pain stabbing into his chest of knowing she didn't love him anymore?

How would he survive again if she remembered she didn't love him anymore? After this taste of Katie's love as a full blown woman.

As they drove through the open front gate to his property and rumbled across the cow guard, or cow-stopping grate as Katie had always called it, it felt like old times. Her hanging around, while he did his chores before they were free to go out on a date.

She'd always waited patiently, doing her homework, getting ready for that scholarship at the big University of Georgia.

When they reached the house, they walked up the front walk, his hand on her lower back, her scent whirling around him. Gardenia-scented perfume wafted off her, something she'd found as a child in her Aunt Mamie Lee's chest of drawers and had claimed as her own.

Everything was as if nothing had changed.

He opened the door letting her inside. She let out a little gasp, glancing around, taking it all in with an expression of awe, as if at a museum, a museum of their earlier life together.

She walked around, looking at old photos of him and his parents, then just him and his aunt. There was a class photo from first grade, a group shot with the entire class.

She picked it up and smiled, running her finger over the spot where he stood.

Then, she wandered to a side table, to a hand thrown pottery bowl. The bowl where he kept his medals from Afghanistan.

She picked up one, put it down, then picked up another. Setting that one down, she drew out a set of dog tags.

A jagged knife ripped through him, with pain so fierce he could hardly breathe for a moment.

She lifted the tags close, as if reading the words. Then, she turned to look at him, tenderness in her eyes. "I read about your heroic acts," she said quietly.

So, she remembered that much.

As if she'd realized the same, she gasped, "Oh!" Her eyes met his with the recognition of the breakthrough.

She carefully placed the dog tags back into the bowl with a gentle reverence. The respect that the remembrance deserved.

Then, she looked back up at him, her clear, blue eyes meeting his. "Why do you keep these dog tags together like this with your medals?" she almost whispered, so softly that he could barely hear her.

Could he talk about it? He sucked in air, wondering could he force it out into words.

Joey. The man who hadn't come home, the man who'd given everything.

His jaw muscle twitched and he walked over to the bowl. He lifted the set with Joey's name engraved on them, softly fingering the words that identified a man who'd lived on the earth only a little more than two decades. Such a short period of time. Too little.

"Because," he forced out, "when I start believing all that hero talk about myself, I just look at Joey's tags. His mother gave them to me because I was there when he died. Said I ought to have them."

"Joey was the real hero." A pain in his gut worse than the bullet wound almost made it impossible to go on. "He gave his life. Me, a little bullet wound. Both of us got hurt that day, but I was the one who came home. So, I keep his tags there in the bowl with my medals to keep it all in perspective."

A mist rose in her eyes, and she took the tags from him, set them back into the bowl, then wrapped her arms around his waist. "You are a hero," she whispered. "Just like Joey. Only you're an alive one. And for that I am so grateful. I was so afraid when you left, afraid I'd get a call from your aunt one day, telling me you were dead."

So, she remembered that, too, as if everything was beginning to bubble up from her memory. He held her, waiting for more, waiting to see what might burst free from the claws of amnesia.

She gripped him tighter. "I'm glad you've

come home, Grant."

He held her, as if this was his real homecoming, home to the arms of the woman he'd loved, and in one sense had fought for. Feeling that if Al-Qaeda could reach its deadly tentacles into his country that it could one day hurt the people he loved, could hurt Katie.

He'd fought for her and, on some level had wanted her recognition for what he'd done. Finally, this felt like it.

She pulled back to look at him, her eyes welling with emotion. He sensed there weren't any more connections coming out of the recesses of her mind.

He decided to break the moment, to lessen the dramatic mood.

"I need to milk my cows."

She laughed slightly, stepping back. The distance felt like miles, and he wanted to yank her back against him, to hold her there forever.

"I can't believe you still keep cows." She wiped at her eyes.

"Yeah, just a couple for the heck of it."

"Like old times," she said.

"Exactly. I love the smell of them, the look of them, with those big eyes, the way they moo when I call them in."

"Milk cows are a big responsibility." She nodded her head, sagely. "What do you do when you can't get home?"

He smiled at her immediate concern for the

animals' welfare. "I have a high school kid who helps me out. If he can't do it, then his dad will fill in. These cows don't go hurting, believe me.

She laughed. "I believe you. I wasn't saying anything about your character."

"I didn't think you were." He tilted his head toward the barn. "You want to come with me."

She nodded with a distant smile. "I remember all the times I'd watch you milk them back in the day."

The cows had helped him and his aunt make ends meet. The mortgage had been paid off long ago so they'd just had upkeep and day-to-day living expenses.

"Where's your aunt these days?" She looked up the stairs as if his aunt might come down and catch them necking on the couch, telling Grant he needed to get her home.

"Tomorrow will come mighty early, kids," she'd say. "You've got the cow milking tomorrow before school, you know."

He'd known, 'cause he'd done it every day. With a whole lot more cows back then.

"My aunt lives down in Gainesville. A little condo with no upkeep. Just how she likes it, she says. No cows, no chickens, no property to maintain."

He'd gotten a new mortgage on the farm so he could give his aunt a nest egg to pay her back for all the years she'd supported him. She'd immediately moved out of the county.

"Love ya, babe. But, I've done my time in this county. I'm gone," his aunt had joked as she'd headed out.

Somehow, he'd felt it wasn't entirely a joke to her.

Together, he and Kate walked down to the milking shed. Immediately, they fell into their old rhythm. Usually, he'd done other chores while Kate studied, then when he gotten to the cows, she'd help.

She rinsed down the area with a hose, while Grant went to herd in one cow. Then, Kate rinsed off her udders while Grant readied the old milking machine.

"What do you do with all this milk?" she asked. "No big companies are gonna want to worry with this small amount, are they?"

"Sell what I don't use to a lady up the road, who gives me cheese, ice cream, butter, or any type of dairy product I could want. And some vegetables and fruit that other people give her in exchange for her milk products."

"A whole barter system going on."

He nodded. "I like it, being a part of the community."

She laughed. "If being the sheriff isn't enough for you."

He smiled. This had always been how it had been, a back and forth as they worked to get the milking done.

Katie closed her eyes and smiled. "This smell. It really takes me back."

Straw and cow mixed together into a warm, comforting scent. It felt like home to him.

Katie, standing there in the shed, was a visceral memory for him as well. They'd often gotten into more of their serious conversations here in the milking shed. It was where he'd talked about them getting married and having kids, continuing to live on the farm with their own family.

As if she also remembered, Katie's eyes opened, and she looked at him, misty eyed.

He stopped the milking machine hookup and drew her into his arms, holding her there, nosing into her hair, relishing the closeness after all these years.

Here in the milking shed, where they'd shared so many kisses, so many intimate conversations as he'd milked the cows, with that half-occupied mind that allows people to talk about difficult things.

"Ah, Kate," he said, pulling back to look into her eyes. "What became of us?"

She tightened her grip around his waist. "We're still young, Grant. There's still time. Nothing's *become* of us, yet."

Thank God. Thank God for this second chance. If she didn't suddenly come to herself and remember that she wanted nothing more to do with him.

Wanted a richer, classier guy, as he'd always figured their breakup was really about. Not the richer part, but the classier part.

When she'd learned he didn't plan to go with her to the University of Georgia, to pursue higher learning, to take up that football scholarship that had been offered him with all the future possibilities of the pro football career so many believed he could have, with the name recognition and connections it could give him, it was obvious he was on a different path than she'd hoped for them.

He should have been more up front, made sure she'd understood what his goals were. The promise of honor, integrity and the service of country that the military had offered had swirled inside of him, growing into a need he couldn't resist.

It had also fit into his life plan of police work, coming back to Hawk's Peak in a role that would allow him to investigate his father's death and his mother's disappearance.

He should have included Katie in his thought loop more. Then, maybe they would have stood a chance when he joined up.

He'd known she wouldn't like it, since them at UGA was all she'd talked about. So, when the need to go military became too strong, and he knew he wasn't going with her to Athens, to the university, he'd kept that surety to himself, just throwing out references every now and then, hoping she'd come to the realization that UGA wasn't going to happen for him.

He'd been a coward.

"Stop," she demanded. "Stop this thinking. It gets us into trouble."

He laughed and looked down at her. She knew him too well. "Yeah, no thinking." Then, he pulled away from her. "Gotta milk the girls. Don't want them getting uncomfortable."

She laughed quietly and stepped back. "The girls. You always called them that."

"My girls," he agreed. "They depend on me."

"Emm," she murmured, settling down to watch him milk. The quiet swirled around them, the sounds of the cow as she munched hay, as Grant relieved the pressure on her udders.

Outside the little barn, night settled in, an owl hooting in the woods, a reminder of all the land surrounding the house, spreading out as it had when they'd been children.

Only now, the land seemed as though it could hide bad things, people who wanted to hurt others. Provided hiding places for them to sneak up and a sound barrier to prevent cries for help from being heard and help from coming.

She reached inside her purse, touching the gun she'd made sure to tuck there since she'd gotten out of the hospital.

CHAPTER NINETEEN

Later, after the milking, and a dinner of sautéed vegetables, rice and beef, Grant and Katie settled into the living room. A fire roared in the fireplace, and Katie cuddled next to him on the sofa.

She seemed content to relax until she looked up at a photograph of him and his parents. He saw her eyes fasten on the framed photo. It had always been one of Grant's favorites.

He'd stood only about waist high to his parents, squished between them. They had their arms around each other and their other hands on his shoulders so that he was secured into a loving triangle of parents and child. He was wearing a cowboy hat, and the biggest, happiest grin possible.

She stood and took the photo, bringing it closer to her face as if to get a good look at it, then she turned to him, holding the photo out toward him. As if it weren't burned indelibly into his memory. One of the last happy moments in a happy childhood.

Happy until ...

"These aren't parents who would leave their kid," she said definitively.

He sighed inwardly. And pain nicked at him, as it always did when he really stopped to think about his parents leaving.

"That's what I would have thought," he said.

He reached for her hand to draw her back to the couch. "It's bugged me my whole life, Kate. If I were to be honest with you, it was one of the motivating factors behind me becoming a cop, readying myself for coming back here as the sheriff."

He narrowed his eyes, trying to see her face as it was backlit against the fire. "I've known my whole life, Kate, that one day I would be back here, checking into their disappearance. And my father's murder."

"Really?" She slid backward to snuggle into his arms. So good, her there so close again.

"Yeah." He tightened his arms around her, nosing into her hair, the gardenia perfume comforting in its familiarity. He sucked in a long breath, inhaling her all the way down to his soul, taking him back to a time when he'd never believed he could lose her love.

Then, he continued with what she wanted to discuss. Needed to talk about? "A loss that great as a child, you never really get over it."

He didn't say he knew she'd felt the same

way about her mother, that she'd been equally traumatized. She waited a beat. He could feel her waiting.

"There were always rumors about the governor's involvement," she said, quietly.

He'd heard them, remembered the whispers when he'd been a child. And how the talk had always stopped when people realized he might be listening.

So, he'd learned to listen without being apparent, to continue playing with his guns and soldiers, but all the while listening to the adults on the other side of the room.

"I know," he said. "But rumors don't cut it in court. Gotta have evidence."

"Right," she agreed. "Like the SUV and whoever shot into your car the other day. We know it happened, but being able to prove who did it are separate things."

Like her dumping him more than ten years ago, and him understanding it, also two separate things. But, she was in his arms now, and as much as he would like to understand her exact reasoning, he was just happy to have her with him, and didn't want to bring up old issues.

Then, she sat up halfway, on alert again.

It wasn't looking good for just relaxing.

"Grant, where do you keep your old memorabilia from early family days, like that box of old photos I was looking at from my dad's?"

"All of this looking backward." He shook his head. "Not good."

She looked away quickly, refusing to make eye contact. "I think it's a good thing, Grant. So much is clicking lately, things locking into place that I never noticed before."

She turned back to look at him. "It's like that knock on the head loosened up things that were buried deep inside."

He didn't want to ask her if she was sure she was remembering correctly, or if the blow had jumbled her thoughts into something she couldn't trust. He didn't want to introduce that sort of paranoia into all of the other mixture of fear, confusion, and lost memory.

"You want to go upstairs?" he offered.

She met his gaze for a long heated moment, desire swirling into the air around them with a simmering heat. Then he could almost see her getting a grip on her feelings. "Nice try, cowboy. Where's the old stuff? Under there?" She pointed at the built in cabinet next to the television.

His body wanted to deny it, to scoop her up and carry her up the stairs for a repeat of the night before. But the insistent look in her eyes couldn't be denied. He nodded.

"Can I look?" The hopefulness on her face tore at him, jagged little razor blades cutting into his memories, forcing him to think about the most hurtful moments of his life.

"The past is a scary, scary place. Are you

sure you want to keep going there? Isn't forward a better direction?" He tilted his head toward the stairs.

Her smile softened. "In a bit, I'll come on up. Okay?"

He nodded. He just couldn't face it though, looking at all of those documents of a long ago ruptured childhood. "Knock yourself out. I'm gonna go take a shower."

"Probably a good idea." She held her nose with a grin.

"I meant a cold one."

She laughed. "No need to start talking like that. I'll be up later." Her eyes met his with a promise, of heat and passion, connectedness. A return to the *them* of the old days.

For one night? Or more?

Could they get back to what they'd had as teenagers, when he'd thought nothing could separate them?

Was he crazy to even go down this twisted path? As mentally mixed up as she was? Wanting her permanently, expecting it, might only lead to more pain.

Because, once upon a time, she'd decided he wasn't good enough for her. She'd wanted a college guy, the type of guy who would end up like Hamilton, doing *great things*.

Not some army guy. Not some local law enforcement guy.

He sucked in a deep breath. He needed to accept this wasn't going anywhere. She'd made it clear for many years that she wanted something different than him.

And he didn't want a woman who didn't want him.

At least that was what he'd told himself all those lonely nights in the Afghan mountains.

He pushed up out of the couch and headed toward the stairs. Before he reached halfway up, she was already opening the cabinet and pulling out old dusty boxes.

He'd concentrated his attentions since he'd become sheriff on criminal evidence, instead of emotional evidence, because looking at old photos of when they'd last been a family was just too painful.

The past with his family was gone. For whatever reason, his parents had decided to leave him, and there was no use looking back at false evidence that seemed to indicate they loved their little boy and would never leave him.

Twenty minutes later, he was asleep when Katie climbed into bed. He woke to a sweet smelling woman. Warm from a shower, she seemed so innocent and young.

"Grant," she whispered.

"Mmm," he murmured into her neck, wrapping her into his arms, pulling her close, her warm, moist skin against his sleep-warmed skin. He woke up enough to pull her on top of him, her hips against his, thin cotton all that separated their bodies.

She pulled away, sitting up, thus allowing him even closer access to her center, her legs on either side of his hips.

"Grant, I found something." She reached over to the bedside table, and as she did so, she slid across his hips in an excruciating tease.

As if she didn't even notice his arousal, she lifted an envelope. "What is this doing in there? Do you know who might have sent this letter?"

The only way to get past this and on to what he was really interested in, he knew from long time experience with Katie, was to deal with this letter.

Then, they could get back to what really mattered. He took the envelope. It was postmarked Gainesville, Georgia.

He held it up closer to the light. A shock of recognition shook him to his core. The handwriting... The handwriting... His father's handwriting.

As distinctive as a face or a fingerprint, the writing was so familiar from his childhood, from old farming accounting books in his father's handwriting, and from a few postcards home to his grandparents when his parents had been off on their honeymoon down in Panama City Beach, Florida, the one time his father had ever left the state of Georgia, and ever left his beloved mountains for more than a day trip.

Grant sat straight up in bed and took the envelope from Katie. "Where'd you find this?"

"In that box in the cabinet."

The letter's postmark was after his parents had abandoned him. Turning it over, he slipped open the envelope and pulled out a single sheet of paper.

No salutation or signature, the letter was only two sentences long.

This is all the money we could scrape together. So grateful for you taking care of Grant until we can manage to come get him.

A rush of emotions filled him, happiness that his parents hadn't forgotten about him, that they'd wanted to return to him. That had been all he'd wished for as a little boy, praying his mommy and daddy would come back for him, that they'd wanted him, hadn't really abandoned him.

Here was proof that his wishes had been the same as theirs. They'd wanted to come back for him.

A hot, moist heat of happiness and nostalgia flooded his eyes. For all that might have been. And the proof here in black and white that his father had wanted the same thing as little Grant had ached for, every day and every night after he'd been abandoned.

Then, a flood of sadness flashed through him. Because it hadn't happened. That little boy had waited and waited. And his parents had never come.

He looked up to find Katie staring at him. Her eyes reflected back the same watery, powerful emotions filling him. As if you'd just been allowed to speak with a dead parent.

He breathed in hard, sucked in cooling air, pushing back the overpowering feelings. Maybe there was more.

"Is this all you found in the box?" he asked.

She nodded. "Of any importance."

No more letters. No more words from the dead.

He pushed back the disappointment and tried to just be thankful for the one letter. Still, the disappointment was almost debilitating.

"I haven't looked in that box for years," he forced out the words. "My aunt must have put it in there before she left, for me to find one day." He looked at Katie. Her eyes glistened with unshed tears. "You read this?"

She nodded, and a tear slipped down her cheek. He thumbed it away, then kissed her softly, drying the trail with his lips.

"They wanted me," he said softly. "Wanted to come back for me." A huge slashing knife stabbed into him, releasing a reservoir of hurt and anger he'd held back since he was five.

A jagged sob ripped from deep inside of him and Katie pulled him into her chest, wrapping her arms around him and her legs around his hips, so that he was encased in a warm, loving woman.

He held onto her, feeling her, smelling her, hearing her soft murmurs in his ear.

He rubbed his face into her neck, just savoring her, the woman he'd lost so long ago, now back in his bed, in his arms.

Asking questions, digging into corners, bringing up so much that he'd pushed back for so long.

Emotions of a thousand different types rushed through him, two lost loves returning at once, the love his parents had taken from him, and this woman, the only woman he'd ever loved, ever wanted so fiercely, ever burned for.

All he could think about now was her, because to think about his parents was too difficult tonight when nothing else could be done.

But Katie?

There was a lot that could be done about his feelings for her.

They had a lot of lost time to erase. Years worth of lovemaking to make up for. And he was starting now.

He slipped the T-shirt over her head then pushed the panties from her hips. She pushed his underwear down over his hips, and he kicked them loose before pulling her back to him, loving the sight of her naked there, wrapped around him.

Lifting her hips, he positioned himself, then slowly slid into her, allowing her to control the speed of entry by how she lowered her hips.

She groaned as he filled her. "Grant," she called out his name, her eyes closed, her head thrown back.

"I'm here."

She opened her eyes, and looked down at him as he slowly slid fully into her. The passion, the desire, the naked want in her eyes almost undid him.

He gripped her hips, holding her in place, wanting to just look at her there with him inside of her, the two of them locked into place as one being.

The way it should have always been, the way he wanted it to always be from here on out.

"Ah Jesus, I want you, Kate. Like I've never wanted you before."

She tightened herself around him. "You've got me. Do what you want with me."

Like a flash, his control slipped, and he flipped her over onto her back, without ever breaking their connection, then began to slide in and out of her, so tightly around him that he could think only of one thing. Her.

Her hot, tight center squeezed onto him as if to say that she would never let him go, that she was his for life.

Then, the memory of all that threatened to take that away from them surfaced, of SUVs that could crush the breath from her, shooters posed on ridges ready to put a bullet into her heart, that heart that he wanted to be his for life.

An owl hooted in the woods, nearer than before, as if the night with all its predatory creatures was closing in.

He pulled Katie to him, as if he could hold her close forever, safe from anyone who wanted to hurt her.

CHAPTER TWENTY

Kate walked into an exam room to see one of her usual patients, a Pomeranian named Lola.

But with a different human accompanying the little dog. Someone who, according to his wife, had little time for such chores.

"Commissioner Gafney, I'm surprised to see you. Your wife usually brings the little pom in. Isn't Lola her baby?"

County Commissioner Buford Gafney smiled. "I thought it was about time I pulled equal duty. Be a good dog daddy." He laughed lightly.

Kate had always liked the commissioner and his wife. She'd voted for his reelection last time.

"I heard you weren't feeling up to snuff." He narrowed his eyes, looking at her closely.

"I'm okay." She smiled down at the little Pomeranian he held on his lap. "More importantly, how's little Lola?"

"I think she's okay. My wife said it was

time for her checkup." His expression was bland. The politician thing kicking in, hiding what she got the feeling was his real objective.

She gestured for him to put the little dog on the exam table and began looking the canine over, patting her reassuringly.

"Weren't you at the barbecue at the governor's the other day?" She launched into the subject she was sure had brought him here.

His eyebrows rose before he caught himself.

He needed a little work on the facial expressions, on not letting them give him away.

"You remembered?" His voice was a bit higher than normal. The guy wouldn't ever be able to pull off anything really crooked, if this was the best he could do.

"No," she answered honestly. "I read it in the paper."

"They really shouldn't print rumors." He harrumphed. "That paper is going to lose all credibility if that's the type of story they want to start running."

She nodded noncommittally.

"What was the rumor part of it?"

His eyebrows arched again but he didn't answer.

She began palpitating Lola's abdomen carefully. "Has she been going regularly?"

The commissioner looked at Kate as if she were speaking a foreign language.

"Going poop?" she clarified.

"Oh, I guess so. I haven't heard any different."

Just like she thought. This man never interacted with this dog, except perhaps to pet it once in a while.

Just an excuse to come talk to her.

"Her teeth look good. You guys are doing a great job with that."

Buford looked at the dog like he was surprised teeth were even a concern for dogs.

"Are you putting that dental stuff into her water, like I told your wife?" She was just yanking his chain now. Enjoying watching him squirm and trying to pretend he knew anything about what she was talking about.

"Yeah, yeah. I mean Janie really does take care of most of Lola's daily needs. I just thought it was time I saw what this whole vet business was about."

"Emm," she murmured as she listened to the dog's heart. She dropped her stethoscope. "I think she's just fine. But, it is time for her heartworm test so I'm going to send her back to the clinic and get some blood drawn."

"A tech will bring her back out to you." She picked up the dog. "It was good to see you, commissioner."

He stood, his hand rubbing along the edge of the exam table. "Katie."

This was his dog and pony show, short one pony, she'd let him run it. She didn't say anything.

"If you remember anything from the barbecue involving me that seems," he hesitated, "unpleasant, you'll come to me and discuss it, won't you?"

His face was kind and unthreatening, but he couldn't hide the anxiety peeking out from around his eyes and mouth. His eye twitched just a bit and his smile kept heading toward the nervous end of the spectrum. "I wouldn't want you to have the wrong idea about me. I would never do anything illegal or that would violate the trust of my constituents."

She gazed into his eyes as he smoothed out his face into a genial expression meant to win votes.

Could she believe him? Or had he just gotten control of his facial features, putting on the best show of all, a politician pulling one off?

What had she heard the other night?

Well, veterinarians had their own professional face they put on with clients, aka pet daddies and moms. "Sure, Buford. I've got nothing to hide. As a matter of fact, I have no memory of the barbecue. But, I appreciate the offer, because if any memories do come back, maybe you can help me straighten them out. The doctor said things might come back in a jumbled form and that I might need help understanding them."

His forehead bunched between his eyes into

the beginnings of a frown.

"*If* I ever do remember anything. They said I might not."

His forehead relaxed and a smile grew on his lips.

She smiled back at him, her best professional smile. "I appreciate the concern."

Uncertainty still played around the edges of his eyes. If she'd ever been asked to describe him, bland would have been the word she would have come up with. Nothing about him had ever really caught her attention.

But, with this new era of uncertainty and danger, everyone seemed in question. Even, bland Buford Gafney.

He smiled overly wide and nodded as she retreated out the door into the safety of her clinic where the biggest danger was an unruly dog trying to bite someone who wanted to give it a shot or get a little too personal with it.

Dogs were pretty straightforward that way. People could learn a thing or two from them.

Don't touch me there. Don't stick that needle into me. You always knew where you stood with dogs.

"Doctor Taylor, you have a call," the front desk clerk yelled back.

"Okay, I'll take it in my office."

She handed the dog off to one of the vet techs in the back clinic and went down the hall to her office.

"Doctor Taylor," she answered the phone.

"Katie, it's Wade over at *Hawk's Peak Daily*."

"Hey, Wade. I wondered when I'd get this call."

He laughed easily. He was a few years ahead of her in school but she'd known his little sister, had hung out at his house on occasion, ogling the older Wade and his buddies.

"I would have called sooner," he said. "But it's generally considered bad form to get quotes from people who've had head trauma while they're still in the hospital or not back at work yet."

She laughed. "Spit it out, Wade. Let's get this over with, then you can tell me how your sister and her new baby are doing down in Athens."

His sister had been a casualty of her college days, falling in love and marrying a local guy, settling down in Athens.

"Okie dokie," Wade said. "Here goes. Can you comment on the fact that several people said they overheard a heated exchange between you and your fiancé about something to do with the road proposed for the governor's property? They said you were very agitated and walked off into the woods afterwards."

"Off into the woods?"

He didn't say anything.

"That seems strange, doesn't it?" she queried him as if he'd know all that had gone on that day. As a newspaperman, she suspected he often knew more than he said. Was under some sort of code of ethics to keep a lot to himself.

People told him a lot of things, things that never made it into print.

"Is it?" he asked back.

"We're not gonna get anywhere with that type of answer, Wade, so I'll just cut to the chase. I don't remember being at that barbecue. Between you and me and not for print, please, I don't even remember being engaged to Hamilton Avery."

"Wow." Wade dropped the professional façade. "Yeah, that won't be making it into the article. But that's heavy. How's Ham handling it? Do you think he could have made these two attempts on your life?"

"Wow." Said so flat out like that, it really hit home. "Wow."

"Sorry, Katie. I didn't mean to sound like such a cold fish. About your possible death and all." He laughed darkly. "We news people just get so matter of fact about stuff, even when they might be the worse moments of other people's lives."

Wade had worked down in Atlanta before coming back to work on the Hawk's Peak paper. He'd gotten street cred, as a big city reporter. And seen stuff. Wade's sister had often talked about the stories he'd covered.

"It's okay, Wade. I know what you mean. I

have to be there at some of the worse
moments in people's lives, too. When they
have to put down a beloved pet." She coughed
huskily, remembering the recent tears of a dog
owner.

"Then, we try to put it behind us," she
continued. "Doesn't make us terrible people,
just normal. You can't really let all of that
infiltrate your mind to the degree that it does
the person most closely affected by the death
or disaster, or we'd never be able to get out of
bed and go back to work."

"Gallows humor helps, too," he added.

Kate laughed for real then. He'd always
been a funny guy, probably one of the reasons
people confided so much in him.

But, she suddenly wondered what else he
knew about that night, the night her car was
run off the road.

"If you knew something really vital to me,
you'd tell me, wouldn't you, Wade?"

"Oh, yeah, Katie. I'd go right to the sheriff,
too. I'm not in the business of covering up for
criminals. In fact, I'd put it on the front page
in big headlines, right along with an exclusive
photograph of the jerk being arrested. *Alleged*
jerk," he corrected himself.

"But, Katie." His voice dropped in tone.
"Watch your back. I haven't seen anything
like this in a long time. The names of people
like ex-governors, county commissioners and
sitting Georgia House of Representative

members being bandied about along with two attempts on the life of a local girl?"

He laughed harshly. "Watch your back, Katie. I don't want to have to report on your murder."

A cold shudder ran through her. His warning wasn't meant to intimidate. It was meant with the best of intentions, but it was even more frightening coming from him, a man with pure motives.

A man who heard a lot of talk and knew so much more than he felt at liberty to say.

*****

Kate locked the front door of the vet clinic, determined not to let everything that had happened recently affect her mood.

The crisp fall air exhilarated her and thoughts of a night ahead with Grant filled her with anticipation, memories of the night before heating her blood.

Flashes of Grant pulling her to him, insistent, male.

It was like it'd always been between them, only better. Though she would never have dreamed that was possible.

He was a man now and brought a lot of testosterone to the table. Or bedroom, as the case may be.

She'd never known she possessed so much estrogen, activated by his hands. He brought out the woman in her, made her feel desirable, beautiful, wanted. All the things a man should make a woman feel.

Yet no one had, except him.

She hummed as she hit the car unlock button to her SUV, which was now parked on the street in front of the clinic because her staff said it was safer. They'd wanted to wait around while she caught up on paperwork, but she'd said that was ridiculous. She couldn't live like that.

They all had families to get home to, or in the case of the single people, gyms or bars or dates to get to. She'd sent them on their way.

She walked to her car, sniffing the faint odor of wood smoke that always lingered in the air of Hawk's Peak in the fall. A heady, exciting scent that evoked exhilaration, along with the brisk breeze that whirled leaves along the street, swirling through the pools of orange light thrown by the late afternoon sun.

She tossed her hair, letting the wind cleanse it of vet clinic smells, taking away the worries of the day, with the sick pets and their owner's fears and concerns.

Every day, she and her staff and the other vet did everything they could to extend the lives of beloved pets and to make their illnesses and injuries better. Her life's work held real meaning for her. And satisfaction.

Thank God, she'd realized early on that she wanted to be a vet.

Like Grant was a vet, a niggling little guilty part of her mind prodded. Just a vet of a different kind, a veteran.

Apparently, he'd realized his calling as well. She'd just been unwilling to accept it.

She turned her face up to the wind. How strong was that breeze? Could it wash away her regrets for her behavior and all the time it had cost her and Grant?

The wind whistled through the trees, as if answering her question. *Yes, yes, yes.*

A sense of peace filled her and she continued on to her SUV.

Then, a man walked out from the side alley across the street.

As if he'd been waiting for her.

A kick of nervous apprehension flashed through her.

The man was large, hulking.

CHAPTER TWENTY-ONE

Big and burley, his sheer physical bulk intimidating, his face hidden in shadow, the man took a few steps closer.

The air tightened in her lungs, ready to explode if she ran. She couldn't get to her car door and get in without being within arm's reach of him.

Despite his size, the man looked like he could sprint as fast as a pit bull, his bulk seeming all muscle.

Her heart began pounding, and she looked back toward the door of the clinic. He would pound across that street and snatch her up like a little Pomeranian before she could get the key into the lock.

He could swing her into the air, like a small dog in the mouth of a bad pit bull, slam her into the pavement, and crush the life from her, before a single yelp escaped her lips.

She reached into her purse, searching for her pistol. It wasn't there. She'd left it in her car earlier, thinking it was safer not to have a loaded gun in her workplace. With all the children who frequently came to the clinic with their parents and pets, she'd decided to leave it in the car rather than risk an accident.

That was earlier when employees and early clients were coming and going from the clinic's parking lot, when this street had been busy and felt safe.

She pulled out her cell phone, hitting the button to bring it to life. The light flashed on the ground, bouncing up into the air as if attempting to illuminate the face of the bulky man.

He stepped forward into the sunlight and his face became visible.

Jocko. The man who'd been part of the governor's personal security detail when he'd been a state senator, then the governor. And now, his private bodyguard.

Jocko had come back to the mountains with the governor after he'd left office and provided security for the governor and his wife.

You never saw the governor in town without Jocko nearby.

His eyes locked on her and an animal instinct told her to run. But, she'd seen predatory reactions in animals - the chase and kill impulse that often took over when prey fled in panic.

She smiled at him, forcing the grimace to her lips, although every nerve in her body wanted to scream in fear.

They both hesitated, he on his side of the road, she on hers, in that moment when two creatures realize they've been spotted. Fight or flight. Which would it be?

He smiled back at her, the smile only on his lips, not making its way to his eyes.

A chill seeped through her.

Just then, Jason, Grant's youngest deputy, pulled out from his spot down the street from the clinic where he'd sat all afternoon, probably thinking she wouldn't see him, but where he could watch the comings and goings at the clinic and wait for her to head home.

In her panic, she'd forgotten all about Jason, only seeing Jocko.

Jason pulled up between her and Jocko, stopping, the windows down on both front windows.

"Hey, Jocko. What's up, man?" Jason smiled like it was just another day on the streets of Hawk's Peak.

"Jason," Jocko called out, jovially, raising a hand.

When he took his eyes off her, she felt like she'd been released from a paralyzing grip. Quickly, before he could turn his gaze on her again, she stumbled toward her SUV.

As the two men continued to talk, she got in, hit the door lock button and turned the key in the ignition.

With her eyes darting back to check Jocko's

whereabouts in her mirrors, she put the car into gear and pulled out.

A sigh of relief whooshed out of her lungs as she put distance between herself and that large man. His mere presence had felt a warning.

A threat?

Just by showing up at her work place unexpectedly. A dark harbinger sent by the governor?

The night of the crash flashed into her head.

The bulk of the man who'd looked at her from the black SUV fit Jocko's. Had he come after her that night? Overreacted to something he'd heard her say?

Would the governor and Hamilton be furious if they'd known it was him? Had it been him? The face of the man in the SUV wouldn't come into focus.

She pressed her foot on the accelerator, putting more distance between herself and Jocko.

The town vanished around the last curve out of town and she drove purposefully, with intent.

A minute later, Jason appeared in the distance behind her, tailing her close enough for it to be obvious to Jocko that he was doing so.

No one would be running her off the road on Jason's watch.

Sweet little Jason. She remembered him in middle school when she'd come home from college one year, coming round her dad's place, selling popcorn for the Boy Scouts fundraiser.

Grant had assigned Jason to watch her since he'd gone out to a man's house who'd seen the article in the paper about Katie's crash, and had called, saying his son had been playing with the camera on his new smart phone, recording along that road that night around the time of the crash.

Said he thought he might have caught the SUV on video, that there was something on the recording that looked like it.

Kate drove slow enough that Jason could follow her along the route to Miss Sally's place, just like she'd told Grant she'd do after work.

Memories of Grant flooded into her mind. The two of them making love last night as if for the first time, with the passion of new lovers, but also the intrinsic knowledge of each other's bodies born of their teenaged lovemaking, with such a powerful connection that, even now, the thought of what they'd done in the night heated her, making her want him.

Without thinking, as if driven by the arousal Grant's body elicited, she picked up speed. Along the road outside of town, her car flew around the curves. Soon, there were several turns in the road between her and Jason.

As she came around the last turn before Miss Sally's house, the driveway to the governor's house appeared. On impulse, she turned left up the driveway.

The lovemaking she'd shared with Grant last night had made her anxious for her new life to begin. For that to happen, she needed to put to rest all of the leftover debris from her relationship with Hamilton. She also needed to resolve the matter about what had instigated the attacks.

If that was what they were, instead of two separate incidents. Then, she laughed harshly at herself for wishful, naïve thinking.

Something told her the answers to what had been happening lately and the ability to stop all of it lay up this driveway. She needed to know, to refuse to run away from bad memories, as it appeared she'd done so often in her life.

If she were ever to have a chance at a life with Grant, she needed to face things head on.

Her car disappeared into the trees that almost hid the driveway from the road so that Jason would never know she'd gone this way. It wasn't like she'd planned to deceive him, just that at the last moment, something had drawn her up the hill.

What was she going to do when she got to the house? Say *Hey*, like nothing had happened the last couple of days? Mrs. Avery would invite her to supper? Then, maybe all of them could put this behind them with a civility that would allow them all to remain friends?

Right.

Just then, her phone rang. Her friend's number popped up. "Hey, Callie. What's up?" They'd bonded in Callie's store, where Kate had always stopped for coffee and a bit of town *information*, as Callie insisted on calling the gossip.

"What's up with you?" Callie's impertinent little voice snapped through the cell phone. "I hear you've changed your name?"

"Oh, Callie. Callie, Callie. You've been over to the diner again?"

Callie laughed her wild laugh. "I don't need to go to the diner 'cause the gossip comes to me at the store. People say you're not yourself." She waited a beat. "You did seem off when I came to see you at the hospital."

"You came to see me?"

Callie didn't say anything for a moment, then she let out a long breath.

"Some of what happened right after the crash is a complete blank, Callie." Kate laughed awkwardly. "Pretty disturbing, wondering about all I said in those hours."

Callie laughed lightly. "You were fine. Just a little dazed acting. Are you back to normal now?"

What to say to that? "I guess. But, my memory is so odd. Some things are a complete blank, while others I remember like nothing happened. I remember things about my business and who I interacted with a few days before the crash. But, things right before and right after the crash are quite blank."

Callie murmured sympathetically. "I hear you're back with Grant. That Hamilton Avery is history?"

Kate wanted to make light of that, to smooth it all over, but something about Callie always invited her to confide in her. "I don't even remember being *with* Hamilton in *that* way. *And* I don't remember ever breaking up with Grant. My last memories of him are as my boyfriend in high school." She sucked in a deep breath, willing it to get to her brain, to help make sense of everything. "Yet, I remember coming into your store and hanging out with you and your boys. So bizarre."

"Where are you now?" Callie said in a no-nonsense tone. "Why don't I come pick you up and take you out to the house to eat with me and the boys?"

"That sounds so good. Just like old times."

Callie laughed a bit funny. "Real old times. You hardly ever had time for me when you were Hamilton's *Katherine*," she said the name with an affected British accent, like she was talking about the princess.

She'd blown off Callie? That just didn't

sound like her.

"Really, Callie? I don't even remember that either. But, listen, I can't talk right now. I'll have to take you up on that dinner offer later."

"Where are you, Katie? What's going on?" Callie had always been able to read between the lines with Kate, sensing when there was something she wasn't telling her.

Ahead, a dark tunnel-like opening appeared on the right. To the unknowing eye, it was just a gap in the trees. But, she knew it slipped into an almost hidden driveway.

She knew that because of a flash of memory of herself, Grant, and Ham going down that driveway as kids.

Face it, face your past, a voice called to her. *Take control of your life. Do what you need to in order to deserve Grant.*

"Where are you? Tell me." Callie's voice penetrated her thoughts.

"I'm out at the governor's," she answered.

Callie let out a gasp. "Katie, what are you up to?"

"Nothing." But, suddenly, she turned right into the almost hidden dirt road that led to an old abandoned barn, where she, Ham and Grant used to play as kids during barbecues at the governor's house.

"Why does everybody think I'm *up to something* lately?"

Callie let the question hang in the air. Then, finally, she said, "Because you've been run off the road, shot at, ended up in the hospital with amnesia. If that's the truth. Is it, Katie? Can't you remember anything about being engaged to Ham?"

Kate silently shook her head at all of the questions, causing the beginning of a headache. "I can't think about all that right now. I've got to figure things out."

"Please, please, be careful," Callie echoed what so many people were saying to her these days.

"Be careful, be careful, be careful. I feel like I've been too careful, Callie. I'm tired of being careful."

Callie didn't say anything for a minute, then finally said, "Call me when you're leaving that place, girl. I want to know you're out of there before it's dark. Okay?"

"Okay, I'll call you."

"You know what they've always said around here, Katie. 'Don't mess with the governor.' They say it with a laugh. But I've always known deep down, underneath the joke, they meant it."

A deep foreboding welled up inside Kate, followed by a little kick of anger. Don't mess with the governor? He shouldn't mess with her.

Ahead, the barn loomed, dark, the wood blending so well with the forest around it that it almost disappeared into the dusky landscape.

That barn? What was it about the barn that called to her?

"Gotta go!" she said, hanging up before her friend could try to talk sense into her.

The time for thinking was over. She needed answers.

*****

Grant watched the image the fourteen-year-old kid had downloaded to his computer from his smart phone. The boy's father stood right by Grant's side, peering intently at the screen, excitement bouncing off him.

Grant's phone rang and he pulled it out of his pocket without taking his eyes off the computer screen. "Sheriff Campbell."

"Hey, Grant." Luke's voice was intense. "Got the report back from the GBI."

"Yeah? Speak to me, Luke, whatcha got?"

"Here it comes," the father said. "In just a minute."

The boy's attention was all on Grant although the father leaned closer to the video screen.

"Hold on, Luke." He nodded at the boy. "Got to take this on the front porch. Can you pause that video?"

The father nodded distractedly, still looking at the screen, while the kid stared avidly at Grant, seeming to realize something was up.

"You're a cop in the making, kid," Grant said with a nod, acknowledging the kid's observant nature, then walked outside for privacy.

He walked out onto the front porch and closed the door behind him.

"Did the bullet from my patrol car match the bullet found in that guy down near the county line?" he asked.

"No, it didn't," Luke answered.

The words disappointed him more than he could ever have imagined. He wanted an end to this, an end to the threat to Katie.

"But something else came up, Grant. Something you're not gonna believe." Luke paused, sucked in a deep breath that Grant could hear even over the phone. It wasn't like Luke to get so excited. "Man, I can't even believe I'm about to say this."

Grant just waited.

"The bullet from the dead guy near the county line matches the bullet that you sent down to the GBI. From your dad's murder," Luke elaborated.

Grant's pulse shot up as blood pounded in his head, beating the tattoo that finally some clue to his father's murder had shown up in the modern world. Almost twenty-five years later, the evidence might connect to a living person.

Murder had no statute of limitations, could always be prosecuted as long as the murderer was alive.

Luke sniffed contemplatively, slowing his rate of speech. "This bullet doesn't connect back to the gunshot up at the governor's place."

"But, the fact that a guy in a black SUV was shot, right while we're looking for a black SUV that drove Katie off the road after the governor's barbeque does," Luke said what he knew Grant was thinking. "The dead guy has a substantial criminal history, which would take the heat off the shooter up at the governor's, make us think we solved the crime."

A blast of adrenalin shot through Grant, with the conviction that someone was playing them, thinking he was smarter than everybody else. A sense of righteous anger blew through Grant.

The black SUV found with a dead guy in it tied the shooting to the governor's place in his mind, and the bullet in the shooting of the driver of the SUV was tied to his father's shooting.

So that made that son of a bitch ex-governor tied to his father's murder. Just needed more evidence, more hard proof to take to the district attorney to present to a jury.

Someone was gonna finally pay for his father's murder. Grant's money was on the governor being the perpetrator. The man behind the shooting, who'd ordered it.

But, was it really justice when Jefferson Avery had lived a full life for so many years, watched his son grow up, while Grant's father had been in the ground more than twenty years? It was like the man had been dancing on his father's grave.

If it was indeed the governor, as he'd suspected for so many years, then the man's fall from grace would be harsh. That pain might be punishment enough.

"I've got to go, Luke. Don't do anything yet. I'll call you when I'm ready to act, when we've got a few more loose strings tied up."

He turned to go, then remembered the video and went back inside.

"We got it paused right before the moment the car comes around the corner," the father said. The excitement in the room was palpable. They knew they had something good.

"I can't believe I never looked at this before, didn't think about it till Joey here brought it up."

"Good going, Joey," Grant said. "Could tell you had cop instincts."

The kid puffed up a bit with pride. But Grant wasn't blowing smoke up his ass. In the short time Grant had been at the farm, the kid had shown the personality traits that made a good cop.

"Play it, Joey," Grant said.

"Play it again, Joey," the father said with a laugh. "He's looked at it multiple times now."

Just hit the play button, Grant wanted to yell. He needed to get out of here. This was probably nothing because people called all the time with false leads, thinking they had something that usually turned out to be nothing.

The video began rolling, Joey and his father's car headlights flashing onto the road ahead.

Finally, they came around a curve and a large black SUV, with visible front passenger side damage loomed toward the car.

The SUV came closer and Joey hit a button that slowed the video down. At the snail's pace that Joey had given to the video, it was easy to study the vehicle.

It came closer, and closer, until finally Grant had a close up view of the car. The father's car's headlights flashed momentarily onto the driver side.

It still didn't show the driver, just the vague impression of a white man. Maybe the image could be enhanced.

He looked closer at the image. It was a Chevrolet Suburban. The dead guy's SUV was a Ford Expedition.

Grant stepped back, shock shooting out from his heart to all parts of his body. So, here was proof that the SUV with the murdered felon in it wasn't the same one that had run Katie off the road.

Someone had gone to a lot of effort to make it look like the case was tied up with a bow. Maybe even killed the felon who'd never done anything that Grant knew of to deserve the death penalty. Except hang out with the wrong sort of people.

People who killed easily.

He needed air, felt as if he'd been sprinting for miles uphill.

Because the person who'd done that was still out there. Maybe still gunning for Katie.

He looked at the boy, then up at the father. "Good stuff," he said as a way of a thank you.

"I know, right?" the father said, his eyes intense, knowing exactly what his kid had caught on video. "It doesn't show his face exactly, but still."

"It shows that sticker right there." Joey pointed toward the driver's side. "Probably a dealer sticker. Maybe you can check with dealers around the area. It's good enough to use in court, or to get a warrant," the boy said. "If you can find that SUV. Right, sheriff?"

"He watches a lot of cop shows," Joey's dad said with a laugh.

Grant peered closer at the screen, then laughed harshly. He'd been so intent on the driver's face, he hadn't even picked up on the decal. "See me when you get out of high school, kid. I got a couple of recommendations where you might want to study criminal procedures."

Then, he looked at the decal again. "Can you blow up that part with the sticker?"

The boy nodded decidedly. He did something to grab an isolated image from the video then dragged the image wider until Grant could make out a state seal, with a blurry number underneath it. Where had he seen that sticker before?

Suddenly, he remembered. And the realization blasted through him like a gunshot.

On Ham's car.

That was a parking decal for the capitol. A steel hard anger surged through him. Someone was going to jail for trying to kill Katie.

Hamilton Avery was going to jail. All sympathy for his childhood friend blasted away like a bullet exiting a body, exploding with a violent force.

Grant pulled a flash drive out of his pocket and handed it to Joey. "Can you put a copy of that onto this? Also, I need you to email this back to me at the station as well. And I hate to say it, Joey. But your phone is now evidence. I gotta take it."

The boy's face dimmed for a minute then flashed excitement again. "Do you think I'll have to testify in court?"

Grant tilted his head. "I think so. But, it's very important that," he met Joey's eyes, "that neither of you say anything to anyone about this until I tell you it's okay. All right?"

He looked into the father's eyes and saw it settling in just how dangerous this could be for his family if anyone knew they possessed this type of evidence.

"Sheriff, get that phone out of here right now, and believe me, we will not tell a soul. Not a soul." He put his hand on his son's shoulder and squeezed.

Joey winced and tried to pull away. "Okay, okay. I get it. We could wind up dead." The kid laughed like it was a joke, until his dad squeezed his shoulder again. "Oww, I was just kidding, really."

Then, as if he realized the truth of what he'd just said about winding up dead, his face turned serious and he swiveled back to the computer and began copying the file to Grant's flash drive and emailing a copy to the email address on a card Grant produced.

Now, Grant needed to convey the information to Luke and get him to go to a judge and get a warrant to search the governor's property for that SUV as well as Hamilton's place in Hawk's Ridge and down in Atlanta as well.

Hamilton could have driven up Mountain Ridge Road to the side road through his dad's property to take that potshot at Katie. He could have hidden the car somewhere on the vast grounds that the ex-governor owned.

That could also be why he and Katie had been shot at the other day. Someone had wanted to keep him from going up that road and finding the SUV.

The SUV might still be up there somewhere

since it had become too hot to move it around the county easily.

And Katie was just across the road from the governor's property at Miss Sally's house.

He had to get a hold of her.

CHAPTER TWENTY-TWO

As Kate got out of her car, the woods closed in around her as if they would strangle her with the vines that climbed over everything, eventually hiding all structures with its green clawing mass if the vines were not cut back, held at bay.

A silent, timeless quality emanated from the forest, both reassuring and dismal at the same time, with a reminder that one day she too would be gone, and other people, other little girls would roam these woods, roam this property, having heard tales of the governor who once owned the big house at the top of the hill.

She sucked in a deep breath, praying for strength, the fortitude not to run.

Were the crash and the shooting into Grant's car unconnected incidents, a road raging person, shots fired to keep nosey people off a contested piece of property? Or were they threats on her life? Failed attempts to silence her forever.

The dead man in the decoy SUV down near the county line reinforced that theory.

She looked into the dense overgrowth for anyone lurking nearby. Then turned back and reached into her purse for the gun her father had insisted she might need one day. The cold steel of the weapon felt good, with an empowering promise that she could protect herself.

She tucked it into her waistband and pulled her shirt over it to hide it. The headlights from her car automatically shut off, and the creeping darkness overwhelmed her like a blanket thrown over her head.

Somewhere in the distance an owl hooted. A branch crackled nearby and she jumped, looking into the dense undergrowth that could hide many types of predators.

Tangled, twisted vines covered the ground.

Soon, all the leaves would fall away leaving the skeletons of the crawling, smothering vines.

She shivered at the reminder of the circle of life, from birth to death. Though sometimes, like this morning's murdered SUV driver, that cycle was cut short.

With a quick glance around, she walked toward the barn, driven by instinct, premonition. She was like a wild animal in the woods these days, living on instinct, ideas coming to her from a source she didn't understand.

Slowly, she crept to the barn, and looked inside one of the old windows, so covered with dirt and grime that it was almost impossible to see through.

She wiped at the dirt, clearing a small spot.

There it was, a large black SUV. Shock surged through her, generating a sense of panic throughout her entire body as the reality of what she saw hit her.

Someone had tried to kill her with this vehicle and hid it here, on the governor's property. Ham? The Governor? Or someone who worked for one of them? Jocko?

Someone from this house wanted her dead. The newspapers and television carried stories all the time of spurned lovers trying to kill the other.

It just didn't seem like Ham.

She moved to a side door and tried it. It was locked. So, she looked in the hiding place Ham had shown she and Grant as children, where Ham's daddy hid the key.

It was still there, the same hiding place more than twenty years later. A little hole in one of the barn's wooden planks.

She unlocked the door and went inside. Using her cell phone to light the darkened barn, she circled the SUV until she saw it. On the right side, a huge scar on the vehicle's body showed the damage done when the mammoth car had hit her tiny car, sending her spinning into the ditch.

She moved on around to the driver's side, to the front windshield where a small ancient sticker, so like the ones on Hamilton's cars flashed light back at her phone. The metallic shield was aged like the governor and also like him crusted in dirt, like the governor's metaphoric dirt from politics.

It was a sticker from the days when Jefferson Avery had been governor. And all-powerful.

As if this sticker served as a reminder to everyone of just how much power he'd once wielded. And maybe like this vestige of those days, he still did possess great power. And connections.

Her stomach roiled with the knowledge that someone from this house had deliberately tried to kill her.

Someone in her fiancé's family had tried to kill her. Staggering back, she turned toward the door, wanting to get off the property as fast as possible.

But, she bumped into one of the barn's large supporting pillars and dropped her phone, the small thing sliding off into the dirt underneath the car.

The light died, as if it had gone facedown. Suddenly, the dark closed around her. And her breathing became so loud that she wasn't sure there wasn't someone else in the barn as well.

She glanced carefully around, then kneeled

and reached for the phone where it had slid far underneath the SUV. Her heart beat loudly in her chest, pumping fear throughout her body.

She was alone on the property where murderers dwelled.

Frantically, she swept her hand along the dirty barn floor, desperate to find the phone in the growing dark underneath the car. If she left it, it might be discovered, then they'd know for sure she'd been there.

And discovered this incriminating evidence.

They'd have to kill her then.

Why had she come here like this? Did she want to die?

No. No, she didn't. She wanted to live. To live and remember everything that happened to her from now on. She wanted to remember every moment she and Grant could share together in their future.

Something rustled, and she whirled to look over her shoulder. A skittering in a corner announced some small animal scurrying away.

As if it, too, sensed the danger living in the barn. Sensed that it wasn't safe to be here.

She swiped her hand along the ground in an ever- increasing circle. Until finally, finally, her hand touched her phone. She grabbed it and struggled to a standing position.

Sweat and dirt and dust covered her, and

she felt as if cobwebs were stuck to her hair. Almost as if she were already a part of history.

Just another dead person connected to this SUV.

She had to get out of here. Make it look like no one had been here. The floor of the barn was so covered in dirt and dust. Was it disturbed enough by her kneeling that it would be apparent that someone had been down in the dust? Had she touched the vehicle, leaving fingerprints?

It didn't matter. She just needed to get out of there alive, get off the property. She ran toward the door.

Outside, she locked the door, replaced the key and started toward her car.

Then, a feeling came over her, a feeling from deep in the woods, calling to her with a voice from somewhere in the deep murky mists of her childhood.

It sounded like her mother's voice. When she would call her in for the night, call her away from the lightning bugs of summer evenings, into the safety of their home.

Kate looked out into the trees. Why did she feel drawn down there, in the direction of the ridge overlooking Miss Sally's house.

Slowly, she looked around. If the wrong person found her here . . .

What might happen?

Nothing good.

But, the draw from the woods called to her so powerfully, as if everything would end, all the questions, all the mystery of her loss memory.

If only she were brave enough to head down into that wooded property. The property where she'd seen the governor stalking and muttering.

With that rifle so close and ready at hand.

If she and Grant were ever to have a chance, a chance at a life where he could trust that she wouldn't suddenly *forget* that she loved him ...

She had to face whatever was calling to her from the woods. She had to.

*****

Grant's cell phone rang and he didn't even have time to spit out his usual greeting before Callie started rattling into his ear. Breathless, high-pitched, the woman meant business.

"Grant, Katie didn't want me to tell you, but you have to know."

"Tell me," Grant prompted.

"She's going to Jefferson Avery's. Like she's going to confront him or something."

"She's what?" Grant clutched his cell phone tighter, as if it were Katie and he could force some sense into her. "The governor's property? Man alive."

"I know," Callie's voice went into a high-pitched, panicked range. "Something's going on with her, Grant. She's seems so ... different."

"You could say that."

"Like she's on a mission. Like something's driving her and she can't control it."

Like Katie had ever needed a reason not to do something once she'd made up her mind to do it.

Even if it led to her death?

"How long ago did you talk to her?"

"Just a minute ago. Grant, you've got to get up there. It was like she was going to find out what's been going on. No matter the consequences. Cause what sane person would go up there after all that's happened?"

"Yeah." He needed to get to the governor's fast. But, Katie had been right. The answers to all that had happened the last few days lay with someone connected to the governor.

And the blame for at least one dead man. And attempts on Katie's life. He had to reach her fast.

"Callie, please call me if she calls you again. Try to make her get off the governor's property as quickly as possible. And thanks."

He had to get up there before something happened to her. Something else. And this time the person who'd tried to kill her twice before might be successful, might get lucky. The thought of Katie alone up there gnawed into his gut.

He hung up and called Katie's phone. Voice mail. "Get off that property now! You don't know what you're dealing with. Someone up there is very dangerous. I have more proof. Kate, get off that property."

Then, he called Jason.

Jason who immediately sputtered out words so fast that Grant could barely understand him.

"I lost Katie, don't know where she is, she went around a curve. I drove on out to Miss Sally's, seen she wasn't there, went back to the right turn in the road, doubled back."

"Slow down, Jason."

Jason gulped in air, then continued at a more understandable pace. "I lost her. I don't know if she kept on up the road, or went down that road that leads to Dahlonega. Sheriff, I am sorry."

"Listen, Jason, go to Miss Sally's, park, and wait for a call from me. Don't do anything else. Got it?"

"Got it, sheriff," he stuttered out. The confusion in his tone said he didn't get it but he'd spent time in the army after high school and got the don't-argue, just-do-it tone.

Grant put in a fast call to Luke and Travis, then drove as fast as he could, praying he was in time, praying Katie knew just how much danger she was in.

Someone had gone over the edge, into the deep end of the psychotic pool.

His money was on the governor as the one taking that dive. Though it could be Ham as well.

The governor could have stumbled over the edge when his son's pride had been damaged when Katie had dumped Hamilton. Jefferson Avery put so much store into that boy and his political career, might have thought it wouldn't look good for his run for senator.

It was like he lived through that boy, pushing him, wanting him to fulfill the dreams the governor hadn't achieved. He'd always said his boy was destined to be president.

People had thought Jefferson Avery was going to make a run for president after his stint as governor, then for whatever reason, he'd not run.

This sort of rage was ridiculous because of a broken engagement. Whether it was the governor or Ham. All sorts of women would want a man like Ham, with his money, good looks and connections. Ham would have bounced back in no time.

Or had Katie heard or seen something transpire about the state's change of route on the road through the governor's property? That could impact Ham's senatorial run. Not to mention sending people to prison.

He picked up his phone and called Katie again. "Pick up, damn it," he cursed at the phone.

Where was she right now? Confronting the governor, a man with an ego bigger than his bank account.

Or confronting Ham?

Either way, it might be someone who'd already tried to kill her twice.

Finally her voice mail kicked in and he left another message. "It' me again. Get off the governor's property right now. Call me, but get off his property this instant!"

Someone wanted Katie dead. He had to find her before someone made that a reality.

CHAPTER TWENTY-THREE

Grant turned onto the governor's property. Why had Katie come up here? It was foolhardy. Nothing could be accomplished this way.

He drove through the wooded drive, the forest clutching at his vehicle from all sides, branches lashing at his windshield, whipping around the wheels and top of the car.

Then, he came up on the almost hidden drive to the right, the woods seeming to win the battle to reclaim the man-made entry into its guts, closing around the drive so you wouldn't see it unless you already knew it was there.

Instinctively, he turned right, realizing that was where she would have gone. To that barn, to check for a hidden vehicle.

Why hadn't he thought of that earlier? Because the memory of that old barn was hidden so deep in his memory, it was like he'd almost forgotten it.

But, the visual cues in the afternoon light

reminded him of what he hadn't noticed on his last nighttime visit to question the governor and his wife.

So much seemed to bubble up from the depths of his memory, almost like Katie's new way of thinking, with the past leaching up into the present. Memories from so long ago, when he and Katie and Ham had played here as children.

As he rounded the last curve, his gut clenched. Katie's car sat parked outside the barn.

He pulled up and got out, drew his gun immediately, then slowly circled the area.

*****

Like a dream, the small trail took her back to another time, to the landscape of her childhood, running through these woods, with Grant and Ham · her buddies, her friends. The three of them together had been invincible, unafraid, because the other two were always there to help if something happened.

Together in the woods, they were safe. Because of their friendship, because of each other.

A small creek rushed down the mountainside, its sound like a thousand librarians shushing her, warning her to be quiet, urging stealth.

Her blood pulsed at the same rate as the creek, pumping adrenalin through her. She descended the mountain, rushing perilously toward her destiny, the same as the creek.

She came up over a ridge and looked down at the little area below. The small valley was separated by just one more ridge before the property ran down to Miss Sally's land on the other side of the road.

Something about the little valley was distinctive, memorable, with so many dogwood trees lining the bottom of the low-lying land.

Dogwoods grew everywhere in Georgia, wild and planted. Now, in the fall, their leaves shimmered, reflecting back the last sunlight with a coppery glow, some bright red, others a muted shade of pink.

Here, the dogwoods formed a tribe of sorts, hiding among the larger trees, ready to spring forth with their cotton-colored flowers in the spring.

Suddenly, a memory flashed forth. This small dogwood strewn area was where it had ended.

Another memory appeared fully-formed in her brain of the last time she'd been here - the governor's barbecue only a few days ago.

What had possessed her to come out into these woods by herself that early evening? As if with no control of her own, after a fight with Hamilton, she'd headed down here. Drawn to the woods.

That day, she hadn't realized what had driven her down here. Now she realized why, the memories bubbling up faster and faster.

Slowly, she crept forward, closer and closer to the spot where she'd experienced a psychotic break as a little girl.

The sight of her mother being gunned down had been enough to drive a child crazy. Her mother had been shot elsewhere on the property but Katie had followed the governor as he carried her mother's limp body here and buried her.

He'd put her mother's body into a shallow grave then covered her with dirt. Katie had run away, crying softly so the monster wouldn't hear her.

The image of her mother being covered with dirt was already being pushed back into the recesses of her mind.

Little Katie had pushed the horror of that moment back into the depths of her psyche because her young mind couldn't handle such a terrifying concept.

Her mother lying motionless as dirt was shoveled on top of her.

But, Kate wasn't that little girl anymore, little Katie. Now, she was grown. And Kate could handle anything she needed to handle.

It was time.

Steadily, surely, she approached the area. The little circle of trees where she'd seen her mother buried, put into the ground with no casket, no consecration, no memorial stone and no loving family around her to wish her into the next world.

Kate stepped inside the sheltering trees and looked at the exact spot where she was convinced the governor had buried her mother.

The desire came over her to claw at the earth, to scratch it away and reveal the truth that her mother hadn't willingly left her. But, had been ripped from her life.

By the former governor of Georgia.

Kate shook herself out of her memories, concentrating on the now and what she needed to do. She stuck her gun into the waistband of her pants and her shirt fell loosely over the hard metal. She pulled her cell phone from her pocket and snapped a few identifying photos to show investigators so they would be able to find the exact spot.

Then, she heard the crushing of leaves behind her and twirled.

To a rifle pointed straight at her heart.

"Oh, it's you, Katherine Shelby." The governor dropped the gun to his side. "You've come back to me," he said, his voice dreamy, as if he weren't really there with her, but back in another time.

With the woman who looked so like Kate in photos.

He squinted his eyes, searching her face. "Is it really you?"

"It's me," Kate's sense of self-preservation urged her to say. Then, another idea came to her. Her phone was still on the camera function. Quickly, she pressed the video recorder on her phone, to capture everything that happened. Perhaps to document her own death?

"Where have you been, Katherine Shelby?"

"Why, I've been right here, Jefferson Avery. Right where you left me. All this time, I've been right here beneath these dogwoods."

"Ahh." Remorse tinged his face, crumpling it, changing it from the tough man's man he'd always been to a younger, more tender version of himself, like the man in the photo who'd stared at her mother with such naked longing.

"That shouldn't have happened," he said. "That bullet wasn't meant for you."

"No, it wasn't. It was meant for Grant's father, Tom."

"I'm Grant's father," he protested angrily, the sadness falling away for a moment. Then, he looked back at Kate's face and remorse returned.

"A boy has a right to know his real father," he said with a self-righteous air.

As if he weren't a man whore. Impregnating a woman on the side, while his wife was about four months pregnant.

At the same time, he was lusting after Kate's mother as well, a married woman.

"A boy's got the right to know who his real father is," he said again, as if trying to reassure himself. He swung his left hand free of the gun, swinging it out toward the woods.

"He stood to inherit part of all this one day, as my son."

He blew out a gust of air in disgust. "But, Tom went crazy when Martha told him I planned to tell Grant I was his father. That half-man came out here all full of bluster, like he could tell *me* what to do. Told me I better keep away from his boy." The governor pulled his head back on his neck like someone had just suggested he wasn't the most powerful animal on the mountain, at the State Capitol, hell in the whole state of Georgia.

"His boy? You could look at that child and see me all over him. See my genes written all across his face."

The intensity in Jefferson Avery's eyes was that of a madman, fully convinced his distorted view of the world was the real truth.

If he got distracted enough, she could pull her gun. And do what? Shoot him?

She didn't want him dead, just held accountable finally.

He had to pay, be brought to justice in a courtroom for all he'd taken from her, taken from Grant, taken from her father.

And all the other people who'd loved her mother and Grant's parents.

Slowly, she slid her hand toward her gun.

The governor's eyes cleared and he peered closely at Kate, his other hand returning to grasp the rifle tightly. He brought the gun up a few inches. In a second, she could be dead.

Casually, she wrapped her hands around her waist as if that was what she'd been planning to do when she'd moved her hand toward her gun.

"You're not Katherine Shelby. But, you look so much like her, as lovely as she ever was. I wish you could have seen her."

Could have seen her?

"But, I did see her, Jefferson. For five years, I saw her every day. First thing in the morning, last thing at night, her face was there for me. Her beautiful face."

A burning rage ripped through her. A killing rage. This man had ended her mother's life, taken away a little girl's mama. Slowly, she moved her hand closer to the gun. "You killed her. And then stuck her underneath this dirt."

It hadn't been wise to say but anger had pushed the statement from her, as if she couldn't breathe unless she got the words out.

Jefferson's face twisted with rage. "It's not what I wanted. If that damn slut Martha and that idiot she convinced to marry her while she was knocked up with some other man's child hadn't come out here, raising hell, then none of this ever would have happened."

In his rage, he advanced on her. She backed up, but he took another step closer.

Then, he looked at the cell phone in her hand. "What are you doing with that phone, calling somebody?" He lurched forward and knocked it out of her hand.

When he did so, she lunged for his gun, latching onto it, holding it so he couldn't turn it back at her.

This was her chance to live, to not end up under that ground like her mother.

Jefferson Avery, though getting older, was still powerful. He jerked her around like a toy, like a little girl, that little girl who'd run crying through the woods.

Terror flooded through her but a determination to live gave her strength, so she could make this man pay for what he'd done. She fought to avenge her mother's life, to get justice for Katherine Shelby.

Her mother hadn't deserved to be shot down like a rabid dog. He had to pay for that.

Kate was the only one who could make this man pay his debt for his crime.

If he killed her today, he'd walk away - still *the governor*, still the big man on the mountain.

Damned if that would happen. She held onto the gun, fighting for all she was worth, for all her mother had been worth.

"Stop!" a voice rang out.

She and the governor both whipped their heads toward the voice.

"Thank God," she burst out. Grant stood there with his gun pointed at the governor.

"Drop the gun, governor," Grant said with a hard, granite tone. "Or I'll shoot."

The governor tilted his head. "You wouldn't shoot your own daddy, would you, son?"

Grant's face twisted with fury, almost unable to control his anger. She'd seen that look on his face only once, back in high school when they'd caught some middle school boys shooting paint balls at Grant's family's cows.

Grant had lunged across the fence, dragging the younger boys to the ground. "How dare you hurt those helpless animals," he'd yelled in a voice that didn't sound quite human, certainly not the voice of a high school boy.

The boys, though only a few years younger than Grant, and outnumbering him, had been terrified, the sound of his voice ferocious with an animalistic growl. She hadn't been sure what he might do to them, what he was capable of.

The same uncontrolled fear that had shown on those boys' faces now crumpled the governor's face. Slowly, he released the rifle and she pulled it away, stepping back from him.

Relief flowed through her. She was alive. And the governor was going to pay for all he'd cost her, cost Grant. Cost her father.

Finally, her father would know his beloved wife hadn't walked out on him and their child.

She would give her father that gift. The gift of knowing the love of his life hadn't willingly left him.

Then, a voice behind Grant rang out, "You drop your gun, sheriff, and you too, missy."

CHAPTER TWENTY-FOUR

Kate glanced back over her shoulder.

Jocko. Of course it was Jocko. Who else would it be? Always guarding the governor, always close by when he was needed.

Her breath came in quick pants, gasping at each breath as though it might be her last.

Were she and Grant going to be buried here, at the same spot as her mother, two women who looked so much alike lying so close together in unmarked graves?

Was Grant going to likewise be killed by the same people who had probably murdered his father?

The karmic circle doubling back into a horribly twisted connection?

The governor yanked at the rifle and slowly, she released her hold on it. As if releasing her last chance at life.

Grant set down his gun and likewise glanced at the bodyguard. He gave the man a little nod, almost a professional acknowledgement.

"Glad you're here, Jocko," he said, his voice level and calm. "Looking out for your boss."

"We need to call in the GBI to straighten this all out," Grant continued, matter-of-factly. As if this were just business.

Jocko's face darkened. "Drop your sidearm, too."

Slowly, Grant removed his pistol and set it on the ground.

Jocko looked toward the governor. "What do you want me to do with them?"

The governor shook his head. "This is not what I wanted, Katherine, Grant." He looked between the two.

"I never wanted to hurt your parents. They backed me into a corner. I had to protect myself. All I ever wanted was for you to know that you're my son, Grant."

Grant's face paled and a muscle strained in his neck. As if the thought had never occurred to him that the governor might be his father.

Jefferson Avery's gaze faltered at the shock on Grant's face. That wasn't the look of gratitude of a son finally being acknowledged by his birth father.

Grant's jaw tightened and a hard fury filled his eyes.

The governor looked away toward Kate, his face softening. "And you. You look so like your mother, so like her. I loved her, you know."

"I know." Kate nodded and smiled at him, making eye contact. She had to engage him, get him to think about what it meant to kill the daughter of a woman he'd loved, and the son who finally knew him as a father.

"I would never have hurt your mother. She jumped in the way. I didn't even want to shoot Tom Campbell. I was forced to 'cause he was coming at me, had to protect myself."

His face crumpled. "I would never have hurt my Katherine Shelby." His voice broke and an old man's sob ripped from his lips. The sound of someone crying wailed through the woods, crying for things they'd wanted and actions they'd regretted for decades.

But he'd lived long enough to know some things could never be put right again. Some things you'd lost forever.

"I would never hurt you, Katherine Shelby." His watery blue eyes looked directly at Kate.

He'd called her Katherine Shelby again, her mother's name. He was living in another time, when the love of his life had still been alive.

Before she'd been killed at his hands.

Jocko and Grant both looked sharply at the governor.

Suddenly, it occurred to her why the governor and all his family had always called her Katherine instead of Katie. Her mother's name had been Katherine Shelby. Though she'd always gone by her middle name Shelby, people who didn't know her naturally called her by her first name.

And that impression of her mother as

Katherine, apparently, had stuck with the governor. He'd always called her mother Katherine Shelby, even when he'd learned her preference.

Had it been arrogance, or just pompousness on his part to insist on calling her mother by that name?

And calling Kate by the name Katherine, as if she were her mother would have been a creepy harbinger if she had remembered what had happened with her mother or even known about the governor's fascination with her mother.

"What do you want me to do, boss?" Jocko looked at the governor with a reverence, looked for direction from the man who'd controlled his destiny for decades, the man to whom people said he had complete loyalty, and apparently considered a higher authority than any local sheriff or police chief. Or human code of decency.

Jefferson Avery tilted his head, concern creeping across his face, an expression that didn't ring true, as if acting, as if performing his ultimate political deception. "Just get them out of here, Jocko. Make sure they never come back and bother me again."

"But, don't hurt them." He stuck out his hand, regally, emphasizing that point. "I would never hurt my own son or my Katherine Shelby."

Jocko nodded. If anyone asked in court or

under a lie detector test, he could honestly say the governor told him not to hurt them.

Then, the governor's face hardened and the message that shot from his eyes to Jocko was very different from his words, a silent command that gave his employee complete discretion in how he chose to dispose of them.

Preferably somewhere their bodies would never be found, or at least not traced to him.

"Come on, let's go." Jocko motioned with his rifle.

He motioned away from the road, away from the driveway leading to the governor's house, away from where anyone could hear gunshots or the final dying cries of two people.

A second generation disposed of by the governor, first the parents, now the children.

She looked at Grant, and a silent agreement passed between them. They weren't going down quietly. She still had her gun tucked into her waistband. She also remembered the pistol Grant had strapped to his ankle, a final backup weapon she'd seen when he was dressing this morning.

When they were away from the governor and his gun, when Jocko wasn't paying attention, she could pull her weapon. And maybe Grant would have a chance to also get his gun.

One of them, at least, might survive.

But, before they could act, before she or Grant could take any evasive action, another voice rang out through the small valley.

"Both of you put down your guns."

Jocko and the governor stopped immediately, stock still, and their eyes widened.

Slowly, all four of them swiveled their heads toward the voice.

Hamilton Avery. Kate had known before she looked, had recognized his voice, as apparently had the governor. Dismay swept across his features, softening the determination to kill them that had just sat so harshly upon his face.

"Hamilton!" he cried, as if his boy had just come home from war.

Ham's face shone pale in the late afternoon sunlight, his neck muscles strained, pulsing in his throat as if trying to pump enough blood to his brain for all of this to make sense. "Put down your gun, Dad, and you too, Jocko." His strange expression did more to convince them than his words, his mouth working convulsively.

That *I just don't know what I might do* expression played across his face. Crazy people were unreliable. Jocko dropped his gun into the dirt. But, the governor just lowered his, letting it rest by his side, as if he were walking casually through the woods, ready to go hunting.

Ham pointed his gun at Jocko, ready to shoot him if he moved. Or, Ham's expression said, if he just got ticked off enough.

Then, he turned toward his father. "Your son? Is that what you called Grant?"

"Son, you don't understand," Jefferson Avery blustered, red-faced, for once the roles reversed between him and his son, his role as the infallible elder statesman probably lost for all time as far as his publicly acknowledged son was concerned.

"Which son are you talking to, Dad? 'Cause it's getting pretty confusing here, with a brother I didn't know I had. Or at least had only heard rumors about."

His father's face stilled, his eyes large, fixed upon Hamilton.

"Oh yeah, people threw it in my face that my dad was a whoremonger." Hamilton slurred the words, he was so angry and spit flew from his mouth. He swallowed and looked at Grant. "No offense, Grant. I don't mean your mom. She was lovely, when she came here for barbecues with Kate's mom and dad."

Ham shook his head bemusedly. "It's a strange thing, a small town like this, a rural community where people know each other their whole lives. Imagine the scene. Grant's mother, pregnant with your child." He gestured toward the former governor. "And her husband at her former lover's house for a barbecue."

He grimaced. "And, your mother, Kate, the woman my father was in love with since she'd been a high school beauty queen."

Ham nodded at his dad again. "Yeah, I heard the talk about that, too. But what I cannot believe is that just as soon as you'd impregnated my mother with me, you're out hunting down other women to bed, looking for fun and games while my mother was pregnant with *your* child!"

Ham's voice rose in tone, and he stepped closer to his father, his gun actually trained on him, as if he might shoot him.

"How could you disrespect my mother that way?" he yelled. His face twisted with rage, disgust pouring from his eyes.

"That's not how it was, Hamilton. You don't understand. These women go after men in high places." The governor's face morphed into that of a pleading child. Or a politician making a last stand?

"I understand that you killed three people to protect your own interests, Dad, to keep your reputation intact." Hamilton laughed with a slightly crazed sound, his eyes rolling in disbelief. "To protect yourself, you were willing to murder as many people as it took."

Ham motioned toward Grant with his head. "His father and mother. Kate's mother." He gestured wildly at his father, taking one hand off the gun. "And finally, today, you were going to have Jocko take Grant and Katherine off to be killed and buried somewhere in unmarked graves."

He tilted his head to make eye contact with his father. "Unmarked graves are real big with you, aren't they? As many as needed. Even me, Dad? Would you have killed me, too?"

The governor shook his head, tears running down his face. "No. Hamilton. No. I would never have hurt you, ever."

Slowly, his face crumpled until Kate could see what he would look like as a very old man.

"I love you, Hamilton. And I loved your brother in my own way. That scholarship the university offered him, that he turned down." He gestured toward Grant. "I got that for him. All I wanted was for my son to know he was my son. But Martha and Tom were insane with anger. Said they didn't deserve that."

He pointed at his chest. "What about me, did I deserve for my son not to even know I was his father?"

"Tom Campbell was his father," Hamilton said clearly and distinctly. "You were the sperm donor. A daddy is the man who puts you to bed, takes care of you when you're scared. You?"

Hamilton jabbed a finger at his father's chest. "You may have donated sperm and arranged for a scholarship for Grant, pulled some strings, big man that you are..." Hamilton gestured wildly, swinging one arm high into the air.

He lowered his voice, speaking slowly and

succinctly as if wanting his father to hear every word. "But I'm sure Grant would say Tom Campbell was his daddy."

He pointed at Jefferson Avery's chest. "Not you. You're the man who took away the only father Grant ever knew. Good job, Dad."

Tears streaked down the governor's cheeks, his face twisting into an ugly, distorted version of itself. Almost as if they all were seeing the real him for the first time. He sobbed one long, loud sob, as if he needed to expel the emotion in his chest before he could speak.

He looked directly into Hamilton's eyes. "Just know that I loved you, Hamilton. I always loved you."

Then, the governor raised his gun.

Hamilton's eyes got larger as his father's gun lifted, and Hamilton seemed to tighten his grip on his own rifle. But, he didn't shoot his father, even though he couldn't be certain just what his father intended to do with his own rifle.

Kate's breath caught in her lungs, every cell in her body focused on that gun, ready to leap away from the direction he pointed it. She pulled her gun out and turned it toward the governor.

Who would the governor try to shoot first? Would he shoot his own son even?

CHAPTER TWENTY-FIVE

Slowly, in time delay, the governor's gun swung up. From the corner of her eye, she saw Grant's body coming at her. As the governor's face hardened, he leveled his gun at Hamilton who just stood with a stunned expression on his face.

But, the governor's face told Kate everything she needed to know. He was angry and determined to keep control, even if he had to kill his own son.

Kate tightened her grip on her gun and pulled the trigger, sending a bullet blasting into the governor's chest.

A millisecond later, Grant pushed her to the side, toward a large tree that offered partial cover. Then, he pulled his gun from his ankle and turned it toward Jocko.

Jocko was lunging for his rifle lying a few feet away on the ground. Grant shot toward the gun, sending Jocko stumbling away from the weapon.

Only then, did Kate look toward the

governor. A red stain splashed out on his shirtfront. He staggered like a drunk.

Hamilton approached, his face pale, the shock of knowing his own father had been willing to kill him seeming to spread through him like a numbing drug.

Grant stepped forward to grab the governor's gun. But, a ferocious anger spiked across the governor's face and he lifted his rifle again.

He was going to shoot Grant, the last dying power play of an angry man, attempting to control the world in his dying moments.

Kate pointed her pistol with both hands and blasted another shot at the governor's chest.

The loud explosion shock-waved out through the woods, ricocheting off the trees until it bounced back to blast through the trees around them.

The governor staggered back, his eyes going blank.

"No!" Jocko yelled, with a wrenching howl of pain. Almost as if the governor were his own father. He leaped toward him, catching him before his body hit the ground.

The governor's gun fell away into the leaves.

Jocko paid no attention to the gun, but knelt by the governor's side, placing his hands over the red stains on the governor's chest.

Hamilton slowly lowered his gun to his

side, and Grant stepped quickly over, putting his hand on the gun. Ham jerked it away, then looked up at Grant, seeming only then to realize who he was, and released the gun to Grant.

Grant moved quickly to secure the governor and Jocko's rifles as well as his own and his sidearm. Then, he turned his pistol back toward Jocko in case the man went berserk when he realized there was no hope for the man he worshipped.

Because the gushing blood left no doubt that the governor would be dead soon, if he wasn't already.

Then, some sense of decency and duty as a medical professional kicked in and Kate stepped forward. Grant took her gun just before she kneeled by the governor and began to check his vitals.

She searched for a pulse. When she didn't find one, she placed her hands over his sternum and began to pump, but that only caused more blood to spurt out between Jocko's fingers. She glanced at Hamilton and continued. Grant sensed she was doing it for Hamilton's sake.

Ham met Katie's eyes, then shook his head. But, Katie continued.

"Stop!" Hamilton yelled. "He's dead. Let him lie in peace."

"Nooo," Jocko moaned, rocking over the body, one hand still in place over one of the wounds, and his other hand pressing on the second gunshot wound.

The man who was mourning the governor most at the moment was the man who'd done his dirty work, who'd shown an ultimate loyalty to *The Governor*.

And, the only one of the group the governor hadn't been recently willing to kill.

Suddenly, Jocko stopped rocking. He sucked in a long shaky breath and looked hopefully up at Hamilton through grief stricken eyes. "We have to preserve his image for the sake of history. We can say it was an accident. A hunting accident."

"Enough, Jocko." Hamilton laughed harshly and shook his head. "No more secrets. We're just gonna tell it like it is. Though I know that goes against the apparent politician's credo."

Realization seemed to dawn on Jocko then. That his idol, his protector, was dead and that he, Jocko, was going to jail. For a very long time.

For murder, maybe. Or at least as an accessory to murder or conspiring to conceal a death.

Anger replaced grief on Jocko's face, his own self- interests coming into play. "I only done what he told me. He was the governor, the ultimate boss in the state. Everybody knows the governor got the ultimate say so."

Hamilton looked into Jocko's eyes and pure hatred poured out of Hamilton's eyes. Hatred for this man who had been the hands that enabled his own father to murder, to do such evil.

"Well, I don't think the governor is going to be commuting your sentence," Hamilton ground out. "He's not going to protect you like you protected him. That ain't gonna happen."

Kate looked down at the governor, an empty husk of a man, a shell that had contained so much evil.

She exhaled, letting go of all the grief and horror he'd brought to her life and to so many others.

*****

Kate walked out of the sheriff's office to a dark street, streetlights pushing back against the night. Moonlight filtered vaguely through the trees, shadowing the road.

Before, when someone was stalking her, waiting to get a shot off at her or run her car off the road, she might have described the scene as spooky. But, now, with the danger behind her, it only looked picturesque.

A cool wind blew fresh air across her face, and she lifted it to the sky, letting the brisk air lift her hair from around her shoulders. For just a moment, she thought of nothing but how good it felt that fall was finally here.

She and Grant had given their statements separately to a GBI officer who'd raced up from Gainesville to take charge of the investigation.

Another GBI team was up at the governor's

processing the black SUV and marking out the area where Kate told them she believed her mother's body lay.

Mental and physical exhaustion dragged at her body, but at the same time emotional exhilaration invigorated her. Finally, she'd dealt with the truth she'd buried so deeply inside herself, that she hadn't been strong enough to face.

Until today.

"Hey."

She opened her eyes and looked toward the voice. Grant leaned against his patrol car. He pushed away from it and approached her, looking at her as if for the first time, taking her measure, wonder playing in his gaze.

He strolled to her slowly, placing his hands on her shoulders, gripping them with a reassuring squeeze, gazing into her eyes for a long moment.

"You want to talk about it?"

She nodded. Finally, all parts of her memory fit together into a cohesive whole. She knew why the memories had been pushed so far back into her mind that they were inaccessible to her. But, could Grant ever understand the self-protective measure that had made her forget such a horrific event?

Although it hadn't really been a conscious choice, could he ever make peace with the fact that on some level she'd known?

She had to tell him the whole story, finally

say all that she knew about the day his parents left him forever. He deserved to hear.

Their eyes connected and silently, he urged her to say it, just say it. Finally.

"I remember the day your mother came to our house." Her voice started out weak, but she willed strength into it. "The day it all happened. As a little girl, I didn't really understand what she was saying to my mother. But her arrival made an impression. She ran up our sidewalk, her hair flying behind her, her face all panicked."

Kate sucked in a deep breath, willing away the anxiety that always surrounded the memories of that day. She could feel the gray Jell-O threatening to move in, to cushion the scary thoughts, to *protect* her.

But, no. Not again. Never would she allow any parts of her mind to slip away into the dark recesses where dangerous secrets were buried.

"I was playing with my dolls as my mother sat in the swing on the front porch," she said on an exhaled breath.

Grant just gazed at her, his expression non-committal, non-critical, as if taking a statement from just any other witness.

"She just started blurting out things," Kate forced herself to continue. "My mother took your mom by the elbow and walked her down the steps and down the front walk."

"I knew from my mom's expression that she

didn't want me to hear. So, I pretended to play with my dolls, as I tried to listen in."

Grant nodded. To keep her talking, to encourage her without speaking. He was probably hell on wheels in an interview room with a real criminal.

Not just someone who'd pushed back memories that would have been so vital to him to know decades ago.

God, how she'd let him down, though it hadn't really been her choice. Tears began to well in her eyes for the little boy who'd lost so much.

He gripped her shoulders, with a little shake.

She couldn't meet his eyes, but she went on. Though it came so late, he needed to hear it, to finally know the truth after all these years.

"A child couldn't possibly understand, but now I know what your mother's words meant. The governor wanted to declare to you that he was your father. Your birth father," she corrected herself.

"Your mother said, 'He'll do it too, through *whatever means necessary*.'" Kate shook her head. "I remember those words. They sounded so terrifying the way she said it. I remember my mother looking back over her shoulder at me, and shushing your mom."

"'*You know how he can get when he is determined to do something, when someone tells him he can't*,' your mother said, her voice getting high and scary sounding."

Jefferson Avery had been legendary under the gold dome of Atlanta's capitol building. Don't cross the governor, they'd say, but if you do, don't let him know it.

Then, everybody would laugh like it was a big joke, according to the stories. But, nobody had meant it as funny.

She struggled to swallow, to clear her throat so the hardest words yet could be expelled.

"'Tom went up there to confront the governor,' your mother said."

Grant sucked in a deep breath, hearing the words after all these years that said his father wasn't some deadbeat dad, that he'd cared more than could be imagined.

Going to confront the governor? That said a lot and everybody around here knew it. Knew what the consequences could be if you crossed that man.

But murder? Tom Campbell probably hadn't anticipated the former governor was capable of that.

Or had he? Willing to do whatever it took to preserve his son's peace of mind and security in his place in the world?

"Then, what happened?" Grant prompted.

She sucked in another breath and prepared for the final onslaught of memories. Even now, thinking about, it was almost as if it were happening again, with the pounding heart,

THE KILLER YOU KNOW

and the terror and horror of what would happen later that day.

"Your mama said, 'I need your help.' She grabbed my mama by both her elbows and looked fiercely into her face. That's why I remember her next words, because her expression was so scary. 'You know what a soft spot the governor has for you', she said." Kate whispered the words, as if she could sneak up on the memory, not let herself really feel it.

Grant looked down at her, his eyes so gentle, his expression silently acknowledging how much Kate had lost because her mother had fought for his family.

For him, for that little five-year-old boy he'd been.

She continued then, wanting to get it over, wanting to move past the horror that she was only now remembering as something more than just a childhood nightmare that had awakened her every night for months, screaming and running in her dreams, running from the monster in the woods.

At least she'd had her father there to wake her up, hold her in his arms, and tell her it was only a dream.

To lie to her. Until little Katie had believed it was the truth, that she'd only dreamed it. Because when she was awake, she couldn't remember anything.

Until today, when it had all flooded back

full force, the bits and pieces of remembered detail fitting together with the parts of her memory she'd recovered today.

"They drove up that dirt road where you and I parked the other day when we were shot at. They saw your daddy's car parked there. Then, they turned around and took me over to the governor's and put me out, told me to go back where Miss Sally was boiling peanuts in the back of the house."

The memory of seeing Miss Sally through the shimmering steam rising from the large pot was as present as if it had just happened.

"But, of course, I didn't stay at the governor's house, didn't even go all the way back to where Miss Sally was working." Miss Sally had waved at her and continued working, probably thinking little Katie would putter around like she always did.

"I took off through the woods on that path that you, me and Ham had traveled on a bunch of times."

Grant stilled as she told the story. She wasn't even sure he was breathing, he was so quiet.

"When I got to the dirt road where your father's car was parked, I saw my mother's car as well. And, I heard voices from deep in the woods. So, I followed the sounds, those scary adult voices. They were yelling at each other. When I found them, I hid in the bushes watching."

She shook her head, willing away the images that she couldn't forget now. "I was very quiet, didn't want them to know I was there, didn't want to get in trouble for disobeying." She blew out a burst of air, even now not believing what had happened next.

"The governor raised his rifle to shoot your father, and my mother jumped in front of him, thinking that would stop the governor, I guess. But he must have already pulled the trigger as she was jumping because she flew backward, into your father. Your mother screamed and ran to my mother. There was blood everywhere." She shuddered and Grant pulled her into his arms.

She relaxed into him, feeling so safe in his arms, inhaling his goodness, his kindness, his honesty.

If the governor was Grant's biological dad, Jefferson Avery's twisted need to control and to get what he wanted at any cost had skipped a generation.

Grant was so good, so kind. Was that old story about the governor being his father even true?

Maybe all that had happened was because of an old lie.

"I can't believe I didn't remember this for so long, because now, it's like I can't forget it. It's a movie that plays over and over in my head, like in my dreams after it happened. So many nights, I relived it." Kate took a deep breath and leaned back to look into Grant's eyes. "The three of them really tried to save my mother, the governor, your mother and father, working over her. Finally, your mother said it wasn't any use, she told your father they needed to call the police."

"That's when the governor picked up his rifle and chased your parents. The three of them ran back toward where the cars were parked."

What came next was too hard to describe, but Grant deserved to hear it all first hand, once and for all.

After she'd told this story as many times as it needed telling today, to Grant, to her father, and whoever else had the right to know, she didn't think she would ever talk about it again.

It was the past, and she was going to put it back there once and for all.

"I ran to my mother and shook her, tried to make her wake up." As the old horror and futileness of that moment filled her, a sob ripped from her chest leaving a jagged roughness in her windpipe. As if singeing her vocal chords so she could never talk of the incident again. That would be okay, because she never wanted to speak of it, or think of it ever again.

As if listening to her, the horrific memories and images began fading from her mind, sinking back into the oblivion of her subconscious once again.

But, she inhaled deeply and held onto her memories, held onto the parts of her brain that wanted to erase the past, to save her from the pain. She wanted all parts of her memory, wanted to remember everything that had ever happened to her.

Both good and bad. She wanted her mind intact.

Needed access to all parts of herself.

Grant squeezed her, bringing her back into the moment. In his arms, safe and loved.

Loved by Grant.

"It's okay, Kate. I don't need to hear all of this," he murmured.

"Yes. Yes, you do." She met his gaze. "You need to know everything. Once and for all." She steeled herself for what came next.

"I don't know how long I was there in the woods with the dead body of my mother. I think I fell asleep, pressed up against her side, my arms around her neck, waiting for her to wake up."

A long deep shudder pulsed through her and the only thing that kept her anchored here, in the present, was the feel of Grant's arms around her, reassuring her, pulling her close against him.

"I didn't understand what death was." She leaned back and met Grant's steel blue gaze. "Finally, I was awakened by sounds of the governor coming back through the trees, crying and moaning."

"Katherine Shelby, where are you? Oh, my Katherine Shelby. What have I done?" The eerie keening of the murderer calling to her mother filled her brain. Those were the sounds and words she'd heard so many times in her childhood nightmares.

She steeled herself against the memory of that monster and the little girl's fear. "I hid, then. I had seen what he could do with that gun. But still, I watched."

"Thank God I did." She shook her head hard, emphasizing the point. "I thank God for giving that little girl the strength to do what she did next. If I hadn't, I wouldn't have the final proof today of my mother's murder."

She sucked in a deep breath, pushing back the tears that wanted to spring forth. Just a bit longer and she could cry. She had to be strong just a bit longer.

"He picked up my mother and carried her. To that spot we were at today. And buried her."

Even now, the memory was too powerful, so hard to remember that she wanted to push it away. "I need to hold onto the truth," she emphasized. "If I hide from it again, I will lose parts of myself, never be able to keep Katie, Katherine and Kate together as one. They need to be integrated into one person - me."

If she pushed back the memories, she might never get them back.

Grant's fingers dug into her biceps, anchoring her to the present. "You learned that as a child, that behavior, that self-protective mechanism. And, I see now, you still do it. You've chosen to forget certain painful things even as an adult. Like when I left you to go away to Afghanistan, you just *forgot* about me."

She laughed harshly, the sound ripping from her chest with a painful jerk.

"Freaky to realize that about yourself," she said. "I learned as a child to separate myself from pain. A mental barrier. A wall against hurtful things."

Now, she needed to finish the story of her mother. To get it over with. Because she wasn't really certain that it wouldn't fade back into the gray recesses of her mind.

It had before. What would stop it from happening again?

Suddenly, she wasn't certain of anything about herself. What her mind was capable of doing to protect itself. Was she really in control of it?

Grant gripped her arms tighter, and she nodded at the prompting.

"After he buried my mother, I was horrified, that he'd put her into the dirt, into the ground. Not my pretty mama, with all that dirt on top of her, covering her pretty red lipstick, her beautiful hair, that cotton dress she wore that day with the matching sandals.

Not my mama."

A sob ripped through her. Her mother had been so beautiful, so kind. "She didn't deserve that, Grant. No one does, but especially not my mama."

She put her face into her hands and sobbed. Until she felt the memory receding, going back into the files.

Maybe never to be recovered again.

She jerked her head up and began talking very fast, as though if she could talk fast enough, she might outrun the protective instincts of her mind.

"I sneaked away through the underbrush, hunkering down, scrabbling through the trees as close to the ground as possible so he wouldn't see me. Then, I ran. Just ran and ran and ran. Finally, I got to the main driveway." She sucked in a breath, and blew it out again.

"Miss Sally was walking back down the drive, calling out my name." The image of that moment when she'd seen her, an adult she'd felt would protect her and keep her safe was as real now, as clear as if it had happened yesterday. She'd run into her arms.

"I was a mess, crying hysterically. Said the governor shot Mommy." She shook her head. "You should have seen Miss Sally's face, the fear as she jerked around to look into the woods, as if she thought the governor might come out of them shooting. She yanked me up into her arms and ran, just ran, as if she were terrified. You don't know how frightening it is as a child, seeing the adults terrified. Your whole world turns upside down."

She looked into Grant's eyes, seeing a ferocious anger.

"She was running for her life. And mine," she said.

He nodded and growled, "That man wouldn't have hesitated to kill both of you to protect what he had, the power, the prestige. Today, he was even willing to kill his own son when he crossed him."

It felt so good to tell Grant, to download from her brain all the secrets she'd kept for more than twenty years.

"That's all I remember," she said quietly. "I think I was in shock after that, with a little girl's inability to remember detail. That's all I can tell you about that day."

"I wonder what happened with my mother and father after that," Grant growled, his voice low, thoughtful, even as he held onto her arms, as if to reassure her he didn't blame her for any of this, for keeping the secret from him.

"I wonder if he killed my mother that day?" Grant mused. "My father died later, I know that much from the report. But was he shot that day and died later?"

"I'm sorry." The pain of not being able to give him answers about the fate of his parents cut into her. She'd recovered her memory, answering a lifetime's worth of questions for herself. He deserved the same.

"I wish I could tell you more about your parents. What became of them, and how your father died." She looked up into his eyes, seeing the pain they'd both carried for a lifetime, knowing she couldn't erase it. "I just don't know the rest of the story."

His eyes said he needed to know the rest, that he wouldn't find the same sort of resolution she'd found until he did know.

Night echoed around them. Insects clicked in the dark and an owl hooted in the woods behind the police precinct. The statements were being taken at the police department instead of the sheriff's department, with the GBI taking the lead, giving as much space between Grant and the investigation as possible. So no one would be able to say it was tainted by the prejudice of the son of a victim.

A wind blew through the trees, brushing across their faces with a mildness that belied the fall date. It was autumn but as if nature realized they weren't strong enough to withstand nature's harshness as well as this emotional blow, it had relented with this unseasonably warm weather.

He sucked in a long breath then let it out in a deep sigh. "We may never know the rest." The words faded into the air, into the quiet night, with a hopeless ring.

Not know the rest? That would haunt him

for the rest of his life as her hidden truths had haunted her.

He deserved to know. Damn it. She wished she could tell him more.

"I can tell you the rest," a small voice came from nearby, a woman's voice from somewhere in the dark.

Kate and Grant jumped and turned, staring into the night, searching for the source of the words.

A thin woman stepped into the glow thrown from a streetlight.

Grant gasped. But, Kate had to stare at her before the features of a much younger woman emerged through the changes that time had brought.

Grant's mother.

Kate's lungs deflated, all of the air leaving her body. After all these years, the woman she'd last seen screaming and running away into the woods was alive.

A car was parked at the opposite curb, behind her. An old Ford Mustang.

"That's Hank Ratherford's car," Grant said. "It used to be blue."

Now, it was a nondescript brown, but where the paint was flaking away, blue shimmered from underneath.

"I saw that car across the way at my baseball game. It stopped outside the fence, like someone wanted to just catch a moment of the game. I turned to look at it 'cause it was a

Mustang. There was a woman driving. That *was* you. I thought so at the time."

The disbelief and shock in his voice was tinged with pure happiness, the joy of a little boy who'd always thought his mommy and daddy would return for him one day.

"It was me, Grant, there at your baseball game. I sneaked back here just that once. To see you. I had to see for myself that you were happy." Her face creased with the need to cry, and the desire to laugh all at the same moment.

Grant took a faltering step toward her and she also matched his step with one of her own.

"Your father was coming back to get you the day he was killed. He was coming to the sheriff's office to tell them everything that had happened. But he wound up dead." She raised a shoulder. "Don't know how."

Her eyes carried decades of sadness and loss. "The governor told your aunt that if I tried to come back and take his boy that I'd end up dead."

She looked away for a second then back at him. "I was afraid if he caught me trying to sneak you out of the county that he'd kill me and maybe you, too. My sister begged me to leave you here with her. Said that man promised he would kill her and me both if we tried to take his boy away. Besides, I was afraid I wouldn't be able to care for you, Sugar, with the little bit of money I could make if I had to always be running, looking over my shoulder, waiting for the governor to find us."

"I came to see if you were happy." She smiled sadly, hopefully. "That day at the game, you were running around those bases like a Brave's baseball player. All those people clapping and hollering for you, like you was somebody. Like you was the hometown hero."

Her eyes creased, the wrinkles around them etching deeper, with all that she'd lost, all that they'd lost. The time that a mother and child should have spent together.

"I hope you can see I thought I was doing the right thing. If they'd killed your daddy, they might kill you and me both, if I came for you. I was afraid for you. I couldn't take the risk."

Grant's eyes were fixed on her face, taking in every word. Hearing the sound of his mother's voice for the first time since he was five years old.

Tears strangled Kate, and she wanted to erupt into full- fledged sobbing. Her eyes burned with unshed wetness. But she held them back, because this was Grant and his mama's moment.

Then, Grant's mama looked toward Katie.

"Katie, your mama didn't suffer. It was almost instantaneous, her death after she was shot. She took just a few breaths. We tried to bring her back, us and the governor, too.

Cause he loved her." She shook her head disdainfully. "Married man and all that he was. But, your mama chose your father over him, and that drove the governor crazy for all those years."

She sniffed. "But, anyway, we all cried and mourned around her body. Then," her eyes narrowed, "the governor's twisted point of view decided that Grant's daddy was the cause of Shelby's death."

She shuddered. "He went for the gun again. Your daddy, Grant, he jumped on him. And they fought. The governor had nearly supernatural strength, what with his grief over losing the great love of his life. Finally, the governor got the gun away, but your daddy knocked him over giving us a chance to run. Jefferson chased us and shot your daddy. Just in the arm."

She shook her head as if in disbelief again, then continued, "After Tom got shot, we kept running. The governor chased us to the cars, then he got in your mama's car and followed after us, all the way down the mountain. We drove like maniacs. If only a cop or deputy had stopped one of us that day, everything would have been different."

She shivered in the mild night air, and wrapped her arms around herself. "That gunshot wound to your daddy was probably how he found us, 'cause we had to go to a hospital down in Gainesville to get your daddy's arm tended to. A police officer came to the hospital to take a report on the shooting. I guess it's routine when a gunshot victim shows up at the hospital."

She shook her head. "The police chief down in Gainesville and the Hall County sheriff both came to the hospital, after we told the cop it was the governor who'd shot your daddy." Her shoulders fell and her whole body wilted with the haunting memories she was probably living through as she told them the story.

Kate knew exactly how she felt, how it was to relive traumatic memories that could become more powerful than the present everyday world.

Grant's mother looked up at Grant and Kate and her eyes were wide with shock even now, all these years later. "It was like the governor had so much power nobody would listen to us. They plumb didn't believe us. Oh, they said they'd look into it."

She guffawed. "But, you could see it in their eyes – nobody was gonna go up against the governor."

Kate's stomach clenched, remembering the terror that had kept everyone in her family quiet about their suspicions all these years after the initial investigation turned up nothing. She'd heard whispers that made sense now.

"But, Katie, we were not content to give it

up, to let that man get away with murdering your mama." Her eyes focused on Kate, laser intense, shining blue in the night, with a burning fury that had been lit decades ago.

"Grant, your daddy was going to come up here, show the sheriff exactly where the shooting happened, and get Grant and bring him down to Gainesville. One-stop shopping."

Her eyes glistened with fury. "But, that weren't the way it happened. Your daddy ended up dead. Don't know the details." She gave a long sigh, as if releasing the information had given her a relief that was decades in the making.

Then she raised her eyes slowly to look at Grant, hesitant, taking his measure, trying to discern his reaction. "I'm sorry we all let you down so badly, son."

Released from the power of her voice telling the story he'd waited so long to hear, Grant sucked in a long deep breath, then stepped forward and pulled her into his arms, the thin woman so tiny next to the boy she'd given birth to so many years before.

For a long moment, he just held her. Then, he pulled back to meet her gaze, her hopeful gaze.

"You did what you thought was right, Mama. The only thing you could do, knowing how Jefferson Avery was, what he was capable of. You did the best you could for your son."

His voice broke on the last word and he hugged her again. She wrapped her arms around him, as if this was finally the moment they both had waited for more than two decades. Since that moment in the woods when everything had changed.

Kate didn't move, not wanting to break the power of the moment. Feeling the emotions flowing through them, rising off them like a mist over the Chattahoochee River in the early mornings, like the fog flowing over the Appalachian Mountains just before sunrise.

Emotion shimmered around them, skimming across their skin, finally swirling up into the night air.

Then, as if released from a spell that had held them prisoners for most of Grant's life, they both stepped back, looking into each other's faces with slightly dazed expressions, tears filling their eyes.

"My boy," Martha said, softly, with awe. "Grown up so big."

Then, as if she'd only just remembered Kate, she turned and put a hand on Kate's shoulder. "And you, Katie, you look just like your mama, just like Shelby." She shook her head in disbelief. "Just like her."

The words she'd heard all her life, had always hated hearing, meant something totally different now that she knew the truth about her mother's disappearance. To hear them coming from her mother's best friend, the woman who'd been there when her mother's life had been taken from her.

Grant looked at Kate, their eyes meeting with an understanding that only the two of them could ever have, the two children who'd lived this nightmare.

A slow smile of deep pleasure spread across Kate's lips as she looked at him. Thank God he'd finally had part of his family returned to him. Finally knew the whole story.

Grant's mother looked at Kate. "I saw the article about you getting run off the road, Katie," she said. "And them shooting at you and Grant. That's why I come up here. Then, the clerk at the gas station just outside of town told me about the shooting up at the governor's. So, I come over here to the police department first to tell them my story. And here you all were."

Just then, Kate's father drove up and parked on the other side of the street. From this distance, in the dark, he wouldn't be able to identify Grant's mother. Kate would tell him later, after they'd left.

"I'm going to go on home," she said to Grant. "My dad is waiting over there to follow me home. You and your mama need time to come to grips with all of this. And she'll need to give the police her statement."

Grant's eyes met hers for a long moment before he nodded, a misty screen hiding his thoughts.

What was he thinking?

As she walked away, all she could think about was his reaction to all of this.

Could he ever understand and come to grips with all she'd hidden inside of herself all these years?

Could he trust a woman who'd shown a psychotic break from reality as a little girl? As well as the fact that she'd reacted so extremely when he'd gone away to war. Then, seemed to have another detachment from reality after the car chase and crash.

All of this was so much to take in for him.

Would it become a permanent wall between them?

At least the physical danger was behind. The emotional risk? That lay straight ahead in front of her.

A wall she and Grant would need to climb together.

If he was willing.

CHAPTER TWENTY-SIX

Kate and her father sat on her front porch, both rocking in chairs that had belonged to Kate's granny. So many family problems had been talked out on this front porch just the same as the porch at her father's house.

Night noises echoed around them, an owl in the woods, a dog barking somewhere off in the distance.

"Daddy," she said softly. "I can't tell you how sorry I am that I never told you all this."

"But you did. Miss Sally brought you home covered in blood. She had to take those bloody clothes off you and put you in the bath before you would calm down at all."

"I don't remember that."

He shook his head. "I'm not surprised. I wish I could forget it, too. You were hysterical."

"Really? What did I tell you?"

"Probably the same thing you told the detectives tonight. I told them what you said back then, and they nodded afterwards, like they'd heard it all before. One of them said yes when I asked if that was the same story you had told them."

Kate looked out into the yard. "The cops were told all this years ago?"

"Oh, yeah. We took the bag of your bloody clothes to them."

Kate turned back to him in time to see his eyes narrow into slits. "That bag of clothes disappeared. Never seen again." A muscle in his jaw twitched. "Later, Miss Sally told me she was afraid for me. Afraid I'd end up like Tom."

Kate gasped. "Did the governor say something to her like that?"

Her father shrugged. "She'd never admit as much. But, I figured she knew what she was talking about. That you would end up an orphan like Grant."

Kate stilled her rocking chair, waiting for any more revelations from her father, not wanting to miss a word.

"Katie, I've always known your mother was dead. Martha told me so on the phone. She said Tom was going to come back and make sure the governor paid for what he'd done." Her father laughed harshly. "We all saw how that turned out. Kinda made people want to forget about justice and just concentrate on staying alive, raising the kids who'd been left behind."

Kate looked at her father and realized just

how much strength it had taken to keep on living, to not go up on that mountain and try to kill the man who'd killed the only woman he'd ever loved.

Instead, he'd put his rage into a box he'd shoved back into a deep closet. And been the sweetest, kindest father any girl could ever hope for.

He'd done that for her. She stood up, walked around behind him, wrapped her arms around his neck, and put her head beside his.

They sat there for a long moment, before she whispered, "Thank you, Daddy."

He waited quietly.

"Thank you for not going crazy with grief. Thank you for not turning into an angry, vengeful man who couldn't be happy."

He half-laughed. "You're welcome?"

She laughed wetly, sniffled, then finally stood up.

"What about Grant? His parents never contacted him?"

John shook his head. "His aunt said she was afraid they'd track the calls if they kept calling. I guess only one or two calls right at the first to her and Grant. Then, when Grant's father was killed, his mother really went on the run, afraid of the governor finding her, afraid if she contacted Grant, the governor might be able to track her down."

A fiery spit of anger spiked into her heart, for all the pain the governor's actions had caused that little boy.

"Everyone was afraid of what that man might do, might pay someone to do."

She nodded. "Nobody has to be afraid of him anymore."

Her father pushed up out of the rocking chair and turned to face her. "That's your doing. You finally killed the bad man, made him pay for what he did, what he still wanted to do. That man was arrogant, with the type of ego that denies. Denies that his actions were evil, denies he didn't have a right to whatever he wanted, at whatever cost to others."

Kate gave a half-hearted, broken laugh. "Little Katie killed the bad man."

Her father shook his head and met her gaze determinedly. "No, grownup Kate stopped him from hurting anyone else." His blue eyes met her blue eyes, flashing between them the promise of no more secrets, nothing hidden away, nothing too hard to face.

"He may have hurt you as a child, but as an adult you were his match."

She nodded, deep inside grateful that the little girl she'd been no longer had to worry on some level that the monster on the mountain could hurt someone she loved.

She'd lived in the shadow of that mountain for all of her life, and now, she could fully understand why she'd *forgotten* what had happened.

Because what little girl could possibly live,

knowing everyday that a monster looked down on her from that mountain?

Her father studied her for a long moment. "I guess there were different choices I could have made, too. To leave the area."

"Stop!" She held out her hand. "We are not going to question ourselves anymore, ever again. That evil man is not going to make us feel guilty, inadequate, or anything else bad about ourselves ever again."

She stared at her father with a steely blue intensity, willing him to accept that she didn't question him, or the way he'd raised her.

"Our people have been here since mists first started rolling over these hills," she said.

Her father gave a husky laugh. "Well, maybe not that long."

"You know what I mean. This is our piece of the planet. And we stand on it."

"That's quite eloquent." His eyes narrowed with the humor she'd always loved about him.

A laugh burst from deep inside her. Her father pulled her into a rough hug that ended with him rubbing his knuckles on her head. He let her go, finally.

"Well, I know you need some rest. You sure you won't come on back home for the night?" He softly patted the porch column while he waited for her answer.

"No, Daddy. I'm fine."

He looked back at her and laughed softly. "Me, too. I'm fine."

She watched while he went to his car.

As he walked away, she realized a bit more of the truth. Her father had always been a bit in denial himself, wanting to believe the love of his life wasn't really dead.

There had always been some part of her father's brain that had wanted to imagine that one day his Katherine Shelby Taylor might walk through his door, had imagined she wasn't really dead.

And Kate knew that if that had happened, her father would have taken his Shelby into his arms, and thanked his lucky stars for any time he could have with her.

The way Grant had acted with her? Would that last for a lifetime?

Kate walked inside, shut the door and hit the code to activate the alarm. She went into the living room, turning on the television to the news. They ran video of GBI officers rolling up the driveway at the governor's house.

A young reporter talked earnestly about the day's events.

Kate listened, amazed at how much information the woman had managed to gather so quickly. It was pretty accurate.

When the reporter finished her story and she and the anchors got through with the eye rolling and the can-you-believe-it expressions on their faces, Kate turned off the television.

She headed for the stairs even though she'd

get no sleep in that bed she'd shared with Grant just last night. Would her father get any sleep?

Would anybody in the area who'd seen that report get any sleep, burning up the phones with calls and text messages?

Tomorrow would be a busy day at the diner. Coffee would be flowing the same as it would be at the vet clinic, and Kate would be drinking as much as anybody.

As her foot hit the first step on the stairs, a knock came at her door. She turned and looked. Grant?

Buford Gafney peered in through the glass windowpanes at the side of the door. He held his wife's toy Pomeranian.

He gestured with his head at the dog, his expression tight and worried. She'd seen the same look on other pet owner's faces when she'd visited them in the middle of the night for emergency calls, or when they showed up on her front porch, distraught, panicked.

What about the *middle of the night* didn't pets get? Taking a turn for the worse as soon as clinic hours ended was pretty uncommon.

Kate smiled and walked to the alarm box, hitting the code to deactivate it. Then, she swung the door open. "Hey Buford. How's Lola?"

"Not good." A white pallor shimmered on his face overlaid with a sheen of sweat. "She was walking in circles with a blank look on her face when I got home. My wife was up at the school, still PTA-ing it up. I grabbed Lola, hoping maybe you could fix her up before my wife got home. You know how she dotes on this dog."

"Walking in circles?" Never a good sign. But from one who'd always been as healthy as Lola? "Did you get the usual flea medication? You didn't get a different one, did you?"

"I thought I'd gotten the same one. They said the records showed something different, but I was sure my wife had told me to get that green one instead."

"That might have done it. Set her down on the floor."

Carefully, Buford lowered her to the ground. The pup looked expectantly back and forth between Kate and Buford. As if expecting a treat.

"Let me get my bag," she said, turning toward the shelf where she always kept her bag ready.

She leaned down to pick up the bag, but hands closed on her neck, yanking her back. She screamed and the hands tightened, closing off all ability to make any noise. Instinctively she kicked backward, hitting bone with a hard, solid knock.

Buford yelped and stumbled but kept a grip on her neck. She twisted to the side, letting her weight take her to the floor in a dead fall.

Buford's grip on her neck was broken. She

flipped away, and rolled on the ground. Buford came toward her but Lola got in between them, jumping up on his knee.

"Get the hell out of the way," he yelled, kicking toward the little dog. That only served to make Buford lose his balance. He drunkenly fell toward the bookcase, grabbing onto it in an attempt to break his fall. That gave Kate just enough time to scramble to her feet and run.

She bolted toward the back door. Just behind her, Buford came for her, his feet sounding like a stampeding elephant, heavy, intent, ready to stomp her into the ground. A shriek tore from her lips.

She had to get out that door. She had to.

Yanking the door open, she ran out into the night, slinging the door closed behind her. Buford crashed into the door as it slammed toward him.

"Bitch!" he yelled, and slammed the door so hard that it crashed into the wall, the glass in the door shattering from the force. "Dammit!" Buford screamed again. "Dammit."

Maybe he'd sliced a vital artery.

She sprinted toward the front of the house. As she ran, she felt in her pocket for her keys and found them, hitting the unlock button on her SUV as she came around the corner. If she could get to her car, she could get her gun. She'd returned it to its usual place in the pocket of the car.

The governor was dead and Jocko had been taken into custody. Everything had been over, she'd thought.

But Buford was just steps behind her, yelling at her. She couldn't hear his words because of the blood pulsing in her head.

Buford was too close. If she tried to get into the car now, he could grab her, so she ran forward, rounding the car's hood. She had to put distance between them or he might wrestle the gun from her hands once she got it from the car and use it on her.

He ran behind her like a madman, as if determined to wring her neck like a chicken. Why did *he* want to kill her?

Then, she remembered. The night of the barbecue, she'd heard Buford talking to Jocko, telling him to tell the governor that he'd fixed the land deal, that the vote would go the way the governor wanted.

She'd seen money change hands, going from Jocko to Buford. An envelope thick with green bills.

That was why she'd broken up with Ham. He hadn't believed her, hadn't believed those slurs on his father, paying for votes against the road.

Kate had looked Hamilton Avery in the eye, telling him what she'd heard and he'd sided with his father. Acting as if she was the liar.

Buford was a man who didn't want to go to jail. If it became public knowledge he'd taken money for a vote on a road project, there was every chance he'd spend a lot of time in jail.

Buford Gafney was obviously willing to kill her to prevent that. Panic gave the man speed she wouldn't have expected in such a beefy man.

Instinctively, she turned and ran toward the road, trying to put distance between herself and Buford's large mitts. All those miles she'd run would go to good use.

She hadn't known she was training for a run for her life.

Her arms pumping, her feet kicking dirt up behind her, she sprinted toward the highway. Once she reached the road, there was a chance someone would drive by and she could flag them down.

Someone had to drive by.

"Stop, Katie, stop!" Buford yelled behind her.

Not a chance of that happening.

Her heart beat in her chest from the physical exertion but also from the sheer panic. Third time's the charm? This third attempt on her life just might be her last.

But she wasn't going out without a fight. A serious one.

Headlights flashed up ahead on the road, someone on the highway from town coming toward her. She ran desperately. This was her chance. Perhaps her only chance.

The car turned into her driveway, flashing

its lights onto her, nearly blinding her. Who was coming toward them? She ran toward the light, hoping she wasn't running toward her death if the wrong person got out of that car.

Who was driving up her driveway at this time of night? Enemies seemed to be coming out of the woodwork. No telling who Buford might have enlisted to help him.

The lights came closer. Should she just flee into the woods? Her breath ripped from her lungs like a fiery knife cutting into her ribs.

What should she do? What was her best chance of coming out of this alive?

Then, a blue light flashed and everything inside of her exploded into jelly. She was safe. She was safe. She was safe.

The car skidded to a stop, sending dust flying into the glare of the headlights, like a misty swirling fog of salvation. She ran through it, into Grant's chest, stopped by one of his arms that grabbed her and swung her behind him.

"Who's chasing you?"

She pointed behind her at a now fleeing form. "Buford Gafney."

Grant swore, then took off running behind him. "Halt," he yelled. "Stop or I'll shoot."

Buford skidded to a stop, raising his hands into the air. "Don't shoot. I'm unarmed. Don't shoot."

Kate gasped for air, putting her hands on her knees, looking up the driveway, at the man who had come after her for a third attempt on her life.

The third time had been charmed. As had all the other attempts on her life in the last few days.

She watched as Grant handcuffed Buford and walked him back toward his patrol car.

Had she used up all of her luck? Did she have any left to give her a chance with Grant? Despite the gratitude she felt for her life, a niggling little voice said it wouldn't be worth much if she didn't have Grant to spend it with.

Grant patted down the commissioner then placed him in the back of his patrol car like a common criminal, a guy who'd just been caught breaking into a home, trying to steal valuables.

Guess there wasn't anything more valuable to steal than someone's life.

The reality of what could have happened here tonight hit her, and she began to tremble. When Grant turned to her and took her in his arms, she went willingly, leaning into the comfort of his body, his smell enveloping her, telling her she was safe.

And that perhaps they had a chance?

CHAPTER TWENTY-SEVEN

Kate sat on Miss Sally's front porch, rocking, and drinking a glass of ice tea, half sweet, half plain. The way she liked it.

Little Lucky sat on Miss Sally's lap smiling his best dog smile as Miss Sally ran her hands through the long, silky hair of his ears.

"Yeah, you like that, don't you, Mr. Lucky?" Miss Sally crooned to him.

"I think he's going to be just fine, Miss Sally. He'll be giving you trouble for some time to come," Kate said the words the old woman wanted to hear, hoping they were true.

Miss Sally held the little dog up to her face and snuggled him close to her. "I think so, too. Thanks to you and gas station hot dogs."

"Thanks to how much you love him," Kate corrected.

The little dog looked up into Miss Sally's face with a look of pure love.

Miss Sally gazed back at him for a long moment, stroking him softly, tenderly. It brought tears to Kate's eyes just how much the two loved each other.

Miss Sally pet Lucky once more, then she slanted her eyes at Kate. "I heard you finally remembered everything."

Kate met her gaze and nodded. "Yeah, I did. But, there's something I don't understand, Miss Sally."

"I know what you want to know." The old woman nodded her head. "You want to know why the police and sheriff didn't arrest the governor back when your mama was killed."

Kate nodded. "Grant said there was just a one-page report of a missing woman. And another thin file when Grant's daddy turned up dead." She shook her head, remembering all the emotion that had poured over her father in torrents last night. "I think my father feels he didn't do enough."

"He sure put a lot of guilt on himself when it happened. The thing is, we did go to the police chief and the sheriff. Your father and me. Even though I was terrified." She shuddered.

"The police chief immediately put it off onto the sheriff, said it happened outside of town, so it wasn't his jurisdiction." Miss Sally guffawed indignantly. "Very convenient for him. The sheriff said there wasn't enough to go on, no body. 'Just a little girl's wild tale', as he put it." Her eyes narrowed with anger and she looked off into space. "By the next day, you were almost catatonic, so all we had to go on was your hysterical description from the night before. We gave them the clothes you were wearing so they could use your mama's blood for evidence."

Kate nodded knowingly.

"Your daddy tol't you the clothes went missing later on?"

"Yep."

Miss Sally rocked hard for a second. "When you were telling me and your daddy the story, you weren't very specific about what had happened, where. Didn't know where you'd been when the governor had buried your mama. That property of the governor's goes on and on."

She rocked back in her chair, guilt playing on her face.

Damn that guilt, that guilt that good people felt for somehow not being able to stop bad people.

"The sheriff said, according to your story, Grant's parents were witnesses too, and if so they should appear in town, and tell him what had happened. That never happened."

"But, they did." Kate leaned forward, putting her hand on Miss Sally's. "Grant's mother said they reported it to a police officer at the hospital, then talked to the police chief and the Hall County Sheriff, as well as called up here, too."

"I 'spect they did," Miss Sally said tiredly and shook her head like even now she couldn't believe all that had happened.

"The sheriff hushed it all up." Miss Sally looked like she wanted to spit with disgust, at the bad taste of it all. "Sheriff said he wouldn't ruin a man's reputation based on a five-year-old child's word."

She grimaced. "He never tolt us that the Campbells came forward."

Kate shook her head. "The governor had so much power. Maybe he had something on the sheriff."

"Or paid him off." Miss Sally stroked her dog for a long moment, looking off into the woods beyond the road, where so much bad had happened – on the governor's wooded property.

"Lawd, Katie, your father went just about crazy, went up onto that property and walked it mile after mile. But he could never find anything."

"Finally, your Aunt Mamie Lee begged him to stop, to put it all behind him, for your sake. Cause law, child, you were in a state. Almost catatonic."

"You used to cry and say you had to find your mama before the bad man could hurt her." Her eyes hardened. "Didn't seem to remember that your mama had already been shot by the bad man. Just that you were afraid for her."

She met Kate's eyes, and the memory came back to Kate with a visceral strength as if it were happening now, of lying on her bed, curled up in a fetal position, afraid *the bad man would come back and hurt Mama.* Kate stared up at the property across from Miss Sally's where so many lives had been irrevocably changed that day. Where her mother had lain for so many years.

"The governor paid the ultimate price finally," Kate said. "The death penalty, and I guess we all just have to move on and be happy for what we've gotten back." She tried to smile. "I've got my memory. Grant has his mama. And we all have some type of justice, finally."

"Speaking of Grant." Miss Sally nodded at the driveway. "There's your boy, right now." Grant's car drove slowly down the dusty driveway. Miss Sally stood up and headed toward the door. "I 'spect y'all have a lot to talk about."

Kate almost wanted to call her back, to say she didn't want to be alone with Grant. How would he react to her now?

So much had happened that she'd just swept under a mental rug.

She wouldn't blame him if he reacted with anger or recriminations for how she'd hurt him when he'd gone away to serve his country.

Nearly ten years later, she'd just opened her eyes in that ditch and acted as if she'd never broken his heart.

She wouldn't blame his reluctance to be

involved with a woman with the ability to forget so much. To create such gaps in her memory.

Nearly twenty-five years later, she'd suddenly remembered the day that had changed both of their lives forever.

Even if he understood on a logical level, there was that other level, the unconscious one, that might fear a woman like her, with her mental history. That wasn't the woman you chose to be the mother of your children.

A pounding fear grew in her chest anticipating his reaction, his possible feelings.

She sucked in a long breath, holding it for a moment, before exhaling all the fear and anxiety with it. She'd just have to face it. She wasn't running from reality anymore. No matter how painful.

Grant unfolded his long frame from his SUV and walked toward the porch, the longest walk she could ever remember, as if it took him years to get there, the more than ten years since she'd told him she never wanted to see his face again.

The more than twenty years the truth had hidden in her brain about their parents' fates.

He lifted his hand in a casual greeting. She searched his face for clues to his feelings.

"You want to take a walk, maybe down to Miss Sally's creek side garden?" he said, his voice giving nothing away. He was using his cop face, his cop voice. How he dealt with people who couldn't know his true thoughts.

Oh, damn. Just damn.

She nodded, afraid to speak, almost wanting to run so she wouldn't have to face his words, his possible rejection.

That was Katie's way. Not hers. Not Kate's way. No longer.

She preceded Grant down the stairs and on the path around the house and back into the woods. Neither of them spoke until they reached the pretty area with benches and a picnic table, set there so long ago by a family member of Miss Sally's beside a little creek.

The same creek that rushed so violently down the mountainside of the governor's property, as if anxious to get off the property of a murderer, flowed here. But on Miss Sally's land, it flattened out into a silent pane of glass, peaceful, flowing slowly. As if all its turmoil had been wrenched from it, leaving only this pretty little stream.

Kate sucked in the tranquility of the gentle water, strengthening herself for what lay ahead, to hear whatever Grant had to say.

He deserved to be heard. She owed him that.

She twirled around to face him, ready to get it over with, to know finally. Because she couldn't stand the suspense any longer.

"Grant, I am so sorry. For so many things." She rubbed her hands together, trying not to gesture wildly, thus making herself seem even crazier than he must already think her. "I'm sorry for all the years that I knew on some level, somewhere inside my mind, what had happened that day, knew that your parents didn't just leave you, that they were driven away. I am so sorry I wasn't strong enough to face the truth, the truth you deserved to know."

He started to speak but she waved him off. "I just need to get this out, get it over with."

He nodded.

"I also want to apologize for how I reacted when you went away to serve your country. That was unforgivable. Unforgivable! I am so sorry for so many things. How I flaunted my engagement to Ham. Everything is intact in there now." She tapped her head. "Too many things to apologize for. I'm kind of sorry I can remember it all now."

She ran out of steam then, because anything else would just be repeated apologies.

For something that might be forgiven, but still impossible to forget.

She took a long breath, then raised her eyes for his reaction. His rejection?

He met her eyes for a long moment before saying anything, a moment that held - promise? God, she hoped so. Hoped that was what that look meant.

"Kate, I realize now what my going off into a war zone did to you. The violent images it must have brought up in your mind, a visceral reminder of your mother's violent death. It must have evoked a powerful response deep in your psyche. I didn't know that then, though I do now."

"But, I should have known somehow what my *leaving* would do to you." He looked into her eyes, empathy and softness glowing there. "You lost your mother at such a young age."

He raised a hand when she started to speak. "Basically, she just went away and *left* you. I know what that feels like. I should have been more sympathetic to how you would feel."

She shook her head. "No, Grant. You were honest and open with me. I remember you started dropping hints. I just chose not to hear you. I'd gotten very good at ignoring painful truths. But I've got to admit the idea of you going away into a war zone where you could be killed ..."

She tried to get the image out of her head that had haunted her so much. The memories of him leaving had come back full force, with all the grief and worry of those days.

"I couldn't deal with that." She shrugged. "I know I said it was because my dreams for us at UGA were destroyed when it was really the war thing, the terror of you dying. So I just decided you didn't exist anymore. It was easier than wondering if that phone call would come – saying you were dead."

A long shudder rippled through her, before she sucked in a breath and straightened her shoulders. "I just wasn't strong enough to deal with it."

"Can you forgive me, Grant?" She looked up into his eyes. Hoping for understanding and forgiveness, but wondering if she really deserved those things.

Grant smiled down at her. "That already happened. In the hospital. Before that even, when I saw you lying in that crumpled car, and realized just how quickly you could have been gone, any resentment I'd felt faded."

He stepped closer. "Cause we both know, Kate, that people can be gone. They can leave our lives for good."

He shook his head, pain radiating from his eyes. "I can stand a lot, Kate, But, not losing you forever." His voice broke as he said, "Not that."

He wound his arm around her, settling his hand on her lower back, pulling her to him ever so slightly.

"I also understand why your mind disassociated itself as little Katie, from all the bad you'd witnessed, why you kept that dark secret inside." He looked down into her eyes. "I also get this *Katie* versus *Kate* name change.

"This new person, this *Kate* is strong, strong enough to venture into the past, to uncover the evil that had been visited upon your family, upon my family."

He tilted his head, leaning closer, so that she anticipated the heat of his mouth on hers. Then, he stopped, and looked down at her.

"That's all in the past." His eyes met hers intently. "What name do you want to be called now?"

She laughed slightly. "Katherine, Katie, or Kate. Any one of those is fine with me, 'cause they're all me, all part of me. They've all been integrated into one, one person who is all three."

His eyes crinkled with that expression that she'd always thought of as *just for her*. "So, a Kate by any other name would kiss as sweet?" he murmured.

She angled her lips, aligning them to match up with his. "Why don't we find out?"

"One more thing." His hand teased along the small of her back. "What name do you want the preacher to call you when he asks if you'll take my hand in marriage?"

A little gasp released from deep in her chest, unraveling the tension that had wrapped around her heart. "I don't really care what first name he uses, as long as I get to use your last name after the ceremony. Cause Kate will answer that she does take your hand, to have and to hold from that day forward."

He edged closer to her mouth, and nodded. "Then, kiss me Kate."

She laughed softly at the old joke. And then she did kiss him, melting away the years that had separated them, until she could hardly remember a time when she hadn't been in his arms, when she hadn't wanted him this close.

Maybe she'd stumbled along the path to forever with him. But now, she knew that forever was what they deserved, what they would have.

And she also knew she'd remember every moment of their life together and treasure every memory.

The End

If you haven't read Mick's and Becca's story, you can find **TARGETED TO KILL,** a Men of the Badge novel, on Amazon.

Romantic Suspense at its best, with a keep you up all night reading intensity. Sometimes redemption and second chances at love come with the worst circumstances. Guilt and grief were copartners in the death of Mick Hampton and Becca Jefferson's love. Now, FBi agent Mick Hampton must stop a horrific attack on American soil as well as save the woman he has loved for most of his life.

The undercover operation to stop the attack takes a dramatic left turn when Mick's former fiancé is kidnapped by the terrorists.

Is Becca Jefferson's kidnapping a matter of simple revenge? Or do the terrorists know more than Mick thinks they do?

The operation becomes a desperate attempt to survive for Mick and Becca, while still preventing the murder of countless innocent civilians.

Love is the prize if they survive.

TEMPTED TO KILL
available on Amazon

The chemistry between Alisa and Weston could be as deadly as the drugs that are readily available in the dark underworld of sex and drug trafficking in Atlanta.

An undercover cop, Weston's job is to "blend in with scum," and go after the big guy in the drug ring. Protecting Alisa as she searches for her missing teen sister could jeopardize the mission as well as his and Alisa's ability to keep breathing.

TAUNTED BY A KILLER
Available on Amazon

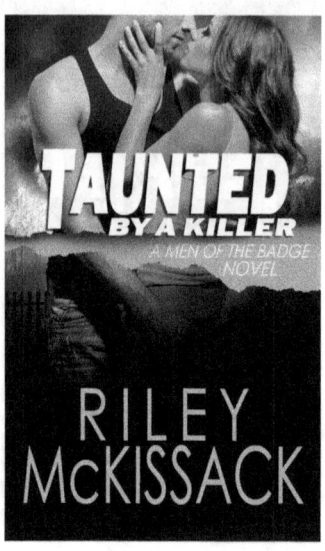

Second time romance? Or second chance at heartache?

Will Cassie and Forrester have their second chance at love? If she survives the serial killer who likes to set fires around his victims, then she can face the fire ravaging her heart. The fire that once burned her badly.

"Oh, yeah, I believe divorce is forever." Cassie laughed, a bit painfully. "Marriage may not be until death do us part. But, divorce? Once someone has crushed your heart between their hands? It's hard to ever look at them the same."

NO ESCAPE FROM A KILLER
Available on Amazon

Men of the Badge moves to the North Georgia mountain town of Hawk's Peak.

Dead Man Stalking. Emmy Bradenton is on the run from a husband who's been declared dead. The day she'd planned to leave him, Atlanta homicide cop Max Weber goes missing. A bloody scene at their home leads cops to the conclusion he must be dead.

But, Emmy knows better. Max knows how to commit murder and get away with it. For whatever reason, he's concocted this maniacal plot to disappear and then kill her.

Luke, one of the undercover cops who worked with Weston in Tempted to Kill, is on sabbatical due to the death of his wife from her long battle against Leukemia.

Emmy sparks his soul back into life. By the time he figures out why she looks familiar, he's already fallen in love with her. Then, it's a flat out sprint to save Emmy from a killer.

ABOUT THE AUTHOR

Riley McKissack is an award-winning journalist. Cornered gunmen, cop killers, a bomb going off in a domestic terrorism incident, Riley's covered them all. Riley spent years chasing stories involving every type of bad guy and cop imaginable, including FBI, Homeland Security, homicide detectives and arson investigators.

Riley sponged up the drama, tension and danger on SWAT operations, hostage negotiations, drug busts and countless other dangerous situations.

That passion and drama spills out onto the pages of Riley's novels, along with the personal stories behind the men and women who stand between danger and the people they love.

Riley can be found at:
https://facebook.com/riley.mckissack
http://rileymckissack.com
https://twitter.com/RileyMckissack

If you liked this book, I would appreciate it if you would help others enjoy the book, too.

Lend it.
This book is lending enabled, so please share it with a friend.

Recommend it.
Please help other readers find this book by recommending it to friends, readers' groups and discussion boards.

Review it.
Please tell other readers why you liked the book by reviewing it at Amazon or Goodreads. Or leave a review wherever you bought the book.

If you leave a review let me know at *Riley@RileyMckissack.com* so I can thank you personally.

Or visit me at *www.rileymckissack.com*

JOIN THE RILEY MCKISSACK NEWSLETTER

Join at:
http://www.rileymckissack.com/contact

Interior format by The Killion Group
www.thekilliongroupinc.com

www.ingramcontent.com/pod-product-compliance
Lightning Source LLC
Chambersburg PA
CBHW062004170626
46813CB00001B/29